Bananas Forever

Bananas Forever

Kenny Everett
and Me

Cleo Rocos
with Richard Topping

Virgin

First published in Great Britain in 1998 by
Virgin Publishing Ltd
Thames Wharf Studios
Rainville Road
London W6 9HT

A catalogue record for this book is available from the British Library.

ISBN 1 85227 762 9

Printed in Great Britain by Mackays of Chatham Ltd.

This book is dedicated to my wonderfully witty, fearless father who died suddenly this year during the time I was writing this book. He never stopped loving us. We will shine for him.

Contents

Acknowledgements

I'd like to thank my strong and beautiful mother, who has been at my side with her love and belief, always selflessly keeping her head above life's tidal waves. And, of course, my four incredible handsome brothers Jerry, Mickey, Dino and Sacha, who I have always looked up to and been proud to be their sister. I would kill and die for them.

I am also hugely grateful to Stevo, a very rare commodity, a manager with honour, dignity and respect from all who work with him. Not only an extraordinary manager, but a true friend.

And a special thank you goes to Richard Topping for all his exceptionally hard work in helping me to make this book all it is.

Bananas Forever

1 She's Quite a Funny Shape, Isn't She?

WHEN I FIRST SET EYES on Kenny two things struck me in a major way: his illegally blue eyes and a smile that made you feel all warm and surrendery. I was standing at the back of Studio 7 in the BBC Television Centre, hidden in the half-light because they were preparing for the next sketch. I was watching from the edge in my drum majorette outfit, and was supposed to be on my way to a make-up room, but was instead transfixed by the sight of the special effects men trying to get the props to work.

They were setting Kenny up for a sketch where he had to drive a tank through a showbiz polystyrene brick wall, followed by a troupe of majorettes (one of which was me). He'd then deliver his lines to camera and finish with the big exploding epaulette finale. The only problem was that the epaulettes weren't cooperating in the slightest. I stood watching curiously as three or four men with tools and wiry bits busily attended to Kenny's costume. From where I was standing it looked like a scrum of electricians. After a few moments they all took a step back and one of them pulled a little red box with a flashing red light on the top from his pocket. It resembled the remote control unit for a bomb, which is precisely what it was. He pushed the detonating lever and there was an alarmingly loud bang, followed immediately by a mushroom cloud of grey smoke that engulfed them all.

Once the haze cleared I could see that Kenny was sitting on a cable box wearing an oversized US general's outfit. He was slumped under the weight of his heavy costume, with his legs outstretched in baggy jodhpurs and shiny leather riding boots. His helmet was so big that when he turned to talk to anyone it stayed in exactly the same position and his head swivelled inside. On each shoulder, under his gold epaulettes, was an exploding gun the size of a small wardrobe. Around him buzzed the team of hunky special effects men in jeans and tight T-shirts, furiously fiddling with bunches of wires in an earnest attempt to get both epaulettes to explode. Occasionally one of them would remove a screwdriver from between his teeth and tap the lethal apparatus with a small tutting noise and a shake of his head, like a scientist in a 50s B-movie. One of Kenny's shoulders was still giving off little wisps of smoke, while the other remained stubbornly undetonated. The effects men sighed and scrummed down for a second time, brandishing pliers and gunpowder.

The studio bustled with the usual mix of floor managers, props department people, make-up girls, lighting engineers, scene shifters, clipboard clutchers and comedy foam-brick-wall constructors. Not five yards away, in a shiny red, white and blue drum majorette outfit, was me. I was fifteen years old and getting my first glimpse of the anarchic world of Maurice James Christopher Cole.

Anyone who has been in a television studio will know that the heat beneath the studio lights can be gruelling sometimes. Even though the studio was in half-light getting ready for the next sketch, poor Kenny was still stuck under a fairly hot glow – wearing his knargly costume full of corners and pointy metal bits – in calm, resigned patience. It looked as though it had been a long day for him, with one too many exploding-epaulette disasters.

Studio work was always very hectic for us. Later, when we were working together regularly, we played many different characters during the course of a day, and hardly had time to sit down between sketches. One minute Kenny's rubbery particles would be melting under the lights, the next one cheek of his inflatable buttocks would be growing fatter than the other. All the time I'd be playing whacky characters opposite his, and we'd laugh wildly from start to finish. It was pure exhausting lunacy, and Kenny and I both adored it.

I stood quite still and watched quietly from about five yards away. Nobody really noticed I was there until Kenny looked over. He rolled his eyes, cracked a crooked smile, and mouthed the word 'showbiz!' I laughed, but suddenly found myself wondering if I was being intrusive by watching. As he caught my eye he paused for a moment and smiled at me.

'Hi, I'm Ken,' he said, beckoning me over. I went up to him.

'Hello,' I said with my hand outstretched. 'I'm Cleo.' His face lit up as he extended his hand.

'Have you come to rescue me?' he asked. He firmly shook my hand and took on a cheery, surprised expression that in time I came to recognise as his she's-a-sweet-old-fashioned-thing look. Straight away we knew we would get on, and from that day neither of us ever looked back. As the only two Martians on this planet we'd finally found each other.

This was such a big event for me – not so much my first television work, but my first job that didn't involve climbing a tree or a ladder. Until then I'd spent an inordinate amount of time doing work in my school uniform that nearly always entailed clambering up things. Having four brothers, I flattered myself that the directors had been impressed with my climbing skills (for a girl). It didn't occur to me that my underwear might be of interest to anyone. How that was to change.

The part on *The Kenny Everett Show* had come about – like everything in my life always seems to – through a series of lucky breaks, freak coincidences, and mischievous twists of fate. This particular break came in the shape of Alan Bell, a BBC director I'd met a year before in rather peculiar circumstances when he had come to Corona, my stage school, to scout for some older girls. He was looking for someone to play the small role of a secretary in a comedy series he was directing called *Mr Big*, starring Ian Lavender, Prunella Scales and Peter Jones. That particular day I was late for my ballet class with the formidable Miss Florence – 109 years old and extremely intolerant when it came to lapses in punctuality. I was racing across the school playground in my regulation green leotard and black ballet shoes, oblivious to the world. Alan saw me disappear into a building and gave chase, going from class to class trying to find me. Eventually he caught up with me, and I was duly offered my first opening at the BBC.

I made a terrible secretary. All I had to do was sit and

pretend to type, but I bashed the keys with such enthusiasm that the props people had to keep coming on set to fix the typewriter. To make matters worse, I arrived at the studio in my school uniform and with a chaperone from Corona. This gave Alan a bit of a start. I was very curvy for my age, and he'd assumed I was about eighteen. When I told him I was only fourteen, he went an apoplectic shade of orange and disappeared off set for a while.

I loved that first day, and never wanted it to end. As the filming drew to a close and the studio audience began to drift out, I turned to my chaperone and asked her if she thought I'd ever work here again. She was an old Scottish lady with a scary face. With a heavily bejewelled hand she lifted her nineteenth double whisky of the day towards her wrinkly pink mouth and, before gathering her lips to the glass, said in her strong accent: 'Of course you will child.' With that she gave me a broad brown smile, coughed, went out of focus and began to chortle like an old train. I took her arm and bundled us into a cab, glowing with post-television euphoria.

Despite the shock of discovering my age, Alan seemed genuinely pleased with my first efforts at television. I wasn't to hear from him for a year however, and after *Mr Big* there followed twelve months of stage school punctuated by the occasional climbing role. I was beginning to realise that if I didn't get any constructive career advice pretty soon, I was going to be typecast as The Girl Who Goes Up Ladders. So, almost a year to the day after filming *Mr Big*, I rang Alan and asked him if he had any advice for me. He suggested we 'do lunch' at the BBC restaurant, and have a face-to-face chat instead of talking on the telephone.

I'm always very grateful when I look back. Here I was: fifteen years old and probably one of a hundred young actors with whom Alan had connections, yet he was willing to take time out of his busy schedule to share with me the benefit of his wisdom. I can't remember much about the meal, but Alan's venue choice became the next link in the chain of coincidences. As we sat chatting – me dressed in a very well-fitted (i.e. tight) red dress – we were unwittingly sharing the restaurant with

Jim Moir, BBC's Head of Light Entertainment and director Bill
Wilson, who were also having lunch together.

This was November 1981, a short while after the BBC had
lured Kenny away from Thames Television. He'd been with
Thames for three years and felt he wasn't getting the support
he needed to make the show evolve and move onward. So,
after a brief courtship with the BBC, Kenny switched teams.
Jim and Bill were charged with getting the new show up and
running, and wanted to do it by building on the success of the
original format. As part of the overhaul there was still one idea
they were trying to flesh out. It was Kenny's naughty bits.

At Thames Kenny worked with Hot Gossip, the troupe of
saucy dancers who added the show's splash of earingy attraction. Jim and Bill had decided to change the dancers and have
them mime to Kenny's jingly bits. But they also wanted to
make the show a little bit different, and so, on that particular
day, in that particular restaurant, they'd met up to decide what
to do about it. Lucky for me they were sitting at the table
next to us.

Alan to Me: 'You're a glamorous, exotic young woman who
needs to get a part in a mainstream show. Try concentrating
on comedy.'

Jim to Bill: 'We need a glamorous, exotic young woman for
a part in a mainstream show. We should concentrate on finding
someone who wants to get into comedy.'

If this was one of Kenny's sketches we would have all frozen,
turned to the camera and grinned, as our teeth sparkled with
a little 'tinging' noise like they do in the toothpaste adverts.

Most people in the media are professional eavesdroppers.
You have to be if you're ever going to get any work as most
of the deals seem to be made in about half a dozen London
restaurants. Unless you (or your agent) are there to hear what's
going on, you'll spend your entire career sitting by the phone
wondering why no one ever calls you. In this case, three professional eavesdroppers suddenly leapt into action:
introductions were made and numbers exchanged.

This was on a Friday, and Jim and Bill had already arranged
for auditions to be held the following Tuesday in BBC TV
centre. I was delighted to be invited along and, in all the

excitement, I'd neglected to tell them I was only fifteen, which had quite a bearing on my eventual casting.

When Tuesday came, I borrowed one of my mother's full-length fur coats for extra effect (this was when wearing dead animals was still quite chic) and tootled off to the audition. Corona were very flexible about letting pupils go to auditions, on the strict condition that they were chaperoned. This was another of those occasions when I'd taken the law into my own hands and failed to tell my tutors of my plans. So, while I waltzed gaily down Wood Lane on the way to the audition rooms, the school was under the impression I was bundled up in bed with a bad cold. Whoops arooty.

When I was called in, Jim and Bill were sitting at the other end of the room. I remained standing as they asked me lots of questions about my previous work, my dancing abilities and all the other stuff you usually get quizzed about at auditions. When they asked if I was good at improvisation, we had an exchange of cartoonular conversation, and the room soon filled with curly laughter. I remember thinking that they didn't seem to find me that odd. Or maybe they did, and this was what they were looking for. They also asked how old I was, and knowing that it was a requirement of the job to be at least eighteen, that was how old I said I was.

The following afternoon Alan rang me at home and asked how the audition had gone. I gave him a detailed account, but didn't pass judgment one way or the other, since (in my experience at least) perception of an audition always seems to have absolutely no bearing on whether you've won the part or not. I've had auditions where I've come out utterly convinced the role was mine, only to get the bum's rush a few days later. And I've had others where I thought I'd been so dreadful only a moron would give me a job, later to get a call from said moron saying I'd won the part. I've given up worrying about it now.

Anyway, I probably gave some banal reply, to which Alan then said that he'd heard it had gone very well. And although he had absolutely no idea what the final decision would be, he suggested I stay by the phone that afternoon, just in case. I could hear him smiling. I thanked him profusely for his advice, and stayed right next to the phone as he suggested.

Later that day I got the call from the production office at the BBC confirming that I'd got the job. The part was mine and they furnished me with dates and times for costume fittings. Filming on the 'Kenny Everett Christmas Special', his first television production for the BBC, was due to start in a few days' time.

I was going to be on *The Kenny Everett Show*!

Back on the day we first met, Kenny and I chatted a little more until the special effects guys came back to sort out the explosives problem. He wished me luck and waved goodbye as he disappeared beneath a horde of men carrying small sticks of dynamite. Among the effects men was Ray Cameron, one of the show's co-writers.

'What do you think of her?' Ray asked Kenny.

'Nice,' said Kenny. 'She's quite a funny shape too, isn't she?'

I made my way to the make-up room where the three other girls on the show were being powdered up for the next sketch. I was the only one of the four who wasn't a professional dancer. I could just about string together some basic tap into a routine glued together with glee, but these girls were doing that leg-wrappy-round-the-head thing to limber up. I would have looked pretty silly if I'd tried to keep up with them, so I excused myself and once again crept into the studio so I could watch the bongly chaos.

Eventually the electrical experts declared they were ready to go, and we took our places. The scene all went perfectly according to plan, and in one take we had tank through wall, majorettes following tank, Kenny being manic and epaulettes exploding. By this time it was getting late – at least seven o'clock – so we all went off to grab a bite from one of the studio canteens on the ground floor.

Back in the dressing room I was the only one of the four girls eager to carry on. The others had all been in the business a lot longer than me, and television studios late at night – especially when husbands, boyfriends and TV soap operas beckoned – held little or no attraction for them. You're not supposed to leave the studio until the director gives the all clear so, while the rest of them had their bags packed and were ready to go, I was wondering who I should ask to see if I could stay a bit longer to watch the filming. As we were waiting, the floor manager, Simon Spencer (now director and producer Simon Spencer), came into the dressing room and said he had to pick one of us for a sketch. He glanced around the room – three girls with their coats on and one still in her majorette's outfit – and chose me. This pleased the others no end, and I was sideways with happiness that I could not only hang around the studio, but actually be in a proper sketch as well!

I was whisked off for a costume change and then into make-up. Kenny was sitting in front of a make-up mirror, halfway through his transformation into the character Cupid Stunt. He had the wig on, and was silently enduring the process of having half a ton of industrial-strength mascara applied. The moment I stepped into the room his eyes lit up.

'Thank gooooooodness!' he said. 'You're still here. I thought everyone had gone home!'

'They have,' I replied. 'But I wouldn't have gone without saying goodbye anyway.' We smiled at each other and once again I got this astonishing feeling of connection. It sent a shiver up my already twinkly spine.

I sat and watched as the make-up girl tried to finish, but Kenny had other ideas. He winked at me and wiggled his fingers, which were sporting hugely long false nails. Whenever the make-up girl wasn't watching he would flick them off, one by one, on to the floor, and quietly chortle in a mischievous Just Williamular fashion. In exasperation, she went off to get some superglue, and Kenny nodded towards Cupid's rubber-chested frock, which was hanging on the back of the door.

'I don't know how you cope with those things,' he said in mock horror.

'What things?' I asked.

'Your chesticles of course. Don't they get in the way?'

Chesticles? *Chesticles*? I laughed so hard I folded in two, instantly confirming his theory that most often they *do* get in the way. This gave us a massive giggling attack, and a few minutes later we were roaring with laughter when the door of the make-up room opened and Bob Geldof's head appeared through the gap. This was getting more surreal by the minute.

Kenny's show had become a latter day *Morecambe and Wise*, (or should that be *The Muppet Show*?), with celebrities queuing up around the block for the privilege of appearing on the programme to have Kenny make fun of them. They kept coming back because Kenny always made them feel part of the joke, instead of the butt of it. Quite often – as with stars like Cliff Richard or Freddie Mercury – they were also Kenny's friends, and you could see the affection shine through the sketches. Bob was a big name thanks to the Boomtown Rats, so Kenny had invited him on the show – an invite which very few turned down.

Bob came in and he and Kenny greeted each other like long-lost chums. No matter how well people knew (or didn't know) Kenny, he always approached them with great warmth and generosity of spirit. People felt good in Kenny's company because he was never judgmental or aloof. He loved everybody without prejudice, and was always genuinely unpretentious and full of natural glee. These traits were terribly infectious: you couldn't help but find yourself smiling if you spent more than a second in Kenny's company. Even Bob Geldof, who I'd imagined to be a mightily cool pop star, immediately became mischievous when Kenny was around.

I had no idea what I was supposed to be doing until a script was hurriedly pushed under my nose and I realised my first proper comedy role was to be wrapped around Bob Geldof in a passport photo booth. Kenny went off to do his Cupid Stunt routine, and we were sent to the other side of the set to be photographically entwined. The sketch went well and before I knew it I was back in the dressing room putting on my civvies.

I couldn't believe what a fantastic day I'd had. Not only had the work been great fun, but it was like I'd been admitted into a secret world made especially for me. I had always felt (and still do) that the real world is too serious, with far too many clenchy-buttocks and sharp edges. I've invariably seen myself as an outsider, a lone Martian sent to observe but not get too involved. But here, in this loony universe of foam bricks and exploding shoulder pads it didn't matter that I was a bit weird. Here weird was good. In fact, here weird was positively encouraged. In Kenny I knew I'd met another Martian. It was a very profound feeling: part excitement, part relief, but largely gleeful. I had no idea if I'd ever see him again, but I was immensely grateful that I'd at least established there was other Martian life on Earth.

Before I left, I went to Kenny's dressing room to say thank you and goodbye. He was shirtless, plastered in cold cream as he tried to rid himself of Cupid's benign influence. He seemed truly disappointed that I was leaving.

'It's been such a dreadfully long day for you,' he apologised. 'I hope it wasn't too horrendous.'

'Are you joking? It wasn't horrendous, it was unbelievably perfect. Thank you so very much. Happy Christmas Mr Everett!' (I called Kenny 'Mr Everett' for months; it was a respect thing drummed into me by my parents. Kenny would rib me ceaselessly about it – usually after a hugely cartoonular sketch, where we'd be covered in some phlegmy splurge, squelching our way back to make-up, and I'd still insist on being so dreadfully formal.)

'Are you going to do the next series with me?' he twinkled. I gulped. 'Er . . . well, I mean, I'd love to . . . but no one's asked me.'

He rubbed his eyes furiously with cold cream and fumbled blindly for a towel. He wiped his face, looked up and grinned at me.

'Well, I think we'll be seeing a lot more of you next year. That is if you want to see a lot more of us, of course.' My heart leapt.

'Oh, very much,' I replied, barely able to speak.

Kenny smiled. He stood, kissed me on the cheek, and wished me a Merry Christmas.

'I'll see you next year,' he said as he winked and left the room.

I got my things and went home, my stomach churning and my head full of the most be doingy thoughts. It was all I could do to stop myself from falling upwards into the sky.

2 All Nurses and Actresses are Sluts

CCORDING TO THE TABLOIDS, I'm half English, half Brazilian, half Greek, half Puerto Rican and half Spanish. That makes me a total of two-and-a-half, which is quite an achievement by any stretch of the imagination. To set the record straight, and for the benefit of any sub-editors who might be reading this, I've only got two halves: an English one from my mother, and a Greek one from my father. Thankfully, you can't see the join. I was born in Brazil, the fourth of five children, and the only girl in a very male family.

My childhood was an extraordinary experience. My father ran his own successful shipping company, and his work bounced him around the world like a tennis ball in a spin dryer.* He was a very forceful, principled man, and raised us with equal measures of firm discipline and tender affection. Greeks are big on family, so instead of leaving us behind when he travelled, he took us with him wherever he went. And boy, he went everywhere. North America, South America, Europe, Asia. You name it, we lived there.† For my brothers and me, it meant changing schools, countries – and quite often entire continents – at least twice a year, dipping in and out of formal education with a fleet of harassed tutors in tow. It was wildly exhilarating and gave me a very mature perspective on different cultures and values around the world. It was also an education in itself: far more valuable than all that hypotenuse-

---

* It's fun you should try it.
† Notable exceptions include Belgium, New Guinea and Basingstoke.

11

right-angled-triangle-dooberry nonsense most schools fill your head with.

Growing up in an ever-changing environment, where you never get to put down roots and always have to make friends on the fly, forces you to become enormously confident and self-reliant. At least it did with me. Faced with the challenge of a new school every six months, I simply got on with it, and came to realise at a very young age that the only obstacles in life are the ones you make for yourself. There was another consequence of my unconventional upbringing. Moving from country to country and school to school, each with different conventions and regulations, meant that after a while I developed a healthy disrespect for all conventions and regulations. Rules became things that applied to other people. The only true authority I knew was my father and even then I pushed it to the limits.

All children, no matter what their background, are terrified of one thing: being different, of standing out from the crowd. But I was always different. I was always the new girl: the girl from Greece, the girl from America, and (quite literally for a while) the girl from Ipanema. Unaffected by peer pressure, I grew up content in the knowledge that I was different, and that this was something to be proud of. By the time I was twelve, I was happy, well balanced and pretty well uncontrollable.

I was in this frame of mind, when, in the mid-seventies, our family moved to England from America, and my parents put me into a strict Catholic church school run by octogenarian Nazi nuns.

It could only end in trouble.

School in America is so laid back it makes your average hippie commune look like a military base. America is the self-professed land of the free, an idea embraced by the schools with so much enthusiasm it's actually a bit worrying. Teachers encourage individuality above all else, and treat you with an odd mixture of respect and excessive sincerity. In many schools discipline is largely confined to confiscating handguns and switchblades at the front gates. By comparison, a medieval Catholic concentration camp in England was way off the scale for weirdness.

My parents chose the school not because we're staunch Catholics (we're not staunch anything), but because Mother Superior Cottingham a.k.a. Obergruppenführer was open to the idea of me being taken in and out of school as and when my father's travels demanded. I suspect she was also open to the idea of being paid huge tuition fees even when I wasn't there. The Catholic Church has a well-deserved reputation for looking after its money.

I suppose I did approach the school with this rather negative attitude from the outset. When we lived in Bogotá, Colombia, a year or so before, you could see the city slums from the Hilton Hotel. At the edge of this shantytown was a Catholic church, with walled-off grounds that I could look into from my bedroom window. Even as a child I was shocked by the contrast between the affluence of the priest, who was quite often seen driving around in a Mercedes, and the poverty of the children who scrambled over mounds of rubbish in search of food right next to the church's wall. It wasn't so much the wealth that upset me, but rather the gross hypocrisy of it all. And it was with this residual mistrust of the Church that I entered the convent. On top of this, the culture shock − even for a seasoned traveller like myself − was profound.

For starters, I had to wear a uniform. The only people you see wearing uniforms in America are policemen, burger chain employees and mad loons who run survivalist camps in Utah. Even though I thought it was completely freaky, it was a novelty, so I just went with the flow.

On my first day I was driven to school and dropped at the front gates wearing the uniform: a smart navy blazer; sensible blouse, skirt, and shoes; and a beret. We were running a bit late that morning, so I leapt out of the car, dashed through the gates stuffing my hat in my bag, and legged it for the main hall where assembly was about to start. Unfortunately, my arrival had been watched by Ms Cottingham, who had a habit* of spying on 'her girls' from behind the heavy grey curtains of her

---

* Ha ha.

office window. I made it to the hall just in time, and slipped unobtrusively into a seat about halfway from the back. Little did I know I was about to be introduced to the entire school in a quite spectacular fashion.

Mother Superior and her entourage of 200-year-old, bearded, fumey, gusseted nuns swept into the hall and took their seats at the front. After we'd sung the first hymn, we took our seats. Ms Cottingham then stood up, all wimple and whiskers, to make her daily address to the school.

'Before I begin,' she barked, like a papal drill sergeant, 'I would like to take this opportunity to remind everyone of the rules concerning school uniform. I'm particularly referring to hats which, as you know, are to be worn at *all* times outside the main building, and not removed until the moment you step through the front door.' From her vantage point on the stage she paused and scanned the rows of upturned faces. Eventually our eyes met and she fixed me with a thermonuclear stare. I felt small holes burning in the back of my head.

'That especially applies to *dirty little dagos*.'

Holy Guacamole. Welcome to England.

There are only two truly miserable episodes in my life: when Kenny died in 1995, and when my father died unexpectedly during the writing of this book. But if I were to choose another, my time at Stalag Catholic would come a very close third. In a school where conformity and obedience ruled above all else, I was tailor-made for victimisation. For a start, my background – exotic and interesting in my eyes – was considered a dangerous and subversive influence on all those nice Catholic girls. To make matters worse, I was a very early developer (things kicked off when I was nine!). So, by the time I was twelve, I had all the bumpy curvy bits I've got today. In an environment of complete and utter paranoid sexual repression, the nuns figured I was Satan's disciple, sent to test their mettle with my strange foreign ways and overflowing particles.

Quite often their attempts to be unpleasant simply sailed over my head. After my introduction to the school, all the teachers and children called me 'Dago', but I was oblivious to the small-mindedness because I didn't know what it actually meant. I had a vague notion that it was something to do with polka dots, and therefore thought it some oblique compliment. It didn't take very long for me to realise I was quite wrong.

Yet despite the fact that the nuns devised other, more creative torture methods, each punishment I received simply drove me on to make more and more trouble. It was never serious trouble though, just fruity, jolly trouble. Nevertheless, although it was a game, there was plenty of mutual mistrust. The nuns thought I was odd, and I found them disturbing and scary.

On one such occasion I sneaked up behind Sister Scatological, who was sitting next to a cupboard knitting a bizarre undergarment out of horsehair. I quietly closed the cupboard door so it trapped her veil, and then kicked her ball of horsehair across the floor. As she rose to retrieve the ball, her headgear came off, revealing a highly unattractive, sweaty, stenchy arrangement of tufty grey hairs. She was a miserable old bag, and deserved some kind of prank, if only as punishment for the dreadful way she stank. When she walked, the swinging of her arms would audibly crunch the crystallised salt stains under her armpits. Furthermore, she always left a faint whiff of stale urine behind her in the corridors. Seeing her scrabble about like a penguin on acid was all very gratifying.

They used to fine us a penny for any contravention of the military-style uniform: incorrectly wearing the stupid beret, failing to keep ones socks up ones legs, not wearing regulation knickers – that sort of thing. To give you an idea of how much trouble I got into, by the end of the first term my fines amounted to nine pounds and thirteen pence – that's 913 fines in three months. I'd single-handedly created a mini-economic boom. The Sisterhood SS – strange, eerie women in medieval Darth Vader outfits, who were the evil Empire's eyes and ears – implemented these fines with ruthless vigour. Alarmingly, their surveillance duties also extended to spying on us when we were naked in the showers. What contraventions of the school uniform rules they expected to find there was quite beyond me.

Showers were always disturbing events. We only had freezing water, and as we washed the Sisterhood would pull back the curtains one by one to 'make sure we were washing properly'.

Certain girls would be inspected for some time. However, they never saw me naked. I found the whole idea of being watched so creepy, I kept my underwear on in the shower – despite their orders and the additional discomfort of having to spend the rest of the day in a uniform with wet underclothes.

I had a great fight in the dressing rooms once. One day a whole group of hyper-religious, guitar-strumming, folk-singing, bible-bashing bints started to close in on me as I was changing. The girls in this group were all pseudo-prefects, but they behaved like legalised thugs, seeing themselves as a sort of Catholic Ku Klux Klan. The nuns turned a blind eye when these girls beat up anyone, as it was felt they were carrying out the Lord's work. If the Lord's work was bullying and mental torture, then this lot were on double overtime, with a company car, subsidised mortgage and staff canteen.

They were all ugly, thickset, and looked like failed boys. I think two of them actually were. Apparently they had a lesson to teach me (not algebra, thinks I). So they gathered around me with all the menace they could muster. The head of this charming little group had a big gaping mouth with flappy lips, bell-bottomed teeth and halitosis – and that was the good news. She was excellent trainee-sister material. The other three girls grabbed me and held me against a wall as their bovine leader made the error of slapping my face.

Big mistake. If you're going to pick a fight with someone, it's best not to start on a girl who's got four huge brothers, and has been in a fight more times than Michael Jackson's seen his plastic surgeon. Not only that, but I'd once met Mohammed Ali in New York, (when I was eight), and had asked him how to fight back against my siblings. He said 'punch first, punch hard, punch straight.' I couldn't have been better prepared.

I struggled free and dealt with Slapper first, by means of a satisfying right hook, then set about the rest of them. It all got very messy, and I was so pumped up to the eyeballs with adrenaline and righteous anger that I must have scared them quite considerably, because they went scuttling away to try to find a teacher to rescue them. They found the RE teacher I'd dubbed Old Rubber Dinghy Legs, but the evidence was so overwhelmingly in my favour that, alas, she was powerless to condone their attack. They didn't bother me again.

Things hit a real low after I committed some minor misdemeanour in Sister Sadist's geography lesson and got a rap on the knuckles. But of course this was no ordinary rap on the knuckles. It was a Spanish Inquisition rap on the knuckles. She'd caught me committing some hideous crime during class: I can't remember what it was exactly, but it probably involved something heinous like breathing, blinking, or simply existing in the same universe. Actually, now I think about it, I had thrown my boater out the window to see if it would fly like a Frisbee (a valuable exercise in the practical application of aeronautics I'd have thought). She called me to the front and grabbed my hand.

'Achtung Rocos! You vill behave. God vill not put up with zis any longer!'*

Her wimple suddenly reminded me of a Gestapo uniform and I could see her whirling dervish moustache twitching madly. She grabbed a plastic ruler from her desk and made me extend my clenched fist. Then she hit my knuckles. But not with the flat side of the ruler – with the edge. The sharp, pointy, painful edge. And she continued to hit me for some considerable time, and with obvious gusto. I tried not to flinch, but it really did hurt.

By the time I got home that night, my hand and arm had swollen up so much that I had to cut open the sleeve of my blazer so that I could take it off. I told my mother I'd caught it on a fence, and hid my hand from her. A few months later I committed a crime too far, and the school told me to leave (horray!).

It was Christmas, and we'd been asked to think carefully about what we intended to buy for our form nuns, and to ensure our gifts were useful and not frivolous. I had given it a lot of thought, and, shortly after the ruler incident, decided on my present for our form nun, who, even by hairy-nun standards, had the kind of chin growth you usually only see in ZZ Top videos.

---

* She probably didn't say it like that, but that's how I remember it.

I bought her a pack of disposable bic razors.

As far as the nuns were concerned, it was the final straw. Although it wasn't planned that way, I'd earned my parole for Christmas by getting myself chucked out. That afternoon I took my ruined school blazer, beret and tie to the corner of the convent playing fields, and, with a can of lighter fluid and box of matches, ceremonially burnt them. The fire gave off thick wads of black smoke and made a terrible stench, but watching the flames melt the hated uniform made me feel a whole lot better.

Freedom!

We were now living in Kensington, and playing a favourite game in the Rocos household: Finding a New School for Cleo and her Brothers. Having had such a horrific time at the convent, I was adamant that my mother put me in a normal school: an unclenchy-buttocked place that didn't come straight out of a Roger Corman film. Nothing in the way of being private, nothing that was primly single sex and nothing that had teachers in penguin costumes. She tried her hardest to get me into the Lycée, but there were no places available. So the only option open to us was the local comprehensive – in my view anyway.

My mother was mortified, and tried her hardest to persuade me to go to a nice private school, but I had the wind in my sails and was insistent I go somewhere normal. And what could be more normal than a comprehensive? Okay, so the children still had to wear a uniform of a sort, but it was nothing like the convent. We locked horns for a while, but eventually she gave in. I got to go to Marylebone Comprehensive.

Talk about jumping from the frying pan into the fire. I couldn't believe that these two schools existed in the same universe, let alone planet, country and city. I had never, ever been to a school where it was common practice for first year students to tell the headmaster to fuck off. Every day was like an episode of *The Sweeney*: fights, foul language and bad haircuts. It was unruly in the extreme and a true case of only the fittest surviving.

When I arrived, I was, as usual, the outsider. Everyone else had established their cliques and circles of friends. They were an earthy bunch, and it took them about two minutes to label me 'Posh Cow' and start the schoolgirl ritual of spitting on your head at all opportunities. They'd forgotten, of course, that I'd just escaped from a top-security Papal Penal Institute and their attempts at intimidation were merely mildly endearing.

When you've changed schools as many times as I have, you get to know all the possible outcomes. This time it was that old favourite, storyline number four: Girl Goes To New School, Girl Accidentally Makes Enemy Of Gang Leader, Gang Leader Bullies Girl, Girl Stands Up For Herself, Gang Leader Fights Girl, Girl Earns Respect, Gang Leader And Girl End Up Friends. Actually, we didn't end up friends, but after a few fisticuffs where I showed I could look after myself, I was grudgingly accepted.

I didn't learn much at Marylebone, but I honed my survival skills and learnt some valuable lessons about friendship and fitting in. In fact, it was the only school I've ever been to where – when I left – some of the girls actually cried as I said goodbye. This meant more to me than anything, especially since they weren't really given to being soft or overly sentimental.

I don't know what it is about me, but I seem to have been born with a Loony Magnet in the back of my head or something. I attract them like train-spotters around Crewe Station. There was one teacher at Marylebone who was a Class 'A' Certified Bongo, and sure enough he latched on to me within about a week of my arrival at the school. He was a round, chubby fellow in his mid-forties who sported a waft of bright red hair. Initially he just used to follow me around during the lunch hour, suspiciously diving into corners and hiding behind textbooks if I turned around to look at him. But then he got braver, and actually started chasing me from room to room. In a school where kids were routinely chased for setting fire to the rubbish bin, or a little light lynching, this hardly raised an eyebrow. The alarm still wasn't raised when he cornered me in the art room once and started clambering over the desk, his tongue lolling out of his mouth. He looked like a deranged bloodhound. I managed to escape and went straight to the headmistress. I asked if this was normal behaviour and would if it be possible for her to ask him to stop chasing me. She told me to stop being so silly, and to get out of her office immediately. So I began concocting a fiendish plan for revenge.

In class, later that week, the troublesome teacher handed me a glass and ordered me to go to the lavatory to get him a drink of water. Which is exactly what I did. I bypassed both the sink and the drinking tap, and filled the cup from the toilet bowl. When I came back, I handed him the cup, watched him drink it in front of the class, and then calmly told him where the water came from. He went an odd shade of green, which clashed with his hair, but said nothing. He never chased me again.

My time at Marylebone was tough, but it wasn't scary like it was in the convent. I have strangely fond memories of my time there, especially since it was during my days at Marylebone that I discovered my future. In an unexpected Damascene revelation, I stumbled across film cameras.

For the first time in thirteen years I knew exactly what I wanted to do.

Near the end of the Easter holidays, when I'd been at Marylebone for about three months, my mother, younger brother and I were walking along Marloes Road in Kensington on the way to do some shopping (my Mother) and eat burgers (us). We rounded a corner and suddenly found ourselves surrounded by the most amazing sight. The road had been closed off and a wall of intensely bright, blueish lights had been set up to illuminate a nearby building. There was a set of small railway tracks on the road, along which a gang of men pushed a platform that supported a huge film camera. The rest of the street was filled with trucks and scaffolding, and the pavements were smothered in leads and cables. It bustled with people all wearing baseball caps and carrying props, clipboards and cups of coffee from a nearby catering van. It was a completely magical sight, and I was riveted to the spot. I knew instantly, there and then, and without the tiniest shadow of a doubt, that I wanted to work in film. This was it. I suddenly knew with total conviction what I was going to spend the rest of my life doing.

My brother soon got bored, and my mother had to physically drag me away so she could go shopping. I can't remember where we went – my mind was in a daze. All I could think about was the film set. I begged and nagged my mother to let us go back, and on our return – since it was just around the corner from where we lived – I insisted she abandon me there so I could talk to some of the crew.

Once alone, I wandered around the set, picking up as much information as I could. It turned out they were filming scenes for a movie called *The Squeeze*, starring Stacy Keach and Freddie Starr, and for the first time in my life I developed a voracious appetite for information. I wanted to know about everything: the cameras, lights, scripts, actors, set-designers – even the catering vans. I eventually befriended a woman who worked in the production office, and she gave me her telephone number. I persuaded her to let me ring her at the office in the morning to find out where they were filming that day (the location turned out to be Iffley Road in Hammersmith). I couldn't have been happier.

It was getting late, so I reluctantly went home, my heart pounding with the sheer exhilarating thrill of seeing a film being made. I hardly slept a wink that night, and was up at the crack of dawn, ready to make my phone call. True to her word, the woman in the office gave me the address of the location for that afternoon's shoot, and asked me if I wanted to come along and watch.

I was spellbound the entire day. I was introduced to Freddie Starr, who told me slightly naughty jokes and made me laugh, as well as taking a sincere interest in my ambitions. He also introduced me to his stunt man, who told me about the Corona Stage School. He said this was a perfect place to go if you were a young person wanting to get into theatre or film-making.

Real school started the following week, but its appeal was microscopic compared to this newly discovered magicky world. So I hatched another fiendish plan. I would pretend to leave the country.

On my first day back I went to see my new form teacher. I

told him that we would be leaving England on Thursday, as my father's business was taking us to America for a short while. It was all very rushed, but my parents would be dropping by in the next day or so to make all the necessary arrangements and sign the paperwork. He accepted this without so much as a shrug, so I walked straight back out of the school again. It says a lot about the school's chaotic running that no one bothered to check my story. They effectively rubber-stamped my truancy, leaving me free to do what I had to do!

I ran to a phone box just around the corner from the school and telephoned the production office to find out where they were filming. Then it was a short trip to McDonald's, where I went to the lavatories and changed out of my school uniform and into the spare clothes I'd brought along in my bag. What an adventure!

Within an hour of leaving school, I was standing in a park, surrounded by film makers, watching agog as the production unfolded before me. It was heaven.

And it stayed heaven for nine weeks. Every morning I would leave home for school in my uniform, ring from the phone box at the end of our road, go to McDonald's to change, and then turn up on location. I became a regular member of the crew – I knew everybody, and everybody knew me. They would invite me to location lunches on the double-decker bus, and gladly answer the trillion questions I had. From producers to make-up girls, each and every one of them was kind, friendly and unpatronising. As the days passed and I learnt more and more, my passion burned brighter and my conviction grew. I knew I was somehow destined for this. For the first time in my life I felt it might be all right being me after all.

When the filming finished I was heartbroken, but I knew that if I was to ever get involved in this work again, I'd need to make it happen myself. (When I want, I can apply myself mercilesssly. Take for example when I took up skateboarding and threw myself into it so much I secured a place on the US female world team, 'The Alleycats'.) I learnt all I could about Corona, even to the extent of obtaining a prospectus, and was determined to earn a place at the school. Armed with the brochure, I told my mother what I'd been up to the last few weeks.

She was not happy, to say the least. I'd been leading a very Secret Squirrel sort of life over the last couple of months, and she was hurt more by the deceit than anything else. But her disappointment was tempered by seeing me so excited about a career (actually excited about anything), so we reached a compromise.

I would return to Marylebone for the rest of the summer term, and, in return, she would enrol me at Corona for the autumn. I was on my way, and in two short years I would be in a mock photo booth, entwined in a knot of limbs with Bob Geldof.

If I'd made it up, no one would have believed me.

3 Two Go Mad in Medialand

A S KENNY HAD PREDICTED AT CHRISTMAS, I did get invited back. BBC Productions rang me in February and offered me contracts for a number of appearances on the show. I wasn't quite ready to leave Corona yet though – I'd learned so much while I was there that I knew I'd be missing out on lots of important stuff if I chucked it in then. So I negotiated to stay at the school throughout the filming of the first half of the series and to have time off as I needed it. I was now one of the older girls at Corona, and didn't need a chaperone anymore. In fact, I was actually considered one of the more responsible pupils (how things had changed), and I quite often acted as chaperone to some of the very young pupils when they had auditions.

On my first day filming the new series, everyone welcomed me back with great warmth. Kenny and I kept catching each other's eye and smiling, I knew that my interpretation of our first meeting wasn't a figment of my imagination. I was relieved and excited. I was also pleased to be working with Ray and Barry again.

Barry Cryer and Ray Cameron were Kenny's trusted lieutenants. The three of them made up an untouchably talented trio that were the power behind the show – the team that had created the show's original format on Thames. Barry Cryer and Kenny had been friends for a long time, and Barry is one those perennial showbiz greats whose expertise always rises to the surface, no matter who he's writing for or to whom he's performing. He's a comedy Moses, a high priest of great gags whose prolific output has been the backbone of many a comedian's show. It says a lot about his standing in the world of light entertainment that, when Channel 4 recently ran a show-case for new stand-ups, instead of choosing a comedic young gun as compere, they gave the job to Barry. He wiped the floor with most of the acts and earned himself a new generation of fans.

When he's away from the crowds and cameras, Barry is a genial, avuncular man with an inquisitive intelligence and a fantastic sense of humour that shoots from the hip. He never misses. He churned out hundreds and hundreds of sketches for the show, and on many occasions made them up with us as he went along.

If you go and see a sketch programme being made these days, you'll probably watch a well-organised production that makes the best use of the studio and the comedians' time. If someone is dressed up as a regular character, the production team arranges it so that a large number of that character's sketches are filmed in one go. It makes perfect sense; otherwise, all the actors spend their time sitting in make-up doing endless costume changes.

We spent all our time sitting in make-up doing endless costume changes. It was chaos. Kenny would be dressed up as the City gent in ladies underwear, and Barry would suddenly come up with an idea for another sketch. They'd write the sketch out on the back of a cigarette packet and then dash off and film it. Or they'd have a living room set made up and then write a sketch in a mad panic before the props people came and took the sofa away. No flat, ink-absorbing surface is safe in Barry's presence – he's continually scribbling down ideas and jokes in a flurry of cigarette packets, train tickets and ten-pound notes. If you ever happen to be lucky enough to have dinner with him, put a huge paper tablecloth down and give him a pen. He'll keep himself happy all night, and you'll prob-ably end up with enough jokes and sketches to start a series of your own.

The only reason the show didn't degenerate into complete pandemonium was the late Ray Cameron, Barry's writing partner. Ray's sheer physical presence and bloody-mindedness kept the whole loony bin in business.

Ray was very good-looking man, a Canadian who, like Barry,

had a background in stand-up comedy. He was one of the funniest people I've ever met, made all the more impressive by his enormous size (he was around six foot four), and the fact that he was built like the QE2.* He also had the loudest, most infectious laugh on the planet – you could be sitting in the canteen having your lunch and hear Ray guffawing two studios away. He laughed like Christmas: big and cheery.

The chemistry between Kenny, Ray and Barry was wonderful to watch. They all played off each other's talents and created a whole that was bigger than the sum of their parts. Kenny relied on Barry's surreal inventiveness and ability to craft good old-fashioned punchlines, while Ray, who wrote many of the sketches with Barry, provided uncannily good judgment on whether a joke was funny or not. In that first series, when they really did push back the boundaries of the humour, Kenny and Barry relied enormously on Ray's bullish gusto with the BBC. He was very American in his approach and simply didn't take no for an answer. We all loved Ray, and when he died a few years ago from a massive cardiac arrest, I was deeply upset. His passing was a loss to us all.

Ray was passionate about the show, and fought hard to make it what it was. He once wrote a sketch involving a guest star (and no, I'm not going to tell you), who during rehearsals turned to Ray and, not realising Ray had written it, complained that he didn't understand the joke. In fact, he was pretty sure there wasn't a joke, and that the sketch simply wasn't funny. Ray put up with about three seconds of this whining and then grabbed the guest by the lapels of his jacket, seemingly lifting him up like a Tom and Jerry cartoon character.

'Actually,' growled Ray, 'I think you'll find the joke *is* funny. It's you who's not funny, all right?'

Kenny, Barry and I stood on the sidelines sniggering with embarrassment, like naughty school children watching a class-mate getting told off for breaking wind in assembly.

Barry was much gentler than Ray, and would walk you through a sketch with a chortling humility that made you just

---

* Except he didn't float, and no one played deck quoits on his head.

want to hug him. Ray, on the other hand, was like a comedy tornado – he'd sweep into the studio and say:

'You stand here, say your lines, turn to Kenny, punchline and . . . woof! – big laugh!' He'd throw his arms in the air and roar with laughter. 'Do you get it?' he'd ask, walking away and not expecting a reply.

Here's a bit of Kenny trivia for you. Do you remember when the show first came on ITV that one of its innovative features was the off-camera laughter that accompanied the sketches and Kenny's monologues?* Well when the show moved to the BBC, the powers that be decreed that off-camera laughter was decidedly un-BBC, and they banned the cameramen from making so much as a titter during recording. Ray took this very badly, and decided, in extremely un-BBC terms, that they could 'go fuck themselves.' Since he was pretty well untouchable, he took the law into his own hands, and for the first two series every roar of appreciative laughter you hear was actually Ray and Barry making enough noise to mask the all-too-obvious cameramen's silence.

On my first day filming the new series, I was shown to a dressing room and there, hanging on the costume rail, was a wonderful display of expensive-looking underwear: frilly knickers, lacy suspenders and matching bras. I was overcome with gratitude for my lovely new BBC bosses. How good of them to buy me all this expensive stuff! I thought it was quite touching. One of the costume girls came into the room and I told her how pleased I was that they'd gone to all the bother of buying me such pretty undergarments, especially since no one was ever going to see them. She gave me a blank look. So I reiterated my gratitude, and watched as an expression of cautious shock slowly crept over her face.

'Ah, the thing is Cleo, that isn't actually your underwear. You see, erm, it's your costume.'

'My *costume*?'

---

* I'm probably going to get loads of letters from television trivia anoraks the world over telling me that off-camera laughter was actually first seen in 1977s hit comedy show *Shut It! I'm A Copper*.

'Well, yes, it's sort of . . . what you're wearing. The only thing you'll be wearing.' She handed me a script.

'I think you'd better read this.'

She hurried out the room, obviously afraid I was going to throw a tantrum or something.

I didn't care. I've always been aware that my shape attracts attention from men, but I've never seen myself as sexual in any way. I'm a bit of a tomboy inside, and have always thought of my bumps and bits in a very cartoony sort of way. I spent a great deal of my time in underwear on the show, but to me, Kenny, and the rest of the team, it was comedy underwear, a costume like any other, and nothing to be sniggery or uncomfortable about. And even as I became well-known, and people pigeon-holed me as Miss Whiplash I was never really concerned or upset about it. I can't imagine Barry Manilow getting touchy about nose jokes. People take sexual matters far too seriously in my book. If you can laugh at yourself, and if you're at ease with your body, then quite frankly I think humour is much sexier than underwear.

The filming started immediately, and Kenny and I began to spend time talking to each other during takes, on anything and everything from cooking to skateboarding (but never, funnily enough, television). We'd catch each other's eye and exchange thoughts like naughty classmates, and over the years this ability to read each other's face and inflections became so acute it was almost telepathic. This mutual understanding was evident from the very beginning, and within a matter of days it was decided that I would be the more prominent of the four girls on the show. This was largely because I'm quite funny and Kenny felt relaxed in my company, throwing himself into the sketches we shared with more silliness.

Lunchtime was the best. The four of us – Ray, Barry, Kenny and I – would often eat together in the BBC restaurant. One particular lunch break we were in the restaurant being served by our regular waitress who, though very pleasant and friendly, would not have died from sweet-smelling armpits or raging beauty. She sported a mouthful of crunkled brown teeth, hairy moles on her face and was propelled on a cloud of stench. Whenever she served food to the table, you had to hold your breath and wait for the air to clear. Eating posed something of a challenge if she was anywhere nearby.

One time Kenny started wickedly teasing Barry, daring him to ask her for a kiss. Barry understandably declined, but after a lot of taunting, and the additional incentive of a ten pound bet, he took up the dare.

'A tenner, eh?' he said. 'Watch this.' Kenny laughingly accused Barry of unashamedly doing anything for a few pounds but, when the waitress returned to our table, Barry chivalrously asked her if she would grant him the honour of a small kiss. She was thrilled, and blushing her way back to a moment of youth, obliged Barry his request. We didn't take our eyes off him as he drew a huge lungful of air before proceeding. Kenny looked on in total horror and disbelief, his jaw clanking around his ankles and his eyes dangling in his soup.

After the waitress walked away Barry turned to Kenny with a Cheshire-cat-sized smile on his chops, and, beaming boyishly with his hand extended said:

'I believe you owe me ten pounds old chap.' Kenny, having reeled in his eyeballs from the soup, declared he had no cash on him and asked if Barry would accept a cheque. Barry was feeling very conquistadory, and, as the waitress floated by with her new found sex appeal, winking towards our table, Barry glowed with good deedness and agreed. Kenny produced a cheque book and with one mighty flourish of his fountain pen wrote a cheque and signed it with great extravagance. Barry plucked the cheque from Kenny's hand, between his thumb and forefinger, and made a great show of wafting it through the air and blowing the ink dry.

'I believe this is mine,' he declared and proudly began to read it out loud to us all.

'Pay Mr Barry Cryer The Sum Of Ten Fucking Pounds Only . . . What? *What*?' he spluttered indignantly. 'I can't pay this into my bank!'

'Why not?' enquired Kenny, shrugging his shoulders. 'My cheques are good. The money's aaallll yours. You earned every penny.'

'But . . . but . . .' Barry tried to protest, but we were all laughing so hard he couldn't get a word in. He gave up, folded the cheque and put it in his shirt pocket.

He never did cash it.

The day I nearly killed Billy Connolly proved to be one occasion my age very nearly got me into big trouble. I was about to get dressed up in a saucy chauffeuse's uniform for rehearsals – all peaked cap and pointy bra – when Ray bounded into view and asked if I could drive.

'Yes,' I replied, in a flutter of mild panic. 'I can drive.'

This was technically the truth, since my brother had taken me out in his car for a run around some deserted country lanes over Christmas. If 'driving' meant bunny-hopping, stalling, and weaving erratically, then I was Queen of the Road. I didn't have a licence of course, as I was only sixteen, but I couldn't possibly admit this for fear of discovery.

Ray took me outside and showed me this huge red convertible Mustang and explained the sketch. Billy Connolly would be sitting at a table on set, having a conversation with another guest star as the build-up to the gag. Then I would drive the car into the studio, with Kenny sitting up on the top of the seat beside me, and stop right next to the table. Kenny would leap out of the car and deliver the punchline. I looked at the car and gulped.

'Listen Clee, I know this car is probably a bit bigger than you're used to,' said Ray, 'so we'll take you out for a practice spin and you can get used to driving it. It's a bit heavy to handle and the clutch is quite hard work, but ten minutes behind the wheel and you'll be fine.'

Ten minutes behind the wheel? I was about to increase my driving experience by 200 per cent. But I wasn't overly stressed. The BBC building is a huge circular thing with a road that runs around the perimeter. I figured I'd just have to drive the car around in circles for a while without having to worry about things like traffic lights, other cars, or the laws of the highway. Ray then called over the man whose car it was (it had been hired from an automotive props specialist) and one of the floor managers.

'Right boys, take Cleo out in the car so she can get used to it. A couple of times around Shepherd's Bush Green should do it.'

Shepherd's Bush Green. Oh my God. If you've ever been to Shepherd's Bush, just down Wood Lane from the BBC, you'll know what I'm talking about. It's one of those London traffic junctions that strikes fear into drivers the city over. Cars come at you from every direction and you have to hurtle around it like some demented Ben Hur, or get squished between the convoys of homicidal buses and sociopathic lorry drivers.

How I made it around that roundabout without killing us all is a mystery to me even now. It was terrifying. Fear concentrates the mind incredibly, and I think I burned up two months' brain-power in fifteen minutes. What if I crashed? There would be an insurance claim, they'd then find out I didn't have a licence, the insurance would be invalid, they'd find out how old I was, and I'd get the sack. The consequences of any screw up were quite enormous.

Fifteen minutes later we drove back through the gates at the BBC and I collapsed. Luckily I was sitting in the driver's seat so no one noticed. I'd made it! No damage to the car, and my secret was still safe. Now all I had to do was get the sketch over and done with. I took the car into the studio and practised the run up to the table a couple of times. It all seemed very simple, and the only thing I had to do was avoid the props people who were still constructing the set.

That evening, when the audience had filled the studio and we were ready to start filming, I changed into the chauffeuse's outfit and Kenny and I went outside and sat in the car. We got the wave from the floor manager and I drove into the studio through the double doors. Only I was a bit excited (audiences do that to you) and drove slightly too fast. As I neared the table, I could see Billy looking out the corner of his eye with increasing alarm. I realised I might not stop in time, so I slammed on the brakes.

Kenny flew past me and folded over the windscreen with an unpleasant combination of squelch and thump. The car continued going forward far too fast, largely because, since the practice run, a rug had been put on the floor and the car was now skidding on it. In a flash Billy leapt out of the way crying:

'Fookinheelthatfookincarsgoonakillme.'

The car slid to a halt an inch from his chair.

There was a stunned silence, and then, once everyone realised there were no injuries, the audience and crew burst out laughing. Kenny peeled himself off the bonnet and gave me a look of pure thrill. Billy picked himself off the floor and gave me a look of pure menace.

Like many entertainers, Kenny was appalling at remembering his lines. On the radio he could lay out his scripts and not have to worry about it, but on television you can't really get away with doing sketches with a clipboard in your hand. It became such a problem that we eventually used to write the lines out on big pieces of paper and Sellotape them on to the backs of doors, inside drawers, underneath hats – whatever it was that Kenny was supposed to be using or looking at in the sketch. Barry and Ray would often write sketches with plenty of 'prop-interaction' in them so that Kenny would have an excuse to open a telephone directory and check what his next cue was. We often ended up with hilarious Burrough-sesque results when Kenny would look at the lines on the props in the wrong order and the sketch would come out all jumbled and nonsensical.

The BBC also had the bad-language police who used to try to intimidate Ray and Barry on set. Actually it was hardly intimidation. The bad-language police consisted of a little man in a grey suit who would stand at the back of the studio like some officious school inspector and make sure we all said 'bum' instead of 'arse', and 'naughty bits' instead of 'genitals'. He was very Uriah Heap, a sallow weasly fellow who probably got home at night and swore like a trooper.

Looking back on any relationship you've had, you can see precise points where things change and move forward. For Kenny and I, our companionship moved forward like my driving: steadily, but with the occasional burst of acceleration. The first time we put the pedal to the floor was when Kenny came down with the flu during filming.

He'd come in one morning looking a bit rough but as the day progressed it became obvious he was harbouring some dreadful bacterial horror. He had a fever, headache, runny nose and all the other classic symptoms of something you should be in bed with. So the production team packed him in a cab and sent him home to make himself better.

Ray phoned Kenny and told him that he'd asked me to bring round some chicken soup, paracetamol, etc. How many men do you know who make themselves better when they're sick? None of course – they can't do it. They need their mum, or a mum substitute, to spoil them by running around making them soup and hot drinks, and filling them with pills. Poor noodles.

So when I finished filming, I too leapt in a cab and went home, stopping off to buy the essential supplies on the way. When I got to Kenny's new flat (he'd moved in the weekend before), I rang his intercom and, slightly nervous that he might think I was intruding (I still called him Mr Everett), announced myself. His little croaky voice went all excited when he heard it was me, and the door buzzed open. I dashed upstairs and he let me in: all sweaty and flu-ridden in a T-shirt and shorts.

In his flat, I went to the cupboard to see what he had and was astonished to discover that in his entire kitchen he had three items: a bag of jellybeans and two bottles of champagne. He'd been living there about a week and hadn't bought a single thing. No milk, no bread, no paracetamol.

Luckily, I'm not a man, so I know exactly what you need when you're sick: Chivas Regal.

Forget Lemsip; nothing takes your mind off the flu better than a raging hangover. We spent the evening mixing increasingly ferocious champagne and Chivas cocktails, while Kenny put on some bongly tunes and talked me through a medley of his favourite acid trips. It was a great day, a break from the formalities of the studio and a chance to really get to know each other. There's nothing like getting drunkipoos when you want to make good friends.

That year, 1982, was a very special one for Kenny. In the space of a few short months he agreed his divorce, started the new series on BBC, and bought his flat in Lexham Gardens. It was a fresh start for him, a chance to wipe the slate clean and create a new life away from the misery of an unhappy marriage, and to throw himself into a career that was going truly stratospheric.

The divorce, the new beginning and the move to Lexham Gardens, proved to be a time of pure liberation. He freed himself from the constraints of compromise and stopped living his life to make other people happy.

The root of much of his unhappiness was his sexuality. Kenny never really came to terms with being gay, and he always felt that he was somehow letting people down by not being heterosexual. His Catholic upbringing had a large part to play in this; most Catholics are brought up to struggle under a mountain of self-made guilt, but for Kenny the mountain was always that bit larger. And on top of this, he loved women. He was a gentleman, and lavished attention on girls in a charismatic Cary Grantular fashion. He adored my mother. He called her Mrs C. (i.e. Mrs Cleo) and would send her tapes he'd made with frilly bits of classical music on them. For him, there was a beautiful and natural symmetry in relationships between men and women, and he was wistfully envious of straight couples who had successful relationships. He also loved children. In later years would often tell me that he would love to have a child, and that if it was a boy, he'd like to call him Max. He would say that he thought I'd make the best mother in the world. Sometimes I could see the torment in his eyes so I would joke and suggest we go to the baby department at Harrods and buy one. He'd laugh and call me a demented banana.

But despite all of this – the sense that he'd failed his family and his ex-wife by not trying hard enough, and the extent to which it haunted him – he simply wasn't cut out to be heterosexual. And like many gay men of his generation who'd entered into marriage in the hope it would 'straighten them out', this ploy clearly hadn't worked. Instead it merely reinforced his feelings of failure. But the imminent divorce and move to his own flat was to prove vital for him because he was no longer under any pressure to try to be something he wasn't.

Of course, I hardly knew Kenny then, and had little idea of the extent of the change that had overcome him. But friends who'd known him for years would later comment that 1982 was the year Kenny started to blossom. Living your life for the benefit of others is tiring and unrewarding, and for Kenny the burden had finally been lifted from his shoulders.

Maybe it was this new found freedom that gave the first series of the BBC *Kenny Everett Show* such creativity and cheerfulness, as Kenny threw himself into his work with zapping energy and enthusiasm. There was a special feeling of magic about the show that spring, and we all felt it.

The chemistry between Kenny and I was obvious for all to see, and Barry and Ray did everything they could to encourage it. Ray especially thought that it would be in everyone's best interest if Kenny and I developed a romantic liaison. So, only a few weeks into filming the first series he started writing more and more bed scenes for us (and by that I mean Rock Hudson and Doris Day in *Pillow Talk*, rather than anything saucy). Perhaps he thought he was doing the right thing by putting Kenny into pseudo-sexual encounters in the hope that it might ignite his latent heterosexuality, but of course it never came to anything. Even so, Ray and Barry would continually tell me how much Kenny liked me, something Kenny was incapable of doing because of his painful shyness.

It's difficult for people to understand how someone like Kenny, who to the viewing public seemed about as brash and upfront as you can imagine, could in any way be shy. But ask anyone who ever knew Kenny beyond the surficular showbiz party circuit and you'd hear the same story time and time again: Kenny was crippled by low self-esteem and a fear of rejection. The net result was that he was always doubting his success and avoiding situations where he might fail or be rejected. This was especially evident in his personal life, where he rarely, if ever, declared his feelings for other people, fearing that these feelings might not be reciprocated.

A perfect illustration of how this manifested itself was the holiday he 'invited' me on after the filming of the first series. He'd booked a three-week trip to Peter Island in the Virgin Islands with some friends, and was due to leave about a week after we finished the show. As we got nearer and nearer to the time, he started saying how happy he would be if he was walking along the beach and I popped out from behind a palm tree with a big fruity cocktail. He'd describe the islands in terrific detail, telling me how much I'd love the scenery and the people. He then started leaving the brochure lying around with the name of his hotel ringed in red. He even wrote the number of the travel agents on a piece of paper and tucked it under the rim of the mirror in my changing room, with the booking reference and holiday dates carefully noted on it.

But he never asked me directly if I wanted to come. He was so concerned that I might say no, he went to extraordinary lengths to invite me without actually putting himself in a situation where he could face rejection. And because I was still very young, and with too many manners, I never asked him if he was trying to ask me to go. All this only came out years later, but at the time I couldn't work out how we could be so close in some ways, and yet very distant in others. We drew the outline of our friendship in great detail within months of knowing each other, but it took fifteen years to colour it in.

As it was, Kenny came back from the holiday after only a week. I think for Kenny the anticipation of going somewhere was more fun than actually being there. Take the case of his trip to Australia. Kenny's relationship with his family had always been tumultuous, and one day he decided, on a whim, to go to visit his sister, Kate, in Australia as a surprise. So he packed his bags and jumped on a plane to Perth. Thirty-odd hours later he's walking up an antipodean suburban street looking for the address, when he finds the right house. So he rings the doorbell and there's no reply. Suddenly all of the wind goes out of his sails and he's plagued by self-doubt. Perhaps she doesn't want to see him? Perhaps she's avoiding him? Is she in the house and simply not answering the door? A whirlwind of emotional paranoia sweeps in, and in an instant Kenny's decided his sister never wants to see him again. So he turns around, goes back to the airport and catches the first flight home. As it was, his sister, who loved him dearly, was only down the road shopping and would probably have cried with joy had she seen Kenny on her doorstep. But his fear of rejection was so deeply ingrained that he couldn't face being in a situation that might hurt him. It was this mixture of external fearlessness and internal fear that made Kenny such a magnetic and interesting man. He had a power over people through his comedy that was transfixing, yet he was so vulnerable he was like a child that you just wanted to protect and take care of.

It was this desire for protection that caused him to hatch the plan for deflecting interest in his divorce. Ray and Barry had already given us a clue as to how others perceived our relationship by their insistence on us doing more than our fair share of the Pillow Talk sketches. So, when the press got word of Kenny's divorce and his alleged homosexuality (he didn't come out until 1985), he thought it would be fitting to orchestrate what the press were dying to print about us anyway. Believe it or not, the tabloids are actually much more respectable than they used to be, but back then they were a law unto themselves. It was quite fun playing cat and mouse with them in the 'spirit of the game'.

As we left the Radio One studios at Broadcasting House one day, Kenny wrapped his arm around my shoulder and declared loudly:

'I would like to put the record straight right here and now and state that stories about Cleo and I having a fabulous affair are completely and utterly untrue. We are absolutely not having a glorious and wonderfully immense relationship.' We smiled and hugged for the cameras then leapt into a cab.

Sure enough, the headlines the next day went along the lines of 'Kenny and Cleo Deny "Fabulous Affair" ', which we thought was highly amusing, and taught me a valuable lesson in playing the papers at their own game, instead of being the victim of their editorial policy. This set the pattern for much of our goofing around in the years to come: whenever we went out together, we weren't ourselves but two cartoon characters that could get away with anything because we both had this sense of other-worldliness. It made for some great nights out, but did get us into quite a bit of trouble.

It was around this time, during the first series, that I met the men in Kenny's life. Much has been written about Kenny's 'gay lifestyle' and the vast majority of it is nonsense. There's often an assumption that because the gay scene has more than its fair share of nightclubs and casual sex, gay males must be out dancing and doing naughty things all night. This is patently rubbish, and you only have to look at how shy and introspective Kenny was to realise that flighty relationships just weren't his thing. He liked security and emotional stability. The only problem was, he was attracted to men who were quite the opposite: those who liked to party, and party big.

Kenny had an inherent sense of privacy about his homosexuality. He was a generation older than me and had grown up in a climate where homosexuality was not only socially intolerable, but also a crime. Even during the enlightened eighties, it took him three years after his divorce to admit publicly that he was gay – it was so ingrained in him that you kept stuff like that quiet. This meant he tended to shield those closest to him – Ray, Barry and myself – from his life with his boyfriends. Kenny did this in all aspects of his personal life: he compartmentalised friends and divided his time between very distinct groups of people. I was one of only a few people he allowed to 'spill over' into other groups, so while we knew his boyfriends well and they regularly joined us on nights out, we never discussed them with him. I say 'boyfriends' very guardedly, as it implies that Kenny had a string of lovers, but in fact there were only two main men in his life: Nikolai the Russian and Pepe the Spaniard.

Kenny himself said in an interview in 1986, the year after he came out, that 'I like my men to be dark, swarthy, greasy dagos,' and you couldn't get much darker, greasier or swarthier than Nikolai and Pepe. Kenny had met Nikolai at a restaurant in London, and like everyone who came into contact with Nikolai, was captivated by his animal magnetism. Nikolai Grishanovich was one of those huger-than-huge characters, with a charisma rating way off the scale, who would walk into a room and immediately take over without having to say a word. He was fearsomely attractive, endearing, very muscly and in possession of great strength of character. He also had a prodigious sexual appetite for both men and women. Before moving to London he'd led a dark and mysterious life, allegedly on the Russian black market.

It was Nikolai who (and don't ask me why) was always trying to get Kenny and I 'fixed up'. I guess because he was so energetically bisexual that he didn't see any reason why people shouldn't abandon themselves to their carnal desires with as much 'gay' abandon as he did. He once came up to me and said (in a heavy Russian accent):

'Ken tok about you orl thee time. He's een loff with you, you not know thees?'

You couldn't help but be taken in by his monstrous charm. He was like an affectionate Great Dane made into man; a perpetually chuckling Bluto whose magnetism hid a ruthless talent for using people and discarding them like a two-year-old throws off favourite toys.

When he and Kenny met up, Nikolai was not yet seeing Pepe Flores, a Spanish waiter who joined the relationship two years later, but by the mid-Eighties they were both regular visitors to Lexham Gardens. They were always such fun to go out with, and Kenny enjoyed their company immensely, although it would be dishonest of me if I didn't admit to finding the dynamics of their relationship just a tiny bit weird. I was an insider, and I found it slightly odd, so goodness knows what the rest of the world thought. When Kenny came out in 1985, at an impromptu press conference outside the flat in Lexham Gardens, he had Nikolai standing on one side of him and Pepe the other. It was, he said, 'wonderful having two husbands.' You can imagine what the tabloids made of that. But, peculiar as their three-way relationship seemed to outsiders, it made Kenny happy and comfortable with himself, which was such a gift for him after the lonely years of self-delusion.

By the time the first series was being broadcast, Kenny and I had been established as a showbiz couple and were having a fabulous time. The show was attracting around sixteen million viewers a week and had propelled us to star status. When things go this well, everyone wants a piece of the success, and we were getting invited to party after party: showbiz gatherings corporate launches, film premiers. You name it, we were there. We both had an unquenchable thirst for champagne and rarely passed up an opportunity to go out until the wee hours.

Kenny sometimes adopted the persona of Concerned Uncle Everett whenever things got out of hand. People often made passes at me in clubs or parties and Kenny would get very courageous and brave and stand up for me.* He hated violence of any kind, or, to be more precise, he hated people being horrible to each other, but he nevertheless got very defensive when lager louts lunged for my particles. It was very sweet, but to be honest, I think there was little need for Kenny's chivalry.

We were also invited on to lots of different shows as a pair, and occasionally got, um, 'confused' about how we were supposed to behave. Kenny had already appeared on Terry Wogan's *Blankety Blank* a few times (remember his microphone-bending trick?) but that summer we went on as a duo.

'I can't face doing *Blankety Blank* on my own again,' said Kenny when Jo Gurnett, our shared agent, proposed the appearance. 'Let's do it together and just have a laugh. It'll be safety in numbers.'

Oh boy, did we laugh. We drank three bottles of champagne before recording started, and I was feeling a little flushed and wobbly when we went on. Kenny wasn't too hot himself, and when Terry came on to get the quiz started, Kenny was already in major-mischief mode. That show must have been a nightmare for Terry. We interrupted everyone, cheated, deliberately wrote down silly answers, took liberties with the props and generally sabotaged the whole thing. I could try and kid myself and say I was being led on by Kenny's bad example, but the truth was that we encouraged each other in equal measure and over time our behaviour became more and more inventive. There was so much fun to be had!

The success of *The Kenny Everett Show* also meant Kenny was able to take more liberties with his own guests – the strand that viewers time and time again voted as their favourite bit of the programme. We had a cast of regulars who loved to be in on the joke, and one of my favourites was always Lionel Blair. He's one of those lovely people who never, ever says a bad word about anyone, is charming to a tee, and has a wonderfully self-deprecating sense of humour.

For some reason Lionel always got to do the torture sketches

---

* Actually, he just got cross, but when you're as small as Kenny was, this was courageous and brave.

(the ones where he was hanging from a dungeon wall, in chains). Ray, Barry and Kenny came to the conclusion that Lionel actually enjoyed being chained up, and decided to put the theory to the test. They strung him up against the comedy-foam dungeon wall and filmed the first half of the sketch.

'You all right up there?' boomed Ray from the producer's booth.

'I'm fine,' said Lionel.

'You quite sure you're OK?' Ray asked again.

'Really, I'm fine,' replied Lionel.

'You all right up there?' asked Kenny, looking up at Lionel as he walked past the set.

'Honestly, I'm OK,' said Lionel, wondering what all the fuss was about.

'Jolly good,' said Kenny. He walked away and without warning, Ray turned out all the lights in the studio, plunging it into darkness. 'We're off to lunch then.'

Kenny closed the big, studio double doors behind him with a dull thump and the set became eerily real. Pitch black, not a soul in sight, the only being sound the menacing scratch of rat claws on stone.*

The entire crew left the studio and when we came back Lionel was exactly where we left him (just what you'd expect from a well-made BBC dungeon set). He'd been nibbled by the rats a bit (they refused to touch the food in the canteen), but was otherwise unscathed.

'You still all right up there?' asked Ray, as he turned the lights back on, with the nonchalant air of a writer who's just strung up one of the UK's most loved entertainers with arm shackles and leg chains.

'Absolutely splendid, my dear fellow,' said Lionel, 'I just love hanging around this studio.'

'There you go,' whispered Kenny conspiratorially. 'I told you he likes it.'

As Lionel will testify, you get asked to do strange things when you've been a part of *The Kenny Everett Show*. And sure enough it wasn't long before other propositions came creeping

---

* Oh all right, there weren't any rats in the studio. They all lived in the canteen.

in, for all of us, that offered the promise of work beyond Kenny's vehicle.

The first of these ventures was *Bloodbath At The House Of Death*, a film that sank without a trace, but at least seems worthy of an entry in this book longer than the usual two lines you get in most video back-catalogues.

4 The Great Escape

WE'LL GET ON TO THESE alternative ventures shortly, but before we do that it's worth taking a look outside Kenny's circle for a short while just to see what else was happening in my life. I did, of course, have a life outside mine and Kenny's world, but I seldom allowed it to intrude rudely into all the fun. In 1983, however, it intruded all of its own accord, in the guise of an innocuous phone call from my father that was to lead to a most memorable experience.

My father was a wonderful man – but incredibly stubborn – and the values he held were an absolute truth for him. He was convinced to his core that on things that mattered (such as moral standards) he was never, ever wrong, although this was tempered by an enormous sense of humour and charm. He loved me very much, but his over-protectiveness and inability to understand my lifestyle often led to quite spectacular clashes between us. He really wanted the best for me (for which I loved him dearly), but like him, I'm very independent and single-minded, so he never felt he had any control. This worried him, and he was greatly concerned about my future. My mother had always protected him from the worst of my excesses, but nevertheless he was still highly uncomfortable with my choice of career. For him there was an unconditional and irrefutable truth: all actresses and nurses were sluts. I was an actress, *ergo* fiddle de dee. This was a difficult conclusion for him to reach, and I think it troubled him deeply.

Being the only girl I was uniquely placed in a family of boys. There is a very strong and unbreakable bond in our family that overrides such things as divorce, and no disagreement would

ever sever our loyalty to one another. I have the best brothers
in the world and we were all lucky enough to have been born
the children of our parents. Bizarrely, because of all his foreign
travel and his dislike of television, my father had never seen
me on Kenny's show, and had got it into his head that I
was working with, as he said, 'some comedian called Kenneth
Williams'. I absolutely shudder to think what would have happened if he had ever seen me on national television dressed up
as Miss Whiplash in all that saucy underwear, and not even
using a stage name!

It was a Friday morning late in August and I was pottering
around the house waiting for Kenny to give me a ring about
our plans for the weekend. When the phone did ring, it turned
out not to be Kenny, but my father calling from Athens.
Although my parents had already divorced a few years earlier,
we were all very much in touch with each other and stayed a
good solid family. My father was now based in Greece, and it
was my brothers who, at that time anyway, saw more of him
than I did. We exchanged a few new jokes and the latest news,
and he told me a couple of funny stories before asking me if I
had any plans for the weekend. None that couldn't be changed,
I replied, feeling curious.

'I'm holding a party here Saturday night,' he said, 'and I
thought you might like to come. It's just a few of the old family
friends, and your mother's going to catch a flight and join us
on Monday. I'd love you to come.'

'Oh yes,' I replied. 'A great idea! What about the flight?'

It was all arranged, he told me. I should pick up the ticket
from the airport and he'd arrange a car to collect me at the
other end. Just bring a change of clothes and an evening dress.

This was so typical of my father: thoughtful and organised,
but utterly in control. So I was off to Greece!

I rang Kenny and told him about my change of plans, which
meant I wouldn't be able to go out shrieking with him that
weekend, but instead I'd bring him back a little something
from Athens. He was terribly envious of course: he loved travelling, and we shared some dazzling holidays over the years. But
this was a family thing and it was much more suitable for me
to go on my own.

The next morning I got a cab to the airport and, with a small case of clothes and toiletries, I caught the flight to Athens. It was late afternoon when I landed and the smouldering heat of a Greek summer's day was beginning to uncurl a little. As always, my father was waiting for me with a bunch of flowers and his big smiley driver. He loved to think the little things were more important to me than the big things. On the drive to the house the sun started to turn the sky pink and very Leonardo da Vinci around the edges. It was just beautiful.

We arrived at the house in time for the final preparations that were being made for the party that evening. All the staff were fussing about while the musicians were gently warming up their violins and pianos. I went to my bedroom and unpacked my case. I had an hour or so to get dressed and ready for the party, so I had a leisurely bath before putting on my yellow silk floor-to-ceiling dress and applying a little make-up. I remember wearing my hair up, as it was so sticky-outy at the time of Kenny's show.

I swept into the reception room, which was now bustling with guests, and more were arriving by the minute. Everything was in full swing and it was all I could do to keep clear of the silver trays full of dead bits on toast, which were revolving around the room between everyone like huge propellers.

I floated around the room doing the usual polite small talk until I turned to see an impeccably well-groomed young man in his late twenties, and someone who was clearly his father, step up on to the podium. The father started making a speech in very dignified tones, which attracted the respectful attention of everyone in the room. While he was speaking I thought I'd seize my chance and find somewhere to sit down. Mighty Greek speeches aren't my idea of a good time, especially since my Greek isn't that good. As I started to negotiate my way across the room I noticed people turning to look at me and smile. I smiled back and tried to appear interested. Suddenly I heard my name mentioned by the man on the podium, followed by applause.

People then began to behave very peculiarly indeed. They bustled around me and started to congratulate me for something. Women wearing more make-up than is generally considered safe kissed me from all angles. I was flustered, and tried to get some sense from somebody by asking them what had been said by podium-man. But before I could get a reply, a woman appeared right in front of me and declared:

'You must have a baby immediately!'

This seemed a very surreal way to be greeted, I thought. Then, at her side, another woman arrived a few seconds after her earrings came into view, enquiring when the wedding was. Then it all started to become strangely clear.

I was being engaged to the young man, a fellow I had never (knowingly) met. Before I could even register the situation my father appeared at my side and led me over to the man and his father, where I had to indulge in a flurry of polite kisses and social embraces. To the outside world I looked calm and collected, but inside all my alarm bells were ringing fit to break, and I was breaking out in a panicked sweat not unlike (I should imagine) an animal that's just trodden in a snare. My brain was feverishly working on a get me out of here quickly plan.

Discretion and poise were to be my trusty allies. I was whisked into the crowd by some animated woman who was obviously a professional; she'd married off three daughters of her own and was very up on wedding gowns, and wanted me to know it. Snippets of advice were pouring in from all sides. I excused myself and went upstairs to put into place Stage One of my cunning plan.

I cut the front seam of my dress between my knee and thigh, and grabbed my passport and credit card, which just about fitted into my evening bag alongside my lipstick and powder. I returned to the party two minutes later to the strains of the orchestra and a lot of happy babbling. My father continued to introduce me to a selection of ambassadors and various dignitaries, all old friends of his, but I took him to one side and in mock surprise showed him my dress.

'I need to find a needle and thread to fix it,' I said. 'I'll have to go to the bathroom for a while. Do you mind?'

'Go and get dressed,' he quipped in a panicky whisper. 'You are almost naked!'

So I went back into the bathroom and effected Stage Two of my crafty plan: climbing out the window and running away.

I couldn't walk out the front door or go upstairs to get my things since the place was swarming with butlers and maids, and goodness knows what my father had told them. By now they were officially the enemy. So I clambered out of the bathroom window in a highly undignified fashion, landed in the flower bed with a noiseless grunt, and ran off – keeping low behind the bushes in case anyone was looking out the window or standing on the terrace. It was all very exciting and I felt like Steve McQueen in *The Great Escape*. The only problem was that I didn't have a motorbike, so I had to make do with hailing a taxi half a mile or so from my father's house. Not quite as glamorous, but eminently more practical, especially when you're wearing a torn yellow cocktail dress and high heels.

The cab pulled up at the taxi rank and a man let me go in front of him in the queue.

'After you,' he said politely in English.

'Thank you,' I replied, dropping my guard and thinking I was now safe.

'Don't mention it,' he said in a heavy German accent, pulling a pistol from his pocket and sticking it in my ribs. Actually, he didn't do that at all – I just made it up. I've been thinking about *The Great Escape* too much. I just clambered into the taxi and asked the driver to take me to the airport, my heart pounding and a bit of a cold breeze blowing through the slit in my dress.

Once I arrived with nothing but a slinky yellow outfit, bits of twig in my hair and my trusty credit card, I walked in and bought a ticket on the first plane that was leaving Athens, preferably in the London direction. I didn't care where it was going, just as long as it got me out of this place as soon as possible. Apprehension mounted as I realised the severity of my situation and the measures I had taken to get out of it. My father was not going to be happy.

As luck would have it, a flight for the UK was leaving within an hour. I bought my ticket and headed for the departure lounge. I got a lot of strange looks from the other passengers, but the English ones recognised me from Kenny's show and thought nothing of my attire, as this must have seemed quite normal compared to the things I usually wore on the show. I tried to phone Kenny, but he wasn't in, so I left a message. I then phoned Edward Duke, the outrageously talented award-winning actor best known for his one-man show *Jeeves Takes Charge*. Edward's response was perfect. In his eccentric, flamboyant, gentlemanly manner he insisted on meeting me at Heathrow. Always one to enjoy a drama to its fullest, and to make it bigger, Edward was very satisfying.

Back in London I arrived with no luggage: just my evening bag and two bottles of champagne. Edward was waiting loudly for me with his arms open, bellowing: 'Darling, well arrived!' He embraced me very visually, and whisked me towards a waiting limo, insisting on being told the whole story firsthand and in paralysing detail.

I was so relieved to be back among the loons. We phoned Kenny from the car and I blurted out what had happened, not forgetting to mention that I was equipped with two bottles of champagne and in need of a major glee. He told us to rush over to his house immediately.

'I'll warm up the gramophone,' he said. 'I need to hear absolutely everything.'

When we arrived at his house he wrapped me in a huge embrace and took me by the hand to his spare bedroom, where he had prepared a towelling dressing gown to wear so I could relax a bit. These were what we always wore when we were going to chat at great length: our yapping uniform. We all started talking at once as we fell into Kenny's all-enveloping comfortable sofas and, after a pause in the story, Kenny said what he so often said when he had to sit through one of my Big Adventure stories.

'Doesn't anything normal ever happen to you Clee?'

5 Beyond the Thunderdome

WITH THE SOARAWAY SUCCESS OF the first series, Ray and Barry were widely acknowledged as 'comedy gods', and were being approached by all sorts of weird and wonderful people with all sorts of weird and wonderful ideas. The first of these that actually came to fruition was *Bloodbath At The House Of Death*, an independently backed, spoof horror film starring Vincent Price, Kenny Everett and a hugely eclectic cast that covered such luminaries as Pamela Stephenson, Gareth Hunt, John Wells, John Fortune, me, and a long list of names I can't remember. Looking back, it was a bit of a misconceived project from start to finish: it was a five-minute sketch over-inflated and stretched out to make a one-and-a-half-hour feature film. But spoof was big back then and everyone felt we had what it took.

Regardless of the outcome (and of course I'll urge you to make you own mind up), the filming was a great romp. It was all done over the course of a couple of months in this rambling old house in the middle of the country. Kenny had to play a mad scientist, all brainwaves, beard and boggle eyes. One scene involved him absent-mindedly dropping his monocle into the open stomach of a patient during an operation. It was such a hammy part: he loved it. The only problem was that the character of the scientist had a limp, and Kenny used to forget: (a) which leg he was supposed to be limping with, and (b) that he had a limp at all. Kenny would deliver some lines and then hobble off the set only to hear Ray scream:

'Cut! Wrong friggin' leg Ken. For God's sake, it's the other leg!'

Ray got so frustrated by it all that he eventually had massive signs made up and stuck all over the set that said LIMP!, and had a clapper boy charged with reminding Kenny to limp before every scene.

Ray's other major concern was Kenny's sleep schedule. Kenny was always such a night owl. He'd come alive in the early hours and often rush upstairs to his studio to do some voice-overs for his radio show, and then sleep through to lunchtime and start all over again. The only problem with doing this during a film shoot is that time is money, and if you're on a tight budget (as this film was), you start work before the sun comes up and you finish work after it's gone down. Turn up for work at eleven o'clock and you've just lost the producers £20,000. This put a heavy price on Kenny's lie-ins.

I, on the other hand, have never had many problems getting out of bed in the morning (and how pious did that sound?). Because I lived just around the corner from Kenny's house, Ray put me in charge of Kenny-sitting, or more accurately, Kenny-rising. My job (apart from the stand-in-front-of-the-camera-and-acty stuff) was to get Kenny into work on time for the duration of the shoot. Ray had booked a car to bring us in every morning from Kenny's house at 6 a.m., so I set my alarm for 5 a.m., and was around at Kenny's by 5.30 a.m., giving me half an hour to rouse him. After a few days of standing on the doorstep repeatedly pressing the door buzzer with little or no effect, I tried a slightly different tactic: appearing at the crack of dawn with a bottle of champagne in my hand. It worked a treat, and what started as a quick tipple before we went down to the car, rapidly progressed to two glasses, then four glasses, then a whole bottle. By the time filming finished at the end of the three months, we were turning up for work in a highly relaxed state of mind. This killed two birds because not only did Kenny see the extra incentive in dragging himself out of bed for early morning tipples, but it helped him begin the day with a good, positive attitude.

As I said earlier, Kenny was never very happy performing in front of people. The radio, by the very nature of its medium, spared him the worst of his self-doubt about his work. However, the move to television was initially a big burden. But after a while he got to know and love the crews he worked with and he felt as comfortable as he could in the circumstances. But a film, a full movie, is a different kettle of anchovies altogether. The crew on a film set is enormous. You have people to get coffee. You have people to get coffee for the people who get coffee. You have people who follow around the people who get coffee for the people who get coffee just to make sure everyone's got coffee. It's madness. If the credits at the end of a film actually reflected the people who really *really* need to work on the film to make it happen, you'd have about a third of the names. But what am I moaning for? It keeps people in gainful employment and means that whenever you go out for a drink with the crew you always force everyone else to abandon the pub so you've got it all to yourselves.

But for Kenny, the huge crowds made him nervous, especially since Ray was always trying to pressure things along because time was so precious. Vincent Price did a great deal to make Kenny feel better about things. Vincent was, after all, a very experienced actor and was gently supportive of Kenny's efforts to 'get into character'. He knew that Kenny wasn't a professional thespian and made very conscientious allowances for him. Even so, there were times when Kenny just couldn't cope.

One scene was troubling him particularly. He had to deliver a monologue in the library of the set and in take after take he kept getting the words wrong. When this happens to a professional actor (and it happens to all of us, no exceptions) it can be stressful enough, but for Kenny the strain was unbearable. Crews can be very patient and understanding when you're an actor, but even the dolly grip's smile can fade and take on a mad leer of clenched teeth and barely suppressed fury when some actor's just made the same mistake for the thirty-fourth time, and his partner in the scene has got a bad attack of the giggles. By the time Kenny got to take twenty-something, he'd lost the ability to laugh at himself and was taking it all very seriously. I was standing at the back of the set – as I always did when Kenny was filming without me – because it made him feel better. Someone tried to come on set and calm him down but Kenny wouldn't let anyone touch him. So I dashed on, and, taking Kenny's arm, led him away from everyone and into the grounds of the house. We found a grassy knoll, sat down, and just chatted for half an hour until he'd calmed down enough to go back on set. It was obviously nerves, because when we returned he did a perfect performance on the second take.

Being a support to each other was very much a two-way process, and on the set of *Bloodbath At The House Of Death*, my turn to become a quivering wreck was just around the corner. In the film I had to do a kissing scene with one of the actors. I've always had a problem with kissing scenes: they're just too intimate for my liking. I was still only young and kissing is such a weird thing when you're of tender years.

What was particularly unnerving about this scene was that the man in question was obviously trained as a method actor, and kissing for a method actor usually means performing a complete dental inspection with the tongue, or, if you're really unlucky, a full-on tonsillectomy. This guy was so method he made Daniel Day Lewis look like an amateur: he went beyond the tonsillectomy and was trying an appendectomy for good measure.

After three or four takes, when it was obvious I was enjoying this kiss as much as a fox loves men with bright red coats and big horses, Ray started to lose his temper. And how much did that help? Not very much at all. Kenny, who was watching the scene from behind the cameras could see something was up. I was getting so tense the tendons in my neck were standing out like ski-lift cables and my eyes had this wild bug-eyed look that you often see in rabbits just before you run them over. My hands were also shaking and I was about to lose it completely when Kenny quietly took my arm and led me off set. The location was a beautiful old house surrounded by meadows and little ponds, and we walked through the grounds until we came to one of the miniature lakes. Kenny sat me down, took my hand and then started making up the most ridiculous stories about the insects on the pond. He did all the voices of the waterboatmen and mosquitoes and created a little world away from the set (and the kissing) that allowed me to calm down and view the whole thing a bit more rationally.

We returned a short while later and filmed the kissing scene in one take.

Bloodbath was a huge joy, and we all had a fabulous time doing it. Unfortunately, it sank like the *Titanic* (on its maiden voyage it hit an iceberg in the shape of a review in *The Times*) and was never seen again except on the shelves of budget-video stores. But no one was that bothered. By the time it had bombed, Ray and Barry were already working on another project, and again they asked me to get involved.

They had their own idea for a new comedy series, and had teamed up with Channel Four and the American entertainment network HBO, who envisaged using the comic talents of Ray and Barry combined with heavyweight performances from 'name' actors and comedians on both sides of the Atlantic.

It eventually ended up being called *Assaulted Nuts*, and had a very diverse cast list boasting Emma Thompson, Bill Sadler, Wayne Knight, Tim Brooke-Taylor, Daniel Peacock, Gail Mathis and yours truly. Because the performers all had acting backgrounds, Barry and Ray took a different approach to that of Kenny's show and focused on clever 'wordy' sketches, with the help of additional material from David Renwick (the genius creator of Victor Meldrew) and Andrew Marshall. From my perspective, I felt there wasn't the same energy and vibrancy that shone through on Kenny's show. Far too much time on set seemed to be spent micro-analysing the gags and talking the jokes to death, rather than just getting in front of the camera and enjoying ourselves. I don't have a classical theatrical background either, so I found the constant 'what's my motivation for wearing this silly hat?' chatter a bit tiring and far too serious. Good comedy mostly relies on the chemistry and communication between the players. Successful sketch shows on television usually spring from groups of performers who have worked together in clubs or radio over a long period of time and therefore understand what they're all trying to achieve. We were thrown together like a prefab boy band, and didn't have enough time to get to know each other and find a common comedic voice. Individually, everyone's performance was very accomplished, but the show just didn't hang together as a whole, I thought. I guess the viewing public came to the same conclusion, since we only did two series.

This all happened in the summer of 1983 (there was a second

series in 1984), after *Bloodbath*, and it had quite an effect on our relationship. Kenny and I had grown very close that first year, and during the filming of his show, he loved having me around even when I wasn't performing with him. I had a calming influence on him and, when things got stressed on set, he would always come and seek me out in a quiet corner somewhere so he could relax and forget all the aggravation around non-performing props and Ray's sometimes over-energetic directing. But when I started to work outside the show, although he was happy for me, he became very insecure. He was always worried I was going to leave him and go and do something else on a permanent basis. The truth was that I was simply trying to get a taste of life beyond the thunderdome, and what I saw actually convinced me that I was never going to work on anything as rewarding as *The Kenny Everett Show*.

By the third series in 1984, I started getting offers to appear on other light entertainment shows as a guest in my own right, but these were generally a very bad waste of time indeed. Whenever I was invited, the format was always the same: a sketch written as a poor parody of *The Kenny Everett Show*. The writers of other programmes tried to transpose the lunacy of Kenny's show on to their own, but to be honest, trying to inject the whackiness of a Kenny sketch into something like *The Little and Large Show* just didn't work (that was one guest appearance I couldn't wait to wash out of my hair). After a number of these appearances I started turning them down, for two reasons. First of all, I felt I was pointing my career down the path of celebrity purgatory: being famous for no special reason other than being, well, famous. Secondly, my independent celebrity status was starting to upset Kenny.

It's very difficult trying to explain this without making Kenny sound petulant and possessive, which he most certainly was not. To understand Kenny you needed to suspend your judgement and get inside his insecurities, and realise how they ran through every fibre of his daily life. They weren't insecurities about his fame, or any supposed competition between us on the show (he was never bothered by being a 'star' and approached the whole celebrity issue with great irreverence), but he needed to have an emotional harbour, which offered him security and unconditional protection. I was becoming that harbour, and his discomfort sprung from a fear that a division in our professional lives would lead to a division in our friendship.

I truly believe that Kenny's comedic talents made him a great man, arguably a genius, and history shows us time and time again that exaggerated talents come with a price: the onus of exaggerated flaws. Kenny's flaws were nothing compared to many in his profession – he was certainly no Tony Hancock – but his insecurity and self-doubt were a heavy burden for him to bear. But the truth is that if you love someone, you have to accept and understand their weaknesses, love them all the more for those weaknesses, and help that person to overcome them in a positive fashion. I felt proud that I was able to help Kenny shoulder his problems, and never once judged him for decisions he made that others misinterpreted.

I never sacrificed any ambitions or plans for Kenny, and I've always felt – then and now – that there's no point in doing anything work-wise unless it's innovative or worthy. And quite frankly, the rubbish I was being offered didn't make me feel for a moment I was actually missing out on anything or hampering my career prospects. *Assaulted Nuts* we all later agreed – was not the right format for me to extend or challenge myself, and so it was back to fun business as usual on Kenny's show – with our friendship taking on a life of its own. My career plan has always been based on perseverance and patience rather than aggressive self-promotion, and I'm a firm believer in things happening only if they're meant to happen. There's nothing cosmic or New Agey about this, just a jovial internal chorus of 'Que Sera Sera'.

6 Friends

DURING 1983 AND 1984 KENNY and I were seen in the papers a lot: at charity do's and at clubs. It must have looked as if we were living the stereotypical showbiz lifestyle. But these things always look glamorous and exciting from the outside, and although we did have our fair share of parties, the truth was much more personal. We spent our time together like any other couple of friends. We'd speak every day on the phone if we weren't working, and Kenny would often send little notes or packages round to the house for no other reason than to say hello.

It was around this time that our lifelong affection for bananas came into being. This was a theme that ran through our entire friendship, and became a metaphor and byword for our relationship. I have Kenny's ring with the word 'banana' engraved inside it on my finger now. The whole banana thing started fairly early on, when Kenny and I were out shopping one day and we walked past a greengrocers in Kensington. We were talking about something very ordinary when he suddenly burst out laughing for no reason whatsoever.

'What's so funny, Kenny?' I asked.

'Bananas,' he replied cryptically.

'What?'

'Bananas,' he repeated. He took my arm and turned us around, back towards the greengrocer's.

'Shut your eyes,' he commanded. 'Now imagine you've never ever seen a banana before in your entire life. You've never seen a photograph of a banana, you've never seen a drawing of a banana, you've never seen a banana in a film. You have absolutely no idea what a banana is, let alone what it looks like. Got it?'

'Yes.'

'Now open your eyes and stare at this.' I did as he said. Kenny was holding a solitary banana in front of my face. I looked at it and started laughing.

'It's ridiculous isn't it?' said Kenny. 'It's so bright and cheery and silly. But best of all, you can eat it!'

And he was right. Bananas *do* look really odd when you think about it. And that was how we saw each other: bright and cheery and silly. From that moment on 'banana' became a code word, a secret symbol that meant me to Kenny, and Kenny to me. Over the years we often simply signed our notes to each other with banana logos, sent each other banana cards, wrote two-word notes on bananas and posted them through each other's letter boxes and made all sorts of enigmatic banana references that nobody quite understood.

But as the master of the grand gesture, Kenny couldn't be beaten, and on one occasion he out-bananaed us both. He'd had to go to the States to pick up an award for his radio show, and had planned on making a short holiday of it by tacking a few extra days on the end of his trip to lie in the Florida sun for a while. After the ceremony he rang me and told me all about the award and what a glitzy do it had been.

'Full of fabulous people, darling,' he said. 'You'd have loved it.'

He sounded excited about his beach holiday and I promised to ring him the following day.

When I rang the next morning, I was told he'd checked out of the hotel early. I figured he'd made a swift start for Florida and that he'd give me a ring once he was sunning himself under the hot Florida skies. Later that day, I was writing a letter to some friends in Spain when the front doorbell rang. I went to the door and opened it to find myself staring at an enormous lorry full of bananas. They were stacked in boxes on the steps of the house, on the pavement, by the railings, in the road. There were more bananas than I'd ever seen in one place in my whole life. Two delivery men stood on the only available place left on the doorstep and handed me a delivery note.

'Can you sign this for us, love?' said one of them.

I opened the envelope and inside was a letter hastily scribbled in Kenny's distinctively illegible handwriting.

'I'm in Hans,' said the note (Hans was a restaurant round the corner from my house). 'I missed you terribly. Come and have dinner right now or I'll just die.' I smiled at the delivery men, grabbed a jacket and dashed round to the restaurant.

I was giving away bananas for days.

Being around Kenny was like being in the company of a child whose wide-eyed enthusiasm for life never diminished, no matter what. His mother once told me a story about Kenny as a child that – for me anyway – summed him up completely. He was about seven years old, and playing with a friend of his near a disused railway line in Liverpool (where Kenny grew up). Like all boys of that age, these two had a fascination with fires and matches, and had got a small camp fire burning in an old derelict railway carriage. A breeze had picked up, and the flames suddenly got out of control, catching the wooden walls of the carriage and rapidly turning it into a box-shaped bonfire. The boys tried as hard as they could to put the fire out, but it was clearly getting beyond them, and they had to retreat to a safe distance and watch the pyre get bigger from a stack of railway sleepers. But then, disaster. Some grown-ups saw the smoke and climbed over the rail-yard fence to see what was burning. Kenny and his friend saw them approach and belatedly realised they were likely to get into big trouble. So they leapt to their feet and started running off.

'Oi, you kids, come back 'ere,' shouted one of the men, giving chase. 'Did you do this?'

'Blimey,' said Kenny's friend, looking over his shoulder. 'They're coming after us, Maurice. Leg it!'

The boys picked up their pace and the grown-ups gradually fell behind them as they raced away, outrun by youthful energy and mild terror.

'What are we going to do?' panted Kenny's friend, still running like mad. 'They might know who were are and go round and see our dads or something.'

'Don't worry, I've got a plan,' said Kenny. 'Let's swap jackets. Then they won't recognise us . . .'

This was so Kenny. The seven-year-old was never far below the surface, no matter where he was or what he was doing. It got him into plenty of trouble throughout his career, and landed us both into some wild situations when we were out and about.

Fridays were always our big night out. I would arrive at Kenny's place around seven. He'd answer the door and greet me with an all-consuming hug. He always smelled so delicious before we went out, as he'd pamper himself with a long, hot bath and soak himself in Badedas. We'd pour ourselves a couple of hearty whisky and ginger ales and then listen to any new music Kenny had stumbled across that had taken his fancy.

With his background in radio, Kenny had a passion for all things musical. Although his true love was still the songs of his youth – particularly The Beatles, ELO, and the Bee Gees – he had a keen ear for fresh sounds. He was still doing his radio show for the BBC, so he often managed to get hold of new tracks and pre-released singles long before the rest of us. If he'd discovered something that he liked, he'd play it for me before we went out.

One of my favourite Kenny and Music stories concerns Queen and 'Bohemian Rhapsody': a truly immortal and magnificent song. Kenny and Freddie Mercury had always been good friends and, in 1975, Freddie turned up at Kenny's house clutching a big demo tape: the first mix of 'Bohemian Rhapsody'. At the time, all pop singles were less than three minutes long because that was all the radio stations would play. 'Bohemian Rhapsody' was about eight minutes long. Freddie wanted to release the song as a single, but everyone in the industry told him he was mad – at eight minutes long no radio station would touch it, and without radio play it would sink like a stone. Freddie wanted Kenny's advice (this was when Kenny was the DJ God of his day, the biggest cheese in radio broadcasting) and so they went to Kenny's studio and Freddie put the tape on. Kenny sat and listened, his jaw increasingly edging towards the floor, until at the end Freddie asked nervously:

'Well, Ken, what do you think?'

Kenny unloaded the tape, put it back in its tin and handed it to Freddie.

'Release it now. It'll be number one in days.'

With that piece of advice ringing in his ears, Freddie left. The rest, as they say, is history. Kenny was very proud of his wise words that day, and Freddie often reminded him of it in years to come.

On our Friday nights – after finishing the drinks and having a chat – we'd go out to eat, usually at this Spanishy place off the Fulham Road. From there we'd go dancing and get home around midnight. Once home, one of Kenny's favourite indulgences was for me to lie on the floor while he walked barefoot up and down my back, making it crack as he held on to the backs of his dining room chairs for balance. Another favourite was me massaging his shoulders and head. (Whenever he got tense it would go straight to the muscles in his back, and it would sometimes take hours to get all the knots out.) When we'd consumed a few more drinks and giggled our way into the early hours, he'd draw the curtains so the night would last longer. By lunch time on Saturday I'd call a cab and go home.

If we were going to a party, we'd invariably leave before the end. We liked to depart on a high note, before it got to that wilting stage when people start drifting off and they play 'Lady in Red' on the dance floor. This sometimes presented a few problems because people often get the wrong idea, thinking that you're not enjoying yourself (which sometimes we weren't). Either that, or you decide to leave and then spend an hour and a half fighting your way through the crowds trying to say goodbye to everyone. So we treated our departure from most parties like escapes from POW camps: inventive, dangerous and all terribly good sport. This quite often entailed climbing out of windows, because walking out the front door meant saying goodbye to the hosts, and back doors were always alarmed. Sometimes we'd manage to squeeze in three or four parties a night by arriving, downing a cocktail or two and then clambering out the window in the toilets and disappearing off to the next venue.

We managed to startle a crowd of tourists one evening with one of our most audacious escapes. We'd been invited to a do in the West End, and after a couple of pina coladas decided that we'd much rather be somewhere else. So we went off in search of a runaway route. I was wearing a voluminous ball gown the size of a small planet, and Kenny looked dashingly smart in a black dinner jacket and bow tie. We couldn't find a way out on the ground floor so Kenny led us up a darkened stairwell until we came to a landing with a small window. We unlatched the lock, opened the window, and looked out. We were in a slight architectural overhang, and not three feet below us, was the open top of a London double-decker tourist bus, full of visitors to our fine capital, all clicking away with their cameras and admiring the sights.

Kenny and I looked at each and grinned.

Kenny jumped first and landed on a seat. He turned around, outstretched his arms, and I also leapt from the window, my dress inflating like some Mary Poppinsesque umbrella.

We sat down on our seats as if it was the most natural thing in the world. The tourists stared at us with their mouths agape and several took pictures of us. Not, I'm sure, because they recognised us, but because it's not everyday you get to see people in full evening wear leap out of buildings into the top of your bus. When the tour operator came upstairs to do the commentary she couldn't quite believe her eyes, and you could see the thoughts slowly crunching into place. 'Er I've been standing next to the stairs, no one's come aboard, and now I've got these two characters on my bus. *How?*' We smiled at her, she gave a little shake of her head and retreated downstairs, quite perplexed.

The bus went near Kenny's house, so we got off a few streets away and commandeered our favourite late-night travel equipment; a shopping trolley. Kenny loved pushing me home in trolleys. He'd get up a good speed and then leap on himself, tucking his feet above the wheels and clinging on for dear life. Since we were often dressed up after our nights out, we earned ourselves some very peculiar looks from cabbies and bus drivers as we whizzed over pelican crossings, or absent-mindedly drifted into their path.

One of Kenny's favourite places was the Isabella Plantation enclosure at Richmond Park. We'd quite often drive there and spend our Saturdays or Sundays in May wandering around the park and looking at the deer before decamping for food and drink in Richmond High Street.

It was during this period (just before we filmed *Bloodbath*) that Kenny was to catapult himself into the public's consciousness in a manner that he had never expected, and which many people still recall with relish.

The Bombing of Russia.

It had all come about the weekend before a Young Conservatives rally. Kenny and I had spent the day at a party held at Lyndsey de Paul's house, which was some huge sprawling castley thing in the middle of the country. On the way back we got a lift from the film director, Michael Winner, who was a committed Tory and had connections with the party. Kenny quite enjoyed Michael's company, not only because Michael is one of those people who propel themselves through life on an Exocet missile of self-confidence, but also because Kenny mercilessly mimicked him and Michael didn't seem to mind. Kenny was a fantastic impersonator, and he would hold entire conversations with Michael, borrowing his trademark nasal bark. It was like listening to two Michael Winners at the same time: extremely funny because you knew that Kenny was about the only person on the planet who would be allowed to get away with it.

Michael was transporting us in his flashy red open-topped sports car, with Kenny and him in the front seat, and 'Twinkle' (his then lady friend) and I sitting on the parcel shelf. We were on our way back from the party when the subject of a forthcoming Young Conservatives rally came up. Michael said that he'd be very grateful if Kenny could come on stage and just say a few words in support of Maggie and the party. Kenny reluctantly agreed, although he admitted that he didn't have a clue what he should do. I could tell he wasn't comfortable about the whole thing – he never got over his fear of live performances in front of people – and he tentatively asked Michael what might be suitable.

'Whatever you want, old boy,' said Michael. 'Just make them laugh.'

I didn't go down to the rally with Kenny, but like everybody else in the universe, I caught it on the evening news. Apparently, Kenny had gone all the way there with nothing but a borrowed costume from the BBC and a pair of big foamy hands that he used for the Evangelist Preacher character. He hadn't put a thought into what he was going to say.

Michael was in charge of escorting Kenny backstage just before he was due to go on, and stood in the wings with him as they counted down his cue.

'What shall I say, Michael?' asked Kenny, suddenly realising what he'd let himself in for. The stage manager gave Kenny the signal to go on and Kenny was overwhelmed with panic.

'You mean you haven't written a script or anything?' asked Michael, slightly incredulous. 'You're on in two seconds. Say something outrageous! You're in the business . . .'

'What?' replied Kenny. 'How about telling them to bomb Russia?'

Michael laughed – I'm sure not thinking for a moment that Kenny meant it – and was about to offer some slightly more sensible advice when a stagehand pushed Kenny firmly from behind and propelled him in front of the delegates. Kenny stumbled on stage, blinked a couple of times, and with an off-the-cuff, sketch-like punchline (with upward inflections) immediately urged the Tories to bomb Russia. He also suggested that the antiquated Mr Foot be incapacitated by kicking his stick away. It was all very funny and the delegates loved it. That's the Young Conservatives for you.

There was an uproar. From Help the Aged to CND, the country heaped condemnation on this 'irresponsible outburst'. But for Kenny, all the outrage was hilarious. It's one thing having half the country watch your jokes on a television comedy programme, but quite another having these jokes as headline news on every television and radio station. Of course, Kenny was no stranger to upsetting stuffy up-and-downy people. When he came back to London that night he was besieged by the press, whom he greeted with bemused innocence. But the best was yet to come. The condemnation escalated, until shortly after the conference, Mrs Thatcher herself was forced to go on television to defend Kenny's 'sketch' against the rabid opposition.

Kenny couldn't believe it. The Prime Minister (*the Prime Minister*!) was in sitting rooms up and down the country defending Kenny Everett! For someone who got sacked from the radio a few years back for making a harmless comment about the Transport Minister's wife, it was pure farce. Kenny thought it was absolutely fantastic, even more so since Mrs Thatcher was infamous for having absolutely no sense of humour whatsoever and probably didn't even get the joke in the first place. For Kenny, it ranked as one of his highest achievements.

It was doubly ironic then that a year after having Margaret Thatcher stand up for him, he should be in trouble from BBC radio for making a joke at her expense.

'When we had an empire, we were ruled by an emperor,' went the now infamous gag, handed to Kenny by his producer right at the end of the show. 'When we had a kingdom, we were ruled by a king. Now we're a country, we've got Margaret Thatcher.'

Kenny just loved getting into trouble.

Being thrust into the limelight at the start of your career comes as quite a shock when you're young (actually, it comes as quite a shock no matter how old you are), but I was never too bothered by the intrusions. It comes with the territory. And if you go into the entertainment business you must want to do well, otherwise why would you do it? And when you do well, you become famous. I'm never quite sure why some actors get so upset when they make the big time and people then recognise them in the street, ask for their autograph or see their photo in the *Sun* when they're looking a bit shabby after a night out.

For me, the only really negative aspect of being famous I've discovered is that you tend to attract the attention of some fairly weird people. I'm quite used to this anyway – as I said before – I seem to have been born with a weirdo magnet on my head that attracts all manner of peculiar folk. But when I became well known on television, my weirdo magnet went into overdrive and I started receiving (and still get) letters and 'presents' from the most bizarre and unhealthy people. I even got a series of letters in blood once, which were so badly written they actually made me laugh. But the only one that ever came close to giving me the heebie-jeebies was Mad-Eyed Man.

After about the second or third series, I started getting letters from a man who simply signed his name Jim. They started off on a very nice and complimentary note, as do most fan letters, with comments about how pretty I was, how he liked my hair, what was my favourite perfume, etc. (His return address was something along the lines of Hanky Panky House, Droopy Ball Lane, Fondleton, Gropeshire).* Then he moved on from polite niceties to making concrete plans for us. We were going to be very happy together, apparently. Our children, allegedly, were going to be very beautiful. Then he sent me his picture and I can't say I was terribly surprised at how awfully sad he looked. It was a photo from a passport booth, and what I remember most distinctly was that he was one of those unfortunates whose eyes point in different directions. But not just slightly different. He could have pressed a newspaper against each ear and read them both at the same time. Having him stand next to a mirror would be the only way you could look at both eyes at the same time. I thought he was Marty Feldman's uglier brother.

Mad-Eyed Man obviously realised he'd jumped the gun a bit with plans of our wedding and future familial arrangements, so he reined things in somewhat and suggested we meet up. I didn't reply to his letters – the last one I got from him said, 'I'm going to be at the south end of London Bridge at 6 p.m. this Saturday night. I think it would be nice if we went to the cinema and had some dinner. I'm looking forward to seeing you again [we'd never met before]. Lots of love, Jim.'

The following week I got into work at the BBC a bit earlier than usual, and was sitting in the make-up room waiting for Kenny to come in so we could go over the scripts. The door opened and, thinking it was Kenny, I leapt up and turned around.

---

* Someone's going to write to me now from Fondleton, Gropeshire, pointing out that it's not a comedy address, actually, and in fact they won Best Kept Village 1973, thank you very much.

It was Mad-Eyed Man. Holding a knife. And looking a bit grumpy.

'You thtood me up,' he lithped. 'I waited for three hourth and you never turned up.'

Uh-oh. I tried to smile as cheerfully as I could in the circumstances.

'I'm sorry,' I ad-libbed. 'I couldn't make it and you didn't leave me your phone number.'

'Got dithconnected.'

'Oh, I'm thorry ... I mean, I'm sorry. Anyway, how would you like to watch the show being recorded? It's quite exciting ...'

He stood and swayed a bit, and randomly waved the arm holding the knife.

'Tho we'll go out afterwardth, yeth?'

'Oh yes,' I grinned. 'That would be nice. But first I've got to get my make-up put on.'

'You're not calling any guardth are you?' said Mad-Eyed Man, looking a bit panicky. 'I don't like guardth. And guardth don't like me.' He waved the knife again.

'Not at all,' I said airily. 'I've just got to call make-up and get some girls sent up here to do my foundation.'

I gulped, picked up the internal phone, and still smiling cheerily, dialed BBC security. The phone was answered two rings later by a man who sounded like he had a doughnut in his mouth.

'Security.'

'Oh hello,' I said. 'It's Cleo Rocos here in Studio 8 make-up. Could you send two of your people up here immediately please.' I smiled at Mad-Eyed Man, who was twitching quite alarmingly.

'You got the wrong number love. This is security. You want make-up.'

'No,' I said. 'I've definitely got the right number. Can you send two of your people up here straight away please. Studio 8 make-up. It's quite urgent.'

'Like I said darlin' we don't do make-up here. This is security. I'll put you through.'

'No . . .' I started, but was too late. The next thing I knew a young girl answered the phone with a cheery:

'Hello, make-up.'

'Hello,' I said, keeping a wary eye on my visitor, who was now flicking through the script I'd left on the table. 'It's Cleo Rocos here in Studio 8 make-up. Can you send quite a few people to check me out please.'

'We'll be right there,' she said, and hung-up.

I looked at Mad-Eyed Man, but couldn't decide if he was looking at me or not. He might have been looking at the door behind him and the ceiling, but it was difficult to say. It seemed an age, full of awkward silence, before the door opened and a make-up girl stepped in with her little tray of brushes and colours. She took one look at the scene in front of her, smiled weakly at Mad-Eyed Man and then slapped her forehead in mock anguish.

'Oh would you believe it, Cleo,' she said. 'I've gone and left the foundation downstairs. I'll be back in a minute.' She caught my eye and immediately disappeared back through the door.

About thirty seconds later the door burst open and a tidal wave of grey uniforms and peaked caps swept in. The security staff grabbed Mad-Eyed Man and dragged him out of the room, just as Kenny appeared in the doorway, clutching Cupid's wig and looking totally nonplussed by what he'd just witnessed.

'What was that, Clee,' he asked, as a pair of feet slid out the doorway and we heard a spittley cry of, 'let go of my legth . . .' receding down the corridor.

I told him the story – I was a little bit quivery but otherwise all right – and he sat there just shaking his head.

'What is it with you?' he said, holding my hand in his and giving it a squeeze. 'Doesn't anything normal ever happen when you're around?'

7 Party on Dude

HERE ARE A FEW ADVANTAGES to being royalty, or at least being related to royalty. You never get asked to pay for drinks when you go to the bar, you rarely get parking tickets, and on your twenty-first birthday you can invite pretty well anyone you want, safe in the knowledge that they won't turn you down. This almost corresponds to some of the benefits of being 'famous': you rarely get bought drinks at the bar, you never pay your parking tickets and you often get invited to birthday parties for members of the royal family.

And so it was that in 1985 – the Chinese Year of Much Partying – Kenny and I received an invite to Charles Althorp's twenty-first birthday party at Spencer House. Charles Althorp (you have to call him Earl Spencer these days), used to keep a low public profile, but his late sister was reasonably well known as the girl who married Prince Charles and ended up as possibly the most famous person ever in the history of famous people; then, now or at any indeterminate point in the future. We had met Charles Althorp before, on several occasions, mostly at the Hippodrome (*the* venue those days for any kind of charity function), but also at a number of dinners and dos where our paths had crossed. In the nineties the film premier became the vehicle of choice for celebrity get-togethers, but in the mid-eighties, at the height of the economic boom and big, brash extravagance, it was all about lavish charity dinners and birthday balls.

I haven't seen Charles for some time, but back then he was quite a shy young man with a sharp, dry sense of humour. He was a big fan of the show, and always expressed his appreciation whenever we'd bumped into him in the past. Now it was his turn to be host and he'd invited Kenny and me to join in the fun and games.

Before Kenny and I arrived at Spencer House we thought we'd warm up with a couple of kir royales in a restaurant in Mayfair. When we arrived at Spencer House the place had all the makings of a top-security prison: our bags were searched, they ran a metal detector over all sorts of interesting body parts and the grounds were swarming with rooftop snipers and very serious-looking, muscly men with suits, short haircuts and non-smiling faces. Having been checked over by Special Branch, MI5, the FBI, the KGB and the RSPCA, they let us in and we were ushered towards the gardens. We grabbed a couple of drinks from a passing waiter and turned a corner only to step bang right in front of Prince Charles and Princess Diana, who were walking around outside getting some fresh air. We greeted each other with unaffected appreciation and humour, although I was initially very cautious about how genuine they were being, since not a week before, the BBC had aired an episode of the new series in which we'd done a major spoof of the royal family. The sketch was very clever (another of Barry and Ray's genius creations): I did an impression of Prince Charles doing an impression of Princess Diana, while Kenny did an impression of the Queen beating up Margaret Thatcher with her handbag. Anyway, what did it matter? Charles and Diana probably didn't do anything as mundane as crash out on the sofa watching television, least of all in front of something so improper as *The Kenny Everett Show*.

Wrong again.

No sooner had we said some cheery hellos than Charles squeezed Kenny's elbow and said:

'By the way old chap, about that sketch where you took the mickey out of us last week.' Kenny gulped and smiled weakly. 'I thought it rather funny,' continued Charles. 'In fact we loved it, didn't we dear?' He turned to Diana.

'Oh yes,' she said, smiling at me. 'I thought your imperson-ation of Charles was brilliant.' She laughed. 'It's the most unusual impression I've ever seen. The best actually.'

This was the first time I'd met either of them face-to-face, although I'd got into the spirit of things by wearing a very noticeable tiara and a ball gown the size of Balmoral. There was no standing on ceremony and no feeling that we had to be awkwardly deferential. And they were both genuinely enjoying themselves. We chatted and made our way down the stone staircase into the garden, where – because Diana and I were both wearing voluminous and highly flammable-looking ball gowns – we guided each other's floaty creations down the steps, to avoid setting light to them on the torches either side of the path. She and I went to get a couple of chairs from another table in the garden, while Charles and Kenny chatted like a pair of old colonials.*

And here was a shock. We started talking and immediately I realised Diana knew absolutely everything there was to know about star signs and birth signs and astrology: the whole shooting match. We were both born in July, although she was a Cancer and I'm a Leo. The conversation got very saucy as she went on to furnish me with her extensive knowledge of which signs were the naughtiest and the sexiest. We also chatted about bands, which led on to questions about where I went dancing and what sort of music I was into. At this point Kenny's ears pricked up and he invited her out dancing with us one night. Not only that, but he enthusiastically promised to make her some compilation tapes of the latest and most dance-worthy tunes in town. Kenny was always ahead with new tunes and was *the* authority on what was hip and what wasn't. Not only did he keep his promise – within a week of the party he'd sent her a tape of his top music – but he regularly sent her tapes he made himself right up until the day he died. Somewhere at Kensington Palace there must be a cupboard absolutely piled to the top with cassette cases – neatly written out in Kenny's precise script – containing tapes with tunes on them spanning Duran Duran to David Bowie.

Charles, as most people know, isn't really a big fan of contemporary music. He'd much rather be in his garden with the

---

* Can you imagine hearing a voice behind you say 'may I have this chair?' and replying 'no' before you turned around and saw it was Princess Diana? 'Ooh, yes . . . terribly sorry. Have the table as well. . .'

stones and roses than listening to The Stone Roses. So, while Diana and Kenny waxed lyrical about *Top Of The Pops*, he got up to have a look at the rose bushes.

'Do you like roses,' he asked, beckoning me to go with him.

'Only when I haven't got any shoes on,' I said. I kicked off my shoes and walked beside him barefoot through the grass around the bushes. He looked very surprised and seemed to struggle with something in his mind for a moment.

'Erm, you . . . er . . . you're very unusual aren't you,' he said as diplomatically as possible. I laughed.

'Everyone's unusual,' I replied. 'Don't you dance in the roses barefoot? I remember that well-publicised samba you did in Rio a few years back. I was very impressed.' He laughed.

'Yes, that was rather fun. Have you ever been to Rio?'

'Actually, I was born there,' I replied.

'Well you must be a marvellous dancer,' he said, perking up and getting excited all of a sudden. 'It's in your blood! Would you like to come and start the dancing off with me? We'll kick things off with a samba, that should get them going a bit.'

'I'd love to,' I said. 'Just let me get my shoes back on.'

We ambled back to the table where Diana and Kenny were still nattering about music, and I put my stiletto mules back on. Charles then took my hand and led us both back up the stairs to the ballroom in the house. When we walked in, the band hadn't started playing yet, so of course there was nobody dancing. The floor looked and felt like it had been covered with Teflon – it was so well polished it was like walking on an ice rink. We had to help each other balance just walking to the middle. Charles went over to the band leader and asked if they could play a samba for us.*

By this time everyone who was in the garden had followed us in, and those around the dance floor gathered to watch Prince Charles and spiky-haired, tiara-wearing Cleo Rocos take the first dance of the evening. By this time Kenny and Diana had returned from the garden and were standing on the sidelines, no doubt waiting for the dancing to 'officially' start so they could

---

* 'Naff off mate, we don't do requests,' is probably something Prince Charles doesn't hear very often.

move on to the floor themselves. The music started and we each took our first steps.

Did I mention how slippy the floor was? Well, I'll mention it again. It was very, very slippy. So slippy, in fact, that we hadn't got five steps into the samba when my stiletto completely lost whatever traction it had and my left leg simply gave way underneath me. I instinctively grabbed hold of Charles' shoulders, which caught him at a similar moment of unsteadiness. He too lost his footing and I plunged to the floor dragging him down on top of me in a tangle of arms and legs. There was a stunned silence. I happened to look out from underneath Charles and saw Kenny standing at the side of the dance floor with his head in his hands, and Diana laughing so hard she was holding on to Kenny for support.

I wondered for one moment if Charles had snapped in the fall, but then I felt his shoulder shake and realised he was laughing wildly as well. He got up and pulled me to my feet to rapturous applause from the guests surging round the dance floor. We took a little bow and then carried on, taking considerably more care with our feet than we had the first time.

If it hadn't been for Charles Althorp putting a ban on all photographers and exercising his personal veto on pictures taken by the one official photographer, that could have been the most famous incident of the year. It wasn't too much of a goof though, because Charles and I danced to another seven songs afterwards, and the four of us spent the rest of the evening at the same table, dancing with each other and exchanging jolly banter.

We didn't stay until the end, but left at about 1.30 a.m. We always jumped ship before the parties wound down – our motto was to leave in a flurry of laughter, or immediately post-punchline before the atmosphere had a chance to droop. We stepped outside to be greeted by a million photographers, hailed a cab and headed off in a happy swirl of frivolity for cocktails at Club 91 (Kenny's Flat).

You get to find parties in the most unusual places if you look hard enough. It was around this time that we discovered a great knees-up behind the scenes of a famous television show, and, like many of the parties we went to, we disappeared before this one finished. Much to Terry Wogan's dismay.

There's a kind of light-entertainment freemasonry at the BBC; once you get membership of this exclusive club, doors open for you all over the place. You get guest appearances, you go on quiz shows, you get to do all the best charity programmes. Being in the inner circle is seen as both a privilege and a responsibility.

One such perennial responsibility is the Children in Need telethon. It started off years ago as a low-key schedule-filler-come-worthy-money raiser, but its increasing success year after year has turned it into an institution in its own right. It's now as irreplaceable in the BBC firmament as *Top Of The Pops*, *The Eurovision Song Contest* and *The Generation Game*. It's a charity industry in its own right, which, along with Red Nose Day, has contributed an immense amount of money and resources to home-grown charitable causes.

At the height of *The Kenny Everett Show*'s popularity, Kenny and I were part of this inner circle, and were duly invited to do our bit for the telethon. Kenny was absolutely thrilled to be invited on, but probably for all the wrong reasons.

'Just think, Clee. It's live television. Live! They never let me do this. We'll be invincible. No editors, no one to cut out the rude words. No one to sack me from the show, because it's not my show. I can shout "bum" twenty times and there's nothing they can do about it. It'll be divine!'

So we agreed to go on and do something suitably showbiz, as well as answering the telephones with all the other volunteers.

It was all good fun, and quite an eye-opener. From the audience perspective, everyone seems to be having such a great time you wonder how they're keeping their flagging spirits up for so long. 'Gosh, they're always so happy,' is the cry in sitting rooms up and down the country as guest after guest keeps reappearing with a jolly smile and news that a scout group in Munchkinshire has just raised two hundred pounds by drowning their vicar in a bath full of stuffed olives.

I found out why they're so happy.

It's all a massive party. Behind the big Children in Need set is a long, long table absolutely filled to overflowing with every single possible drink you could think of. From Baileys to Beef-eaters, the studio is a post-riot off-licence. At the beginning of the evening all the bottles are neatly laid out with plastic glasses and little saucers of sliced lemon. But by the early hours, when everyone's well and truly into the spirit of things, it looks like Oliver Reed's kitchen on a Sunday morning: empty bottles rolling on the floor, bins full of dirty cups and pools of sticky mixers slowly congealing under the lights. When we got there, I turned to Kenny and smirked.

'This is going to be fun.'

We appeared in front of the cameras fairly early on, did a spoof on the show with another celebrity, and then we were dispatched to the phones to take pledges from people who promised to give a million pounds if Terry Wogan stripped down to his underpants (or worse). Kenny and I were sitting next to each other, and it was all good clean fun. We behaved ourselves very honourably.

We'd been taking calls for a couple of hours when Kenny leant over to me and asked if I was hungry.

'I don't know about you,' he said, 'but I'm famished. Why don't we go and get some food?'

We left the phone podium (you're not obliged to stay there all night, thank goodness), and sneaked out the back of the studio. There's a taxi rank outside the BBC Centre, so we left through the security gates at the front and leapt into a black cab.

'Where shall we go?' asked Kenny.

'How about that nice Italian place Edward told us about?'

We gave the cabbie the address and sat back to relax. The cab took us around Paddington station, and dropped us outside the restaurant about twenty minutes later.

We went in and found a quiet corner where we could watch the telethon on a television that the owners had put on to the bar. The restaurant regulars had organised a sponsored pizza-eating contest the night before and had made a pledge of a few hundred pounds, which they were hoping was going to be read out on air during the telethon.

Our food arrived and we tucked in, watching the show to see how Terry and Joanna Lumley were getting on, and trying to see if we could work out which guests were getting the most drunk. They showed one of those repeated films that illustrate how to pledge using your credit card, and then the cameras switched back to Terry.

He grinned into the camera and winked, as only Terry can, and chuckled his way into an introduction.

'Well, ladies and gentlemen, there you have it. You can pledge with all manner of credit cards or simply make a deposit in any high-street bank or building society. And don't delay! We need your money! But anyway, on with the show. Let's welcome back on stage Britain's favourite crazy duo, Kenny Everett and Cleo Rocos!'

Kenny spluttered out a mouthful pizza and I gaped in disbelief at the television. The audience were applauding as Terry raised his hand to the corner of the studio set where the guests emerged. He valiantly kept his smile going and repeated his introduction.

'Well, they're around here I'm sure... Kenny Everett and Cleo Rocos!'

The audience waited, Terry smiled, and Kenny and I looked at each other and shrieked with laughter.

They didn't invite us again.

Some parties stand out from the crowd, and the jewel in the crown for 1985 was the bash at the Berkeley Square Ball. Every year these parties have a different theme, and this year it had been decided that we should all dress up as Elizabethans. For a couple whose professional careers consisted of dressing up in wild and crazy costumes anyway, it had all the trappings of a busman's holiday. But we'd been looking forward to this one for some time and put quite a lot of effort into our fancy dress.

Kenny and I were fitted and dressed by David and Elizabeth Emanuel, those who designed and made Princess Diana's wedding dress (as if you didn't know). My outfit was a beautiful white and gold ball gown, one of the collection that was actually auctioned at Christies in the summer of 1997 in New York. Kenny wore a jestery outfit in black, with a large Elizabethan ruff around his neck. Not only did it make him look like he'd swallowed a large plate (an old *Black Adder* gag that one), but he kept fiddling with it because the scratchy cloth irritated his neck.* As well as taking on the onerous task of going to the ball and sampling a variety of cocktails with all the other guests, we'd volunteered, in an overgenerous moment, to help out with the auction, along with Prince Philip. We were supposed to auction off various things with him and then take part in some 'fun charity games'. These are not to be confused with 'boring charity games', which should be avoided at all costs.

As with any event in which the royals are involved, protocol dictates that you must be officially 'presented'. I must say that when we were presented to Prince Philip, any lingering thoughts I might have had about the royal family being clenchy-buttocked rapidly disappeared out the window, across Berkeley Square and on to the A4. After spending an evening with Charles and Diana, I shouldn't have been surprised really. Prince Philip was in jocular spirits, and seemed genuinely pleased to meet me. He was also absolutely transfixed by the engineering acumen that had gone into the construction of my dress, and conveyed an energetic concern for the stability of my cleavage should I find myself laughing too hard. It wasn't quite the sort of banal 'nice to meet you' greeting I'd expected, and I couldn't work out if he was concerned I might have an accident, or looking forward to it.

'I hope you've come equipped with a couple of warm spoons, should push come to shove,' I quipped, really rather enjoying myself by now. He laughed helplessly. Being the Queen's husband I don't suppose he gets much opportunity to talk to people without them walking on eggshells, so we went on to spend the next couple of hours exchanging anecdotes and jokes. Prince Philip's had a lot of bad press over the years, and has been portrayed by the media in a pretty poor light, but I have to say that I found him extremely witty, charming and, well, normal (from a Martian's perspective anyway). He was marvellous company.

Kenny, as always when I just jumped in like this, looked at me as if I was about to leap off a cliff. He sat to one side –

* Ruff material.

squinting slightly – unsure if I would survive my verbal bungee jumping, which of course I always did. I like being a lemming with vertigo, it's a huge rush. You hurtle like a lunatic towards the edge but then slam the brakes on just before you go too far.

So there we were, the three of us sitting around and swapping funny stories like we'd known each other forever, when a shadow fell over the table. I looked up and, standing behind Kenny, was this officious-looking woman with a walkie-talkie, shoulder pads you could launch a jump jet from and the kind of upper torso that looked like it was made entirely out of elbows. She was also wearing dark glasses, which she was obviously hoping would give her a menacing FBI-look, but actually made her look like someone who's silly enough to wear sunglasses indoors when it's dark. Before I had a chance to see what was happening, she quite literally grabbed Kenny and pulled him away. In an instant he was dragged into the crowd and disappeared from view.

Kenny and I always looked after each other when we were out, and my warning antennae immediately swirled into action. I turned around to Prince Philip and pointed out that someone appeared to have stolen Kenny from right under our noses.

'I really ought to go and see who's responsible,' I said. 'I hope they plan to give him back.'

'Well if you must,' he said, looking slightly miffed. 'But do hurry.'

I assured him I'd be no time at all, since anyone who wears sunglasses at a disco can't really be smart enough to effect a competent kidnapping. I went off in search of Kenny and the Scully-wannabe, but after looking in several of the marquees realised that the trail had gone cold. I thought of contacting the party's organisers, but then I remembered Kenny's abductor had been wearing a walkie-talkie, so there was a good chance the entire security division could be involved in a massive Kenny Kidnapping Conspiracy. What on earth could have happened? Perhaps one of Kenny's sketches had upset some mad right-wing military junta-type organisation and they were going to shave off his beard as an act of international terrorism.

I was just about to start getting genuinely worried when I

heard a commotion and loud laughter (not Kenny's) from behind a fence that was blocking off the entrance to a small well-lit marquee. It had been set up like a coconut shy, and from what I could see there was a small crowd of people queuing up to buy handfuls of sponges full of slimy gunk and water. I couldn't see what they were throwing at (but you know exactly where this story's going, don't you?), so I walked along the fence until I could see into the open marquee. It was like a scene from one of our dungeon sketches that had gone horribly wrong. At the back of the marquee was an old-fashioned set of wooden stocks, through which protruded Kenny's damp and dripping face. His ruff was on the front side of the stocks and it made his head look like one of those stuffed hunting trophies which mad, aristocratic Englishmen decorate their stately homes with. 'Here's the head of a man-eating Kennyus Everettus. I bagged this one in Berkeley Square you know, summer of '85. Damned tricky shot: the blighter nearly got away'. Kenny was obviously trying his hardest to look as if he was enjoying himself (like this would be anyone's idea of a good night out), but I could tell he was quite monumentally uncomfortable, and clearly hating every minute of it. It was, I realised immediately, one of the 'fun charity games' that we had been told about when we volunteered for action.

A wet sponge suddenly erupted into flight from somewhere in the crowd around the entrance to the marquee. It flew masterfully through the air and landed with a dull squelching sound right in the middle of Kenny's forehead. There was more raucous laughter (again, not Kenny's), and as the slimy liquid dripped down his face and into his eyes, he looked up and saw my head poking over the top of the fence. We connected.

He didn't have to say a word. His smile said 'hey everyone, I'm really enjoying this ritual humiliation. Throw some more disgusting wet sponges at me and let's all have another really good laugh', but his eyes were saying 'oh my God, get me out of this hell-hole before I have a complete mental breakdown and actually kill somebody'. It was immediately apparent that some kind of Thunderbirds-Are-Go-type rescue was required. In my huge and expensive ball gown I started ripping and tearing at the fence like some sort of possessed lunatic. You

read in the papers sometimes about how people in extraordinary circumstances find the strength to do things like lift
cars off their loved ones after a crash, and I can only liken
my single-minded rescue attempt to some sort of emotional
adrenaline rush. I tore that wooden fence apart like it was a
piece of rice paper. This was evidently more entertaining for
the crowd than Kenny's enforced discomfort, and they gathered
around to see the admittedly bizarre sight of Cleo Rocos van-
dalising the marquee like some acid-crazed head case. Once
through the dismembered fence, I charged the mass of Elizabethan flunkies and came face-to-face with Walkie-Talkie
Woman, who made a rather pathetic attempt to stop me in my
tracks by holding up her arm like a policewoman on traffic
duty. I slammed her to one side (wow, did that feel satisfying)
and continued to barge my way through.

The mob could smell blood and were baying at me to stop,
but I was on a mission.

'Kenny,' I shouted. 'I'm coming!!!'

By now people were trying to pull me back, but I was
unstoppable. I broke through the ranks and, as I splashed into
view, all petticoats and antique lace, I could see relief palpably
wash over Kenny's face. There were still some gimpy men and
dangly debs making half-hearted efforts to throw sponges at
the two of us, but I undid the catch on the side of the stocks,
dragged Kenny to his feet and pulled the two of us through a
slit in the back of the marquee. This really upset the charity
ball gangsters and our disappearance was greeted with howls
of disgust. It was time to make a hasty retreat.

I'm all for stars supporting fund-raising events and using
whatever clout we have to raise much-needed money, but
there's something about a certain breed of charity people that
gives them the idea they can abuse your goodwill and nail your
knees to their causes. In many cases it's a lot easier all round
if you just write them a cheque and aim to be a bit more
choosy about the ones you actually get involved with. As we
fought our way through the crowd, pursued by fancy-dressed
Sloanes clutching wet sponges and screaming for their pound
of flesh, Kenny and I both wished we'd been a bit more picky
when we volunteered to help out on this one.

As we neared the exit I caught sight of Prince Philip peering towards us trying to work out what all the fuss was about. With one hand I grabbed a clutch of silvery helium balloons and with the other I blew him a kiss. Suddenly we popped through the gates and were standing outside the party, surrounded by a bunch of bemused-looking policemen.

'I say,' said Kenny, still dripping slightly from his spongy onslaught. 'You wouldn't mind rescuing us would you? There's a lynch mob on our trail and I think they want to do unspeakable things to Clee and me.'

The two burly policemen looked at each other, broadly smiled and shrugged their shoulders.

'Why not?' said blond policeman. 'Hop in.'

He opened the door to his panda car and Kenny and I leapt in. The only problem was that there were already two more policemen sitting in the back. So I elegantly draped myself across their laps while Kenny squeezed in next to them. The silvery balloons took up all the remaining space.

'Where to?' said moustachioed policeman, obviously enjoying himself. This must all have been a lot more exciting than watching a costume drama get drunk.

'The Hippodrome,' said Kenny breathlessly. 'We've got a less dangerous party to go to.'*

Hats off to the Mayfair police department. They orchestrated a highly effective escape and delivered us unscathed to Leicester Square. Actually, it was quite literally hats off, because when we got into the Hippodrome, Kenny was wearing one of their helmets.

'Quit while you're ahead' was one of Kenny's favourite mottoes, and I don't think we could ever have equalled the excitement of that year's Berkeley Square Ball.

We never went again.

---

* Believe it or not, there was a time when going to the Hippodrome was extremely trendy.

8 Outcomes

S I MENTIONED EARLIER, WHEN Kenny divorced in the early eighties and moved to his flat in Lexham Gardens, it was a very liberating time for him because he was able to reconcile himself to his sexuality on his own terms. There was no pressure on him to pretend to be something he wasn't, and he was able to express his homosexuality with a little less guilt than he had before. He was at long last able to be truthful to himself.

Kenny made no secret of the fact he was gay, but he was discreet about it, and there is a big difference. For a start he was very concerned about how his family would take the news, especially given the fact that they were Catholic, and for Catholics homosexuality is a mortal sin. Also, despite the naughtiness and sauciness of his television show, Kenny was actually one of those people who thought that people's real sex lives (rather than the cartoonular ones we portrayed in the show) were their own business, and that it was simply bad manners and vulgar to talk about what you got up to in private: whether you were gay, straight or curly.

His homosexuality was often hinted at in the press although he was not 'officially' gay in the eyes of the media. That all changed in 1985 when he was 'outed' in a press article by someone who'd been close to him for a number of years before we met. Kenny was very upset at this indiscretion, and annoyed that he was put in the position of having to make an official announcement in the press immediately afterwards. He felt it should have been his choice alone and not anybody else's. He had nothing to hide, but just didn't see why it should be something that others would be interested in.

I was in Los Angeles at the time, and he called me at my friend Leslie's house on the morning the story broke. It was late at night there, and I'd just gone to bed.

'I just wasn't prepared for it, Clee,' he said, very tensely. 'I haven't worked out how to handle it. I wanted to do this properly and put some thought into what I said, but now they've got me all defensive and I'm worried about what they're going to say about me.'

'It doesn't matter, Kenny,' I said. 'None of it matters. You are who you are. You're kind, thoughtful and funny. You like who you are, don't you? Have you got anything to be ashamed of?'

'Of course I haven't,' he replied.

'Well then, nothing's changed since yesterday. Hold your head high. Nobody's going to be horrible to you. You're not cheating or lying, you're just the same Kenny Everett everyone loves. I promise you, nobody's going to be nasty.'

That day he held an impromptu press conference outside the flat and, in a typical flash of Kenny theatricality, he wheeled out Nikolai and Pepe as a bit of moral support ('my two husbands'!). He threw himself into the press conference with humour and energy, which I think went a long way towards the reaction being mostly positive. After the press conference I was called by some journalists who'd managed to track me down in Los Angeles. They asked me what I thought of it. Did I know? Would we still be friends? Had Kenny being lying to me?

'I love Kenny,' I said. 'It doesn't matter what's printed about him or what revelations are made, he's still the best man in the world. Being gay doesn't change a thing about him.'

Much to Kenny's relief, the coverage was fair and honest, although at the height of the story a couple of over-eager magazine journalists went through his dustbins to try and find something salacious on the pretence of doing a piece on 'famous people's rubbish'.

'I don't know what they expected to find,' said Kenny to *The Star* in an interview about a year later. 'I think they were expecting to see a load of tiaras, wigs, frilly underwear and frocks amongst all the shells and potato peelings.'

Kenny's biggest worry – his parents being horribly upset – proved to be groundless. For years he'd lived under the fear of disappointing and hurting them. He loved them very much, and the wall he'd constructed around himself in the past made it difficult for him to be open with them about the subject now. But on hearing the news from press reporters who besieged her front garden the day the story hit, Kenny's mum rang him up and they ended up having the 'cosiest, most intimate chat' they'd ever had.

'Don't worry about me, son,' she said. 'What about you? Are you all right?'

She didn't care about his sexuality, or, if she did, she didn't let it show very much. The only thing that had truly upset her were 'the nosy people asking all these rude questions'.

As for Kenny's fears about people being different or mean to him – or there being an adverse public reaction – they proved largely unjustified. Bar a few very rare occasions when he'd get shouted at by your common-or-garden homophobes, people treated him no differently. They'd still say hello in the street, they'd still ask him to 'do Sid Snot' and they still laughed and joked with him in the queue at the bank. They could all see that he was the same Kenny Everett, and that he was as loveable as he was on television. And for most people, knowing now that he was gay, so much of his humour and his personality just seemed to fall into place and make sense for them. And as Kenny kept pointing out in all the subsequent interviews, he was not a 'mincing tart' or overly promiscuous. He liked steady relationships, with good people, just like anyone else.

The only thing he did change was that during the next series in 1986 he asked Barry and Ray to cut down on the drag scenes and to drop Cupid Stunt. I don't think he had much fear of being seen as a raving transvestite, but rather it was a good excuse not to wear the costumes or to put on the make-up and glue that he hated so much.

'They're so itchy,' he would say of the sequins, bras and dresses. 'How on earth do you ever manage to put those things on every day?'

9 Pondlife

THE YEAR OF THE BERKELEY SQUARE BALL, 1985, was a busy year indeed. As usual the filming of the TV show had taken up most of the first three or four months, and then it was into the party season. That year was the fortieth anniversary of the D-Day landings and the end of the Second World War, and so you couldn't move that summer for fake trilbies and the sound of Glenn Miller. I had a few other projects come in, notably a beer advert that seemed to take forever to get finished, but my mind was elsewhere. I was planning to leave the show.

From my own perspective, things with the show were starting to take on some unwelcome changes. As my own popularity grew, my sketches started to be cut down. This was nothing to do with Kenny; he was always secure in having me as an ally and was much happier in work and in public when I was by his side. Any work issues we had were very distinct from our private friendship which was flourishing. The problem stemmed from the curious fact that I seemed to be doing my job too well, and was being penalised for it. It looked as if those-in-charge didn't want me becoming too prominent on Kenny's show. They translated my growing popularity as me having too much power.

This put Jo Gurnett, Kenny and mine's shared manager, in something of a situation because she had managed Kenny for many years, whereas I was the newcomer to her stable, and her loyalties were split. So, after much soul-searching, I signed up with the management company ICM. I wanted to work in films more, and this was a step in the right direction.

I needed to be allowed to blossom and have people on my

side, not just there when it was convenient for everyone else. If receiving public support and getting sacks of fan mail was perceived as such a threat to the show, then it was clearly time for me to make a quick getaway. Putting aside all the fun I was having with Kenny, I didn't see that accepting a diminished (and diminishing) role was going to further my career one iota. And besides, Kenny and I had fun socially, so it wasn't as if we wouldn't see each other. I explained all of this to him, and he understood, although he really didn't want me to leave.

Contractually, I didn't exactly have a lucrative deal with the BBC, and so money was hardly a constraining factor. On the show I had earned around three to four hundred pounds per episode. When you take that over an eight programme series, once a year, I was being paid a little less than most school leavers in their first bank job. I made most of my money doing adverts, corporate videos and guest show appearances (I even did an Outspan oranges advert once with Kenny. 'Small Ones Are More Juicy' was the hook, I seem to remember).

I had a clear idea of what I wanted to do and the guys at ICM were full of good suggestions, so when I eventually got all my plans together it all went very smoothly. I planned to write, produce, and star in my own one-woman show. However, because my image in the UK was so indelibly scorched on to everyone's psyche as Miss Whiplash, I really felt I should do the show abroad to see whether I'd be able to make a success of it without the burden of typecasting baggage.

So, in late August 1985, I packed my bags with a small typewriter, a change of clothes and a new toothbrush, and boarded my flight. Ten hours later I stepped off the plane at Los Angeles International Airport with a spring in my step and an idea in my head. I was met by a guy from ICM called Wilt Milkshake* who was short, old and very charming (actually, his real name was Meltnik, but Milkshake just seemed so much more appropriate).

Celebrity management is done rather peculiarly in the States. You don't get one agent, you have an army of managers and representatives who each have different responsibilities,

---

* His business partners were Freddie Fries, Billy Burger and Harold Happymeal.

including contract negotiation, personal management and a whole range of different things that, if I'm honest, I never really understood. It all seemed a very complicated way of getting fifteen per cent out of you, but it boiled down to Wilt as my agent. I was also working with an obsessive producer who proved to be a really weird backdrop to my stay in the US.

I had very clear plans regarding what I wanted to do. Once in Los Angeles I holed up with my friend Leslie Lyon and her then husband at their house in Beverly Glen. I unpacked my typewriter and set about writing the show that had been bubbling around in my head for such a long time. It was called *Le Nuit Noir*, and was about an Italian woman who runs a restaurant all on her own, and is chased by a range of peculiar suitors all after her favours. There were six characters in all, including a man with a glass eye and a wooden leg (my favourite), and I made them all different nationalities so I could have fun with the accents. As there were only two people in the show – myself and Leslie (who was the show's pianist) – I had to write in plenty of gaps for me to go away and get changed off-stage while she continued to play the piano in-between.

I finished writing the show in two months, and the guys at ICM liked it so much I was booked into a small theatre on Sunset Boulevard on the back of the script alone. The theatre was called Carlos and Charlie's, and was the venue where Joan Rivers tried out her new routines.

Things were humming!

I decided the part of the man in the show should be played by one of those inflatable rubbermen you get in, er, inflatable rubbermen stores, but being 6,000 miles from Soho meant I had to go and buy the thing myself from an American counterpart. Having never stepped foot in a sex shop before, I decided to go with someone else, and asked Leslie if she'd join me on a little shopping trip.

The shop was called 'The Pleasure Chest', and was in some seedy part of downtown Los Angeles. Leslie and I lingered around outside for a while, then plucked up the courage to go in. We crept through the tawdry darkened doorway into a small entrance hall, at which point we were feeling pretty pleased with ourselves. We turned into the shop itself and – confronted with some of the outfits and strange dangly things with their names tastefully illuminated in neon – Leslie nearly collapsed laughing. Meanwhile I'd sidled up to the front desk and cautiously whispered to the man behind the counter:

'Hel . . . I . . . loo . . . fr . . . m . . . sx.dll???.'

'What?' he said. 'Speak up, I can't hear you.'

'I'm looking for a male sex doll please,' I said, still barely audible.

'Standing, sitting or kneeling,' he asked. Leslie heard him and burst out laughing again. I dared not look at her as she was fiddling with something far too indescribable for these pages.

'Er, standing, please,' I mumbled. The man behind the counter looked at me then looked at Leslie and grinned.

'You ladies gonna have some fun, huh?' he drawled. I looked over at Leslie and saw an expression of horror slowly creep over her face.

'Oh no, it's not like that,' she said, mortifed at his suggestion.

'Sure,' he snorted derisively, taking a box down from the shelf behind him. 'You English are all the same. All roses and pearls on the outside, but come the crunch, you're as kinky as the rest of them . . .'

Leslie was about to launch into an attack on this dirty-minded shopkeeper when I blocked her. Discretion being the better part of valour, I figured it would be best if we bought our rubberman and left as swiftly as possible. The shopkeeper pulled a tray out from beneath the counter with two neatly arranged rows of, er, battery-operated appendages – all different sizes and shapes – and waved them under my nose.

'So,' he said, 'which one of these do you wanna go with this?'

'Erm, that won't be necessary,' I said. 'You see, I'm an actress and I . . .'

'Yeah, you're all actresses,' he said, smirking. 'But I can't sell this without one of these so you better take your pick.' I looked away and just sort of pointed at the tray.

'OK honey,' he said. 'It's all wrapped up and ready to go! Anything else?'

'Well, actually, there is,' I said. 'You see in my play one of the characters uses a lunging whip . . .'

'A whip? Well you ladies get more interesting by the minute.'

Leslie giggled and I shot her a warning glance. The man came out from behind the counter and opened a long glass case on the wall full of all these leathery studdy things that looked far too torturistic to be anything but a bunch of props from one of our sketches.

'Anything you girls fancy?' he asked. There was a whip which was perfect for what the play needed, so I sheepishly pointed at it and he took it out. It was a stiff whip that stood about five feet tall and had another five feet of floppy whip on the end. It was so big he couldn't wrap it up.

I paid the money and hastily grabbed the bag with rubberman, gave the whip to Leslie to carry and we scurried out of the shop. When we got back to the house, we unpacked rubberman (he was perfect for the job, and so charismatic) but couldn't think what to do with his dooberry. So I wrapped it up in tissue paper and put it in the bin.

The next morning, it had gone – mysteriously disappeared – and since Leslie and I were the only ones in the house, we thought it very strange. Until the following day that is, when Josephina, the maid, floated into the room with a beatific smile, all previous signs of tension vanished from her little suntanned face, her quaking buttocks akimbo.

At least rubberman had made someone happy.

Rehearsals for the show got under way just after Christmas, and by the New Year we were almost ready to go. It was a big step for me because not only was it live theatre work, but I had eight songs to sing. Kenny and I spoke to each other on the phone at least four times a week, and we would write these great long letters to each other. He would include all the silly little presents he used to send me when I lived just round the corner from him, which I treasured, and so our friendship resumed its usual state. My mother came out to visit, and the date for the launch of the show was set for early February. I was very much in the frame of mind that I needed to do this project without any support from my circle of friends, so I invited no one to the first night. Kenny was filming the new series, but he sent me a telegram and a bunch of bananas to my dressing room on the opening night.

The show was a roaring success. Although it was only a small theatre, after a few nights there wasn't an empty seat in the house, and I got some great reviews. I even had some fellow comedy actors in the audience, including Cheech and Chong and also Michael Jackson. When I got back to England a year later, the press ran all these stories about how my trip to the US had been a flop and that I'd slunk back to England a destitute failure, which upset me quite a lot because it couldn't have been further from the truth. The show was filmed by Channel 7 in Los Angeles, and after the initial season it was booked in for a re-run in the autumn. The only blot on the horizon was the strange producer.

After the first season, I was becoming increasingly uncomfortable with this man (we'll call him 'Matty'). Despite being massively gay, he used to come into my dressing room as I was trying to change, to which I took great exception. Eventually his behaviour became so erratic and eerie that I exercised my get-out clause.

I started getting phone calls from Matty's boyfriend, Joey. Joey would ring me up and say how upset Matty was.

'He's real unhappy Cleo,' he'd whine. 'I dunno what to do about it, he's so totally stressed by you. He'll stop at nothing you know, I don't think I can control him.'

These calls became more and more frequent but, as I'm more than used to being pursued by nutters, I didn't give it another thought. Whoopseroony. . . .

It was October, and the beginning of the second lot of shows. I was walking along Rodeo Drive in Beverly Hills, on my way to a meeting with an actress friend of mine. You've probably seen Rodeo Drive on films like *Pretty Woman* and *Beverly Hills Cop*. It's groaning with affluence. The buildings sweat wealth and the shops attract famous and wealthy people like smelly tropical flowers attract big fat insects, while repelling the poor little ones with an anti-poverty pheromone. It is the absolute antithesis of other parts of Los Angeles, where you never walk anywhere for fear of being mugged, and always glance over your shoulder at every noise behind you. It is utterly crime-free, a playground for the rich, protected by their very ability to make not-rich people stand out like a sore thumb. At least it was totally crime-free, until I turned up.

It was a lovely sunny day and I was walking along the sidewalk wearing a tight white dress and stiletto heels. I heard a car or a van pull up behind me but it barely registered. Then suddenly someone had their arms around me from behind and was trying to lift me up. Initially I thought it was a friend trying to surprise me, but the forcefulness of the strong arms suddenly made me realise this was no joke.

Then there was a knife at my neck. Corus Blimus, I thought! This was getting a bit serious. A voice in my ear whispered:

'Scream, and I'll kill you.'

There's serious and there's serious. This was scoring top marks on the clapometer. The arms started dragging me towards the van and two more men leapt out of the back and approached, calling me some very unsavoury names.

I screamed and shouted as loud as I could, kicking my legs and trying to break free. I managed to grab hold tightly to a concrete rubbish bin that was stuck to the sidewalk, and no matter how hard I was being tugged, I steadfastly refused to let go (well, would you?). People in the street stood and stared at us, obviously under the impression it was some kind of avant-garde street theatre. I mean, people don't get kidnapped on Rodeo Drive – it's just not polite. I managed to rake the shin of my assailant with my stiletto (it went in a long way and must have hurt like hell). He screamed and took a swipe at me with the knife, which slashed the back of my neck. It bled really well (so Hollywood), but didn't hurt. Suddenly I had this image of me as Reg Prescott, Kenny's hapless DIY enthusiast who had a talent for cutting off his fingers and stabbing himself in the leg with a Black and Decker. If I hadn't been in the throes of fighting off a psychopathic mugger, I might have laughed. It was all very spectacular, especially because I was wearing a beautiful white dress.

By now the onlookers realised that this was no trendy theatrical experience, but an actual crime taking place in front of their actual eyes in the middle of the day. A group of people swarmed out from a restaurant on the other side of the street, and one guy ran across the street shouting at my attackers to leave me alone. On his cue, more people started coming towards us from all around. The assailants threw me to the ground and scuttled back into the van as the crowd closed in around them. Seeing that their number was up, one of them shouted something in Spanish and they screeched off along Rodeo Drive in a cloud of dust.

Wow! I sat up and checked myself for damage, but all I had was the cut on my neck and a few grazes on my leg. It all looked much worse than it was because of the blood on the dress. This large Iranian woman waddled across the road from the restaurant and sat down next to me, giving me a big hug. Within a few minutes an army of police cars pulled up, and judging by the manpower they threw at me you would have thought there'd been a nuclear bomb threat or something. The cop in charge – who later became a good friend – kept saying how he couldn't believe something like this had happened in Beverly Hills.

'We don't get stuff like this,' he kept saying, more in shock than I was.

After the initial upset I calmed down and tried to rationalise it. It was, after all, not much worse than any of the fights I'd had at school, but on police advice I went and stayed with friends for a while, and kept them all informed of my exact movements in case something should happen again. No one had seen the number plate on the van, and the prevailing theory among the police was that these weren't actually the guys who wanted to kidnap me, but were in fact hired by the real perpetrators for their own nefarious reasons!

Kenny was absolutely horrified when I told him, despite the fact that I left it a couple of days after the attack to calm down, and tried to tell it to him in the style of a comedy sketch. He wasn't taken in by it to be honest, but I didn't want anyone to make a fuss so I told him that there was absolutely no need for him to come out and see me. It was only much later that they discovered the real story. This seemed the best way to cope with it, because if I indulged myself and allowed everyone to fuss around me it would simply take me longer to get over it.

Matty and Joey were the main suspects, but although the police came down on them really hard there was nothing that could be pinned on them. For weeks afterward the theatre was under surveillance with policemen waiting for the attackers to make another move – especially because telephone threats had continued. I even had a policeman standing in the wings of the stage every night. He must have been sick of that show after a couple of weeks.

For a long time afterwards I was very wary of vans and men with Spanish accents. All my friends sensitively worked out that it would probably be a bad idea to sneak up behind me and grab me round the waist from then on, for which I was grateful. Eventually the threats petered out, the police presence dissipated and that was pretty much the end of the incident. I pushed it to the back of my mind and simply got on with things. You can't let events like that affect your life, otherwise you just become another victim, besides there is so much fun to be had.

All during this time, being away from Kenny was very difficult, but we communicated as often and as stupidly as possible. Christmas Day in 1985 stands out as one of our most memorable phone calls. Christmas Day was Kenny's birthday, which meant he got half the presents other people did, but twice as much affection. That Christmas I was with some friends at a party in Vangelis's house, Vangelis being that musical genius and composer of huge anthems and tunes whose many accomplishments include the soundtrack to *Chariots of Fire*. I knew Kenny would be at home, so once all the guests had left we rang him. Vangelis had set up his synthesizer in the living room, and when Kenny answered the phone, he launched into this immense version of 'Happy Birthday'. It sounded like a cathedral of music, an entire orchestra camped out in the middle of the room. The sound was breathtaking. After playing it through from start to finish, he did another chorus and this time I sang the words over the top of this monumental film-soundtrack of a birthday song. When we finished, I could hear Kenny was so surprised he could hardly talk.

'That's the best birthday present I've ever had,' he croaked down the other end of the line. 'I can't believe it. Vangelis playing me "Happy Birthday", and you singing for me. I couldn't ask for anything more.'

He was enormously touched, and in turn, so was I.

10 Home, Jeeves

AFTER CHRISTMAS, WHEN MY SHOW had run to the end of its booking on Sunset Boulevard, I decided I was going to take some time off. I'd proved to myself that I could achieve something entirely on my own, and that I didn't necessarily need the help of anyone to get what I wanted. Although I'd had offers to take the show on tour, I was a bit bored with it by then and didn't really fancy the idea of living with my mad Italian creation for another year. So, from New Year's Day in 1986 it was a time to chill out and take stock. After the roller-coaster of the last few years, I really needed it.

I had no immediate plans during this fallow period, but at the back of my mind I was toying with different ideas for shows. By the summer, I had worked out what I wanted to do next, but was torn between my new idea and an urge to go back to the UK to be with Kenny.

My dilemma was made worse in October 1986, when I returned to the UK for a week. On my first night back I went to a Hallowe'en party arranged by some friends of ours. I can't remember what I went dressed as – it certainly wasn't a witch or anything Hallowe'eny – but I do have a vague recollection of going as Imelda Marcos in something of an outfit. There were certainly shoes involved. Anyway, the party was kicking along very nicely, with lots of people I hadn't seen for a while and a fascinating backlog of stories to catch up on. I didn't feel the slightest bit jet-lagged and was having a roaring time when the party suddenly went quiet. I had my back to the front door so I hadn't seen what had caused the silence. My brain slowly registered the drop in background noise and the person I was talking to just smiled at me. I looked around and everyone was grinning at me. Then I turned right around and there, standing in the doorway, was Kenny.

I screamed, he screamed, everyone screamed and we enveloped each other in a full-limb-entwined curly hug. It was so good to see him again: we hadn't been face to face for months and this was such an unexpected surprise. Kenny said a few hellos and then took my hand and led me upstairs. We had so much to catch up on, and the party was so noisy, he wanted to take us somewhere a bit quiet so we could talk to each other in peace.

We sat on the bed and talked and talked and talked. We'd been keeping in touch by phone and writing to each other, but face-to-face contact just opens you up so much more. We'd been talking for about an hour when Kenny cleared his throat, took a deep breath and then announced that he wanted me to come back and appear on the Christmas special. Things on the show had changed a lot since I left, and the old arguments people had about us appearing to be too much of a double act just weren't relevant any more, Kenny said. They'd had mountains of fan mail for me, all begging that I come back to the show and asking why I'd left in the first place. And although Kenny had taken a move back from the running of the show, he was stepping back in on this occasion to make sure I returned.

I was taken aback by the offer; firstly because I hadn't expected anything of this kind to pop up, and secondly because Kenny seemed so adamant that I return. I was also flattered that the viewers had missed me and wanted me back. So I said yes, I would come back for the Christmas Special. Kenny was overjoyed, and went on tell me about many of the ideas he and Barry had come up with for some of the sketches. We chatted for a while longer and then headed back down to the party. I saw Kenny one more time before I had to go back to Los Angeles, and promised to call him about the scripts for the show.

Back in the US, my feet had hardly touched the tarmac at the airport when I got a call from ICM.

'I've got a great offer for you Cleo,' said Wilt. 'How about putting your show on one last time as a Christmas special? I've got a date provisionally booked at the theatre. It'll be a sell out – not only that but I've got a crew from Channel 7 who are going to film it.'

Oh crud. This added quite considerably to my confusion. Despite agreeing to appear with Kenny on his Christmas special, ever since the party I'd been having increasingly big doubts about whether it was wise or not. Since leaving the UK I'd established a credible career for myself writing my own show, and going back to do a one-off show for the BBC seemed such a retrospective step. And on what basis would I come back? As an occasional sketch partner? With a bigger role than before? As a 'special guest'? It was all a bit half-baked and just didn't seem right. And now with this offer of putting my own show on for Christmas it seemed even more inappropriate than it did before. I loved Kenny more than ever, but the last two years had toughened me up. I now knew in my heart that I shouldn't push my career down the wrong path for reasons of friendship.

So I pulled out of 'The Kenny Everett Christmas Special'.

It took me a few days to summon up the courage to do it, but I rang Kenny about a week later and told him my decision. He was desperately upset. Working on the show just hadn't been the same without me, he said. It was stressful, and empty of glee. But I stood firm. Kenny didn't take it personally – he understood my reasons – but it didn't make it any easier. It was the right decision to make, and I knew – even as we both got very emotional – that I was doing the right thing. It was one of the hardest calls I have ever had to make. It also left me feeling very (irrationally) guilty. I felt I'd let him down, and I didn't like that one bit.

After Christmas, when I'd done my special three-day run of *Le Nuit Noir*, I was feeling replete and relaxed when Kenny rang me up. We chatted about the usual things and then he sprung his question.

'Clee, I know all the business about the 'Christmas Special' didn't work out. And I can see why you didn't want to do it. But we're making decisions for the next series and I really really, *really* want you to come back. I've told this to the producers as well. We'll do it properly. We'll get everyone together and sort out a different contract. *Please . . .*'

How could I refuse? I'd felt so guilty about letting him down at Christmas that there was no way I could even think rationally about my decision this time around. And besides, I loved working with him. So I agreed to come home and negotiate with the BBC, without any firm promise to appear on the show. Kenny took this as a yes, and was thrilled, as was I.

Back in the UK, I entered into negotiations with the BBC, and we tried to look at ways in which my return would work as well as possible for the show. I needed a firm commitment from them about my role, which they seemed unwilling to give. My agents also wanted to see the scripts before I signed up. Unfortunately, they never did. This wasn't anything sneaky by the producers, but simply the nature of the show. Every other series we'd filmed had been written on the fly, on the back of cigarette packets, under tables and on Barry Cryer's shirt-sleeves. Why should this one be any different?

It felt good to have the chance to work with Kenny again – his joy was evident for all to see – but it still didn't feel quite right. It's always a big mistake to try to recreate the past. It's like getting back together with a teenage sweetheart when you're in your thirties. So much changes and so much happens to you that you're a very different person from the one you were before. I had moved on, and so had the show, but ironically Kenny and I were closer than ever.

In the end – of course – I did sign up, and Kenny and I had a wonderful time filming that series. But it hadn't worked out how I'd expected from our negotiations (these things rarely do), and I didn't have the emotional commitment to the series to let this disappointment slide away. A lot of my sketches were changed without my involvement or dropped altogether. In fairness, this was absolutely no different from how things worked when I was on the show previously, but I'd been my own boss for two years, calling all the shots on a one-woman act and making exactly the kind of decisions that were now being taken out of my hands. I'd grown out of the role the show had to offer, despite all the hilarity and bongliness of doing the show with Kenny.

There was also another major factor in this shared sense of displacement. Kenny had tired of it all too. He felt he was getting too old for the intensity of the work and, on the wrong side of forty, the physical toll of all the costume changes, make-up and gruelling studio schedules was simply getting too much for him. And he hated the wig glue.

The final straw came after a week of heavy filming, when we'd been doing a lot of visual gags and highly choreographed routines. We were in a sketch where we both had to be hoisted up into the air on 'invisible' wires–dressed as the Hunchback of Notre-Dame and Esmerelda. It was a dress rehearsal, we'd said our lines and then, on cue, whoosh, we were dragged up high into the cathedralesque rafters of the studio, suspended horizontally like a couple of medieval Superman imperson-ators. It really was a skyscrapingly long way up. We could see all the television people scurrying around below us doing studio stuff and I heard the director shout:

'OK, Brian, lower them down, let's try that again.'

I felt a jerk in the cable as the motor kicked in, and then it stopped. The only sensation a faint vibration in the tight wire. I looked at Kenny.

'Did you feel that?' I asked. But the motion of the cables had sent us both twirling slowly in opposite directions: me clockwise, him anticlockwise.

'What was that, Clee?' he said as he twirled round to face me. Only I'd twirled around the other way, so I had to crunch my head sideways to see him.

'I was just asking if . . .'

From below I heard the director getting a bit irate.

'Come on Brian,' he shouted to the hapless cable operator. 'Get them down, we need to get this one done before we finish tonight. They want to have the bedroom set on here ready for the morning.' There was a distant buzzing of electrical equipment, the cable minutely twanged one last time, and then nothing. I watched as a group of people gathered together below, discussing something in an arm-wavingly fervent fashion, and with much shaking of heads. Brian seemed to be getting the lion's share of the attention.

Kenny swung into view and waved at me.

'Hello Clee,' he said. 'What you doing?'

'Oh just hanging around,' I replied. 'What about you?'

'Well I'm a bit tied up right now,' he said, swinging out of view again.

The director looked up and cupped his hands around his mouth.

'Are you all right up there you two?' he shouted.

'I'm feeling highly strung,' said Kenny, rotating like a man-sized weathervane in a very light breeze.

'Yes, well, the thing is you see . . . we've got a bit of a problem. The gearbox on the cable motor's jammed, and if we put it into neutral you're going to, well, sort of fall.'

'What does that mean exactly?' I asked, still revolving at a leisurely pace. I felt like the restaurant on the top of the Post Office Tower.

'It means, well, it's going to take a while to get you down.'

Kenny and I looked at each other briefly as we swung into view, and shrugged. Nothing new here then.

It took them three hours to get us down. Our rate of revolution was pleasantly varied throughout. We couldn't quite reach out and touch each other to stop twirling, so we'd spin for about twenty minutes in one direction, grind to a painfully slow halt, and then gradually start turning the other way. We were too high up for anyone to reach us with a stepladder, so until they got the motor fixed we were well and truly stuck. It was very hot and dusty up there, and we could only hold snippets of conversation (when our heads were aligned). After half an hour or so, the rest of the crew were sent off (there was nothing they could do), so the only ones left in the cavernous studio were me, Kenny and a bunch of engineers studiously crouched over the cable machine in the corner of the studio. We felt quite abandoned, hanging like a couple of heavenly haemorrhoids.

Kenny's head edged slowly into view. We'd exhausted our supply of jokes, I'd told him all the stories I could possibly think of, we'd played alphabet games, animal games, naughty word games and had now reached extreme tedium fatigue.

'Clee,' said Kenny. 'My shoulders hurt.' (We were suspended

by these braces under our costumes and they were beginning to chafe a little.)

'So do mine,' I said.

'You know what,' said Kenny, 'I'm getting really bored with this.'

'So am I. When are they going to get us down?'

'I don't mean this, although yes, I am very bored with this. I meant the whole thing. The whole show. I just can't be bothered anymore. I'm getting too old for this nonsense.'

'Then don't do it,' I said.

'I've been thinking about it,' he said, floating away. He waited a minute or so to line up again, and smiled at me. 'You know Clee, I've just decided this is going to be the last series. If I ever lose my head and talk about doing another, just remind me of how hot, dangly and uncomfortable I feel right now.' We looked at each other and burst out laughing, hard and loud. The engineers looked up.

'You all right up there?' asked Brian.

'Oh yes,' said Kenny, rolling his eyes and wiggling his fingers in a cartoon wave. 'Just fine.'

Kenny, true to his word, ensured that was the last series we filmed. *The Kenny Everett Television Show* was over. It was the most life-changing project I have ever worked on, and I feel proud to have been part of something that so many people loved. Wherever I go, whoever I talk to, people feel they know me as a friend because of the show, and that's a wonderful legacy with which to be left. The eighties were such a serious decade – so full of money and pomposity for some, and recession and difficulties for others – that Kenny's world was a safe haven of irreverent lunacy that touched people in a very personal way. Genius is best viewed from a distance, and as we look back at old clips from the show and assess Kenny's role in the Comedy Hall of Fame, it becomes increasingly apparent that his was a talent the likes of which we'll never see again. His mark on the entertainment business is as profound as it is indelible.

11 Small Men, Big Mistakes

J UST BEFORE WE STARTED WORK on that last series, there occurred an incident remembered by many – the occasion when I had a slightly physical encounter with the leader of the Liberal Party, Mr David Steele. When I set out to write this book I really didn't want to cover this story, but it got so much media coverage at the time, and put me so firmly in everyone's consciousness for about two weeks, that it would be a bit churlish to paper over it. So here goes.

One of the first parties we were invited to, once I was settled back in the UK, was a charity do at the Hippodrome hosted by Princess Diana, sometime in mid-March. We hadn't started filming the new series yet, and were in fact still embroiled in discussions about my contract. The party itself was one of those high-profile affairs, teeming with politicians and rock stars all in glamorous evening dresses and formal dinner suits. It was also swarming with mega-meaty security guards and secret police who wandered around the VIP tables (all cordoned off with VIP rope, as we ate our VIP food sitting on our VIP chairs) whispering into little mouthpieces and clutching suspicious gun-size bulges in their jackets every time a balloon popped.

Princess Diana, as always, was very talkative and mingly, and we ended up having quite a chat. She seemed pleased to see us, especially after our last encounter, and we hadn't been talking for more than a few minutes when Kenny asked (as only Kenny could):

'When are you going to be queen then, my dear?' She laughed.

'I don't know,' she said. 'But I do wish she'd get off the

throne and give me a go.' This was followed by gales of laughter and the clinking of glasses. If we had been Elizabethan courtiers someone would have dragged us away by now and cut off our heads.

After dinner Diana left the party and went home, giving everyone an excuse to behave a little more irreverently. It was a bit like having a teenage party at your parents' house and waiting for them to go to bed before you raided the drinks cabinet. The moment Diana left, we were invited downstairs to the aptly named Star Bar for a private drink with the other guests.

Being in the public eye can be a bit odd when you're out and about because of the presence of photographers taking your picture at inopportune moments. Anyone with a team of photographers in tow for the evening is bound to end up with a photo of themselves that, out of context, could lend itself to any number of creative captions. You might wake up the next morning and find yourself on the front page, under some giant, misleading headline. As a result, you tend to tense up whenever the press are around, and opportunities to enjoy yourself in a photographer-free zone are not to be passed up. On this particular evening we'd been told by the organisers that no press photographers would be allowed into the Star Bar, so everyone skipped downstairs in droves to find a bit of peace and quiet.

We arranged ourselves around a small table for two in the corner, and Kenny went in search of a bottle of something bubbly. No sooner had he arrived back at the table than a plethora of photographers swarmed into the room, and a collective sigh went up from the crowd as we all realised we'd been duped by the management.

This was the first time Kenny and I had been out in public for a year or so and they were keen to get a picture of us together. It's best to negotiate by giving the paparazzi what they want up front, on the understanding that they leave you alone for the rest of the evening. So, we came out from behind the table and Kenny jumped into my arms. We beamed from edge to edge, there was a blinding cacophony of flashbulbs, the photographers got what they wanted and we'd secured an evening's peace away from their ever-present lenses. Or at least that's what I thought. I put Kenny down and we went back to the table.

Some time later we were still waiting for the waitress to bring over our champagne for us, and rapidly growing impatient. I decided that I'd better go and check its whereabouts. I squeezed through the crowds and on the way to the bar I bumped into David Steele, who that year was doing some fairly serious high-profile election campaigning in an effort to get Margaret Thatcher's job. We had met once before (very briefly) on Dame Edna's television show, and so exchanged the usual hellos and light conversational frippery.

That was until the photographers zoomed in and surrounded us. David (I feel I can call him that now) said something to the effect of 'Oh dear, look at this,' and oh dear it most certainly was. The photographers were barking their usual instructions ('Alwight darlin', move in a bit, gorn Dave, pootcha arm round 'er, stand closer togevver . . .' – all that sort of stuff). It was obvious what kind of shot they wanted, and the headline they wanted to go with it: top politician in 'close conversation' with voluptuous stareen in run-up to big election. All very pseudo-scandal and a bit obvious. This was exactly the sort of picture that David Steele didn't want.

Oh fickle finger of fate.

I suggested we act quickly and make a funny photo into which absolutely nothing could be read. A photo of two people talking can be made to look very suspicious if the caption's right and they catch your eyes looking a little skew-whiff. But something that's obviously staged can seldom be misinterpreted. He looked a bit flustered, so I tried to explain myself.

'Let's do the same pose that Kenny and I just did,' I said. 'They'll have a cheery photo and we can just get on with the evening.' Rather than reassuring him, my suggestion just seemed to make him look even more perplexed.

'Jump into my arms and I'll catch you,' I said, spelling it out. 'I'm very strong.'

He is quite a small sort of fellow anyway – about the same size as Kenny – so I had no qualms being able to hold him up (now if it had been Arnold Schwarzenegger, I might have given it another thought).

So he jumped.

The thing about doing anything with a hint of athletic prowess is that once you've decided to do it, you have to go the whole way or not do it at all. This applies to skiing, high diving and clearly, staged photo opportunities. I suppose politicians have a natural urge to curb any human qualities in front of the press, which is what makes them so up-and-downy sometimes. They can never afford to look even slightly undignified, whereas 'entertainment' people on a night out often strive for quite the opposite. Even so, David made a polite effort to follow my plan, which is quite an achievement for any politician really and worthy of congratulations.

Unfortunately, this was the root of the problem. He only made a *bit* of an effort. Perhaps just as he was about to leap into my arms he suddenly thought he would look silly and retracted his jump. Or maybe, more chivalrously, he thought he might squash me. Either way, he sort of half jumped, half raised his leg, half fell at me. As I tried to lift him he trod on my dress with one foot, while I heaved he hoed, and before we knew what had happened, we'd tripped over and fallen on the floor. It was all over in two seconds and, while I struggled to keep my particles tucked into my dress, David was helped to his feet by Hippodrome owner Peter Stringfellow, who appeared from nowhere. We all laughed, brushed ourselves off and carried on gleeing in separate directions, thinking no more of it (well, I didn't anyway, but then I don't have a politician's highly tuned antenna for scandal).

I could see Kenny standing beside Boy George through the ocean of photographers, with his hands over his eyes slowly shaking his head from side to side as he so often did when these things happened. I made my way through to where he was, and he scooped me up smiling madly.

'I knew that was you behind there with all that fuss going on,' he said. 'I can't leave you for a minute.'

We laughed and set about drinking the champagne that had at last turned up on our table. The evening passed uneventfully, and we went back to Kenny's to dance the night away. I eventually got home in the tiny hours.

The next morning, far too early for my liking, the phone rang. It was Kenny. He was bursting with laughter.

'Have you seen the papers yet, Clee?' he asked.

'No Kenny,' I said, 'I've just got out of bed. Actually, you just got me out of bed.'

'Well Clee,' he proudly announced. 'I don't want to spoil your little surprisey-poos, but I'll just say this. It takes a lot to push Princess Diana off the front pages. But it takes a hell of a lot to push her out of every single paper in the land.'

'What on earth are you talking about,' I said, suddenly waking up.

'Go and buy a newspaper and give me a ring back,' he said. 'And you'd better give your mother a whisky as well.' He laughed again and hung up, leaving me holding the phone and wondering what on earth he was talking about.

I climbed into an outfit and dashed around the corner to the local newsagents, who had all the papers laid out in neat piles on the bottom shelf, which ran the entire length of the shop. Or rather, he had pictures of Cleo Rocos laid out in neat piles on a shelf that ran the entire length of the shop.

'Oh my God . . .' I mouthed, bending down to pick up the first paper I could see.

'Oh good morning, Miss Rocos,' said Mr Shamkar, who owned the store. 'Nice to be seeing you this morning. I see you are being plenty famous today.'

'Apparently . . .' I replied, grabbing one of each in a bit of a daze. I looked at the photos. Someone had taken a picture of the precise moment when David Steele and I tumbled to the ground. Not only that, but for a millisecond in the confusion I had, er, popped out of my dress on one side. In real life I'd 'popped' myself back in again so quickly no one had even noticed. No one, that is, except the proud owner of an Olympus Trip and a phone book that had the number of every picture desk on every national newspaper in the entire country.

I hurried back to the house in a bit of a whirl. When I got home the phone was ringing itself off the hook. Every chat show and radio station wanted a quote from Cleo Rocos: The Girl Who Dropped On David Steele. I even had reporters camping outside trying to get the story out of me. It all seemed so ridiculous. All we'd done was fall over at a party. You would have thought I'd carried out some Satanic baby roasting or something.

I turned down all the offers of interviews until, by early afternoon, it became clear that I had to make some kind of statement otherwise the whole thing was going to snowball completely out of control. I received a call from TVAM inviting me on their show the next morning to defend myself, so I decided to do one interview and put the whole thing to rest.

On the phone they asked me whose fault it was and I (rather magnanimously I thought) took the blame. David Steele and I had been discussing Irangate, I said, and I accidentally tripped him up on the way to the bar. Meanwhile the broadcast media were having a field day with anyone and everyone who felt they had an angle to contribute to this most important non-story. The Liberal Party went on television and said that I'd carefully orchestrated the entire episode as a publicity stunt. But I had nothing to publicise: it was simply one of those things that happened one evening. Kenny knew that this was just typical of the sort of incident that befell me on a daily basis, but conspiracy theorists always have the upper hand, no matter how fanciful their ideas, so there was no point me even trying to tell the truth.

The next morning, TVAM had started running trailers for my appearance later in the show. Within minutes of the first one being broadcast, I had what I can only describe as an intimidatory and extremely arrogant phone call from some gimp at the Liberal Party as I was getting ready to leave the house for the studio.

He was furious, insisting that I didn't make my appearance on TVAM, and that David Steele was not happy since he now had a backache from the fall. I promptly informed him that my dress had been torn and I wasn't happy about that. This nasally voiced man then called me petulant, and continued to say that Mrs Steele wasn't very happy either. I retorted (with blunt razor-blades in my voice) that I found this phone call to be not only intrusive, but also highly irritating. I also suggested that while they were so busy quoting text from the tabloids, they might like to look more closely at the photos, because there were quite clearly two of us in the picture and I was not, as they were suggesting, solely responsible for this moment of frivolity.

This was the Liberal Party. The *Liberal Party*: the one Lloyd George used to run. Liberal, as in 'relating to or having policies or views advocating individual freedom; giving and generous in temperament or behaviour; tolerant of other people'. This geek was acting like a complete idiot!

With that, I hung up, grabbed my bag, and headed off for TVAM.

To warrant an intrusion of this kind, the Liberal Party spin doctors must have been expecting me to go on television and spring part two of my so-called 'fiendish publicity stunt', as if I had some media master plan in which David Steele was putty in my hands. But I had one purpose for that interview and one purpose only: to kill the story. I turned up in a terribly demure pink cashmere sweater and was nothing but marshmallowy. And despite the nasty call I'd received that morning, I actually went out of my way to defend David Steele, who I was convinced had nothing to do with the phone call and who, in all fairness, had been very cool and gentlemanly.

The interview seemed to do the trick, and the coverage fizzled out after reporting my quotes the next day. I came out of the TVAM studio set feeling I'd restored my reputation as a good, wacky, decent and honest person, but not everyone seemed to appreciate this. As I walked away I caught sight of Neil Kinnock, who had also been on the show. He'd just finished doing a political interview, and was collecting his things and having his make-up taken off.

He took one look at me, grabbed his notes, and fled the studio, giving me a very wide berth indeed.

I couldn't wait for the whole thing to be over. All I got was trouble I didn't need. At the time I was still negotiating my contract with the BBC for the next series of Kenny's show, and I was very much aware that the large amounts of coverage left me open to accusations of manipulating the media. But I'm simply not Machiavellian enough to have constructed the accident as a media stunt.

Something else very unsavoury happened on the back of this. Three days after it happened, I got a phone call from a news agency saying they wanted to do a telephone interview with me concerning my time in the States, my plans with Kenny and my thoughts on rejoining *The Kenny Everett Television Show*. Phone interviews are very common, simply because meeting up with everyone who wants a quote would take so long you'd never actually get any work done. So we did the interview and it went as boringly well as it could have done, given the poor interviewer and his general apathy for the subject matter. The reporter asked me a couple of questions about the David Steele episode, which I laughed off with a funny line or two and that was it.

I didn't think of it again until about two weeks after the incident, when a reporter from a tabloid rang me up and asked how much I was making from my phone-line service. I didn't have a clue what he was talking about.

'Look in the back of tonight's paper,' he said. 'I suppose that isn't your advert.'

I got my hands on a copy that night and turned to the section at the back where all the steamy sex-line numbers were advertised. And there, wedged between Doris and her Walloping Doo Daas and I'm Brenda and I Like Big Boys, was an ad with my picture on it, advertising Cleo's Saucy Stories–She's Liberal and She'll Floor You! (no joking). And when I rang the number, what did I hear? My phone interview. Nothing saucy, and nothing naughty. People were being badly conned, including me.

When I rang Kenny I was very upset by it all, and he was massively supportive. He'd had to deal with the real knobbly end of the stick when it came to press intrusion and over time had learnt to be very thick-skinned about it. And as for the phone line, he'd had a similar experience years ago when a transvestite/drag club in a Greek holiday resort advertised itself in the UK using pictures of Kenny as Cupid Stunt, or at least someone impersonating him. At the time Kenny was very sensitive about his sexuality and tried to use the law to get them to stop using the picture. But it simply blew up in his face when the papers found out, and it made the whole thing a lot worse than if he'd just let them get on with it. His advice to me was to ignore it, and it would go away. I did, and it did. Kenny, as usual, was right.

12 Loony Tunes

ONCE WE FINISHED FILMING THE last series, we had to do the usual round of interviews and press conferences before the shows were broadcast. Whenever a new series was due to go out on television, it was standard practice for the BBC marketing machine to kick into action and organise a lot of pre-broadcast publicity. This meant that we all had to commit ourselves to a series of intense, and often quite gruelling, press conferences, which Kenny dreaded. For many performers, their persona on radio or television is something created to entertain, and quite removed from the real person. But at press conferences you can't act in character or hide behind a script, and it's one of those few occasions where you have to expose some of the real person behind the act. For someone as painfully shy as Kenny, this was an ordeal.

Press conferences always had the air of a prison interrogation to them, and reporters *en masse* can be very intimidating, which I guess is part of their job. Most press conferences we did weren't big events like you see on television, with a top table and ranks of polite journalists raising their hands and asking questions in turn. They're more like semi-benevolent muggings, with hoards of journalists closing in, trying to bash you over the head with their microphones and rob you of a good quote.

We'd always start off standing side by side, trying to keep our composure, as the camera bulbs flashed and questions were fired at us from all angles. Gradually the journalists would start to crowd in on us, shoving tape recorders, pads and mikes into our faces and getting more and more excited. A typical tactic was to get us answering different questions, then slowly the press conference would divide into two and we'd find ourselves separated. We'd try to keep our eyes on each other and focus on answering just one question at a time, and I would try to make sure Kenny wasn't getting too stressed, or wasn't struggling at all with the journalists. This often proved quite difficult, and I always knew when I saw a certain look in his eyes that the questions were getting too personal and too uncomfortable for him. If you're in the public eye, it may just be that you view your personal life to be exactly that – personal – but there's an implicit belief within the press that once you're famous, your private life is no longer your own. And if you appear defensive, the journalists think you've got something to hide, so they get even more aggressive, or leap to conclusions. There's generally nothing personal in what they do, it's just how they operate, and in some respects it's like a sport where everyone knows the rules and you play along according to a fixed game plan. Short of simply walking out of the press conference (and that would not go down very well at all) there's not much you can do.

Not much, but there is something.

On a few occasions, when things really got boiling, Kenny and I played our Get out of Jail Free card. I'd shoot him a look that would let him know to get ready, wink, and then – much in the style of a Victorian melodrama – I'd swoon to the ground with a plaintive cry of 'oohh . . . *Kenny.*' As I dropped to the floor, Kenny would break away from his reporters and rush to my side.

The following moments would be full of high drama as Kenny shushed everyone away from me so I could get some air, and then half-dragged, half-walked me away from the crowd and towards the exit. This reverse attention role worked swiftly and effectively, and we'd either make a getaway, or round off the press conference with a few low-key answers about the show.

I don't imagine for a moment the press were even the slightest bit fooled by my Sarah Bernhardt attack of the vapours (if they did there would have been headlines galore saying 'Kenny and Cleo in Fainting Fit Drama – Overwork and Stress Lead to Television Star's Collapse'), especially since on at least two occasions I recognised the same faces in the crowd of journalists. To faint once is unfortunate, to faint twice is clearly unbelievable. But I think they had an admiration and a place in their hearts for the ridiculous lengths Kenny and I would go to in order to protect one another, and they let us get away with it. I suppose in a funny way our press conferences had a slightly different set of rules to other people's. It was all a bit of a wheeze, and we only did it a handful of times, but it was still mightily effective.

The press conference for the last series was no different from any of the others, except that both Kenny and I knew it was going to be our last. We didn't tell anyone else of our decision, deciding that it would simply fuel speculation about our plans and invite scrutiny that we didn't really want. So we soldiered on with the promotion of the show, knowing full well we wouldn't be doing it again next year, and with our focus already fixed on what we were hoping to do next. By coincidence – although we weren't going to work together again immediately – we both ended up going into something musical, me immediately, and Kenny a couple of years down the line.

I'd already been toying with the idea of doing something more tuney during my break in the US, and after deciding not to renew my contract with the BBC, I turned my thoughts to music more seriously. I'd written some musical numbers into my US show, and had enjoyed them so much that I decided I wanted to do a show that was all tunes and big bongly entertainment. Which is when I met Dominic Buggati.

Dominic's one of those people who was beaten severely over the head with the talent stick when he was born. He can write songs, he can perform, he can rub his stomach and pat his head at the same time: it's really rather irritating all the things he can effortlessly turn his mind to. Some of the notches on his success post include writing songs for Carly Simon, putting tunes into the mouths of the Three Degrees, winning Grammy awards – that sort of thing. I'd met him in 1987 through Elizabeth and David Emanuel, and it transpired we had yin and yang ideas. I needed someone to write songs for the show I wanted to do, and he was looking for a vehicle for a selection of songs that he'd already written. So, after I finished filming the last television series, we got together. In a week we'd assembled the Cleo Rocos and Enrico Valdez Orchestra, turning an idea scribbled on the back of an airline ticket into showbiz reality.

The show was designed to get people singing and dancing to big band Latiny songs in the style of Lucille Ball and Desi Arnaz. Dominic wrote the songs and played the bandleader Enrico Valdez, a Bolivian lounge lizard who made Steve Coogan's Tony Ferrino look like an unassuming right-on nineties kinda guy. I played the singer, a mad Carmen Miranda character with costumes that were so big they needed their own traffic system and with more fruit on my head than a greengrocers' hat convention. We got together a twenty-two-piece band, a brilliantly eclectic group comprising talented young black musicians, old jazz buffs, retired classical orchestra members and anyone who could play like the devil and had a costume that looked suitably *ariba*. They were a great band and the show – despite its cobbled together nature – had an energy and fizz to it that was dangerously contagious. In fact, the band went on to live an independent life long after the show finished, with various spin-offs and break-away groups constantly forming and reforming like some vast musical amoeba.

The format was fairly basic; a number of tongue-in-cheek songs with names like 'Blame It on the Bosonova', linked together with a bit of cheery chat and cartoonular characteris-ations. We wanted it to be as over-the-top as possible, and so had everyone wear whatever costume they wanted: from dressing gowns and dinner jackets to scuba gear and safari outfits. After a few weeks of rehearsal we had our opening night at the Paramount City theatre (off Picadilly Circus) and the show went down a storm. I'd always wanted to play Paramount because it was where Stan Laurel and Charlie Chaplin used to do their music-hall acts. Going on stage there was very magicky.

After a few weeks at Paramount, it became obvious we had something on our hands, but unfortunately our booking was nearing its end, so we decided to take the show on the road. By this stage we'd attracted something of an underground following, and people were coming to the show night after night dressing up in their own wild 'n' crazy costumes, much like people do when *The Rocky Horror Picture Show* plays. The dialogue between the songs was becoming enormously interactive with the audience, with the same jokes generating identical responses each night. It was like being part of a cult phenomenon. It was fantastic.

When we took the show on the road, our first gig was at the Mean Fiddler, a venue that is usually frequented by large, greasy bikers and real bands that were the absolute antithesis of the audiences we'd been playing to at Paramount. On our first night, just before we went on, Dominic peered from backstage across the sea of long, lank locks and scuffed, smelly leather jackets and gulped.

'We're going to die, Cleo,' he said. 'And I don't mean theatrically. I mean literally. They will kill us.'

But they loved it. It was so kitsch and over the top you couldn't help but like it. From there we went on to play a host of other venues, all with the same reaction. And the show stayed on tour for almost eighteen months.

Halfway through the tour we were approached by a young guy who wanted to film the show as a pilot, and then try to get a series commissioned for us on television. Dominic and I thought it was great idea, so we went ahead. We called the show *The Cha Cha Club*, to give it a bit more marketability, and set about devising a format that would be more television friendly. It was to be filmed at the famous Nomis Rehearsal Studios in West London.

The week before filming we blitzed all the local clubs and pubs with leaflets asking people to turn up at the studios so they could: a) get on television, and (b) drink free cocktails. It wasn't the done thing to serve real drinks to studio audiences then, but we were convinced that this would create a happy, club feeling before filming, and would add substantially to a warm, glowy atmosphere in the show and so oil the wheels of joviality. And we were right.

The show was similar in format to Chris Evans' *TFI Friday*: three bands playing, music from the resident musicians and chat at the bar with stars between songs. The pilot had some great guests, including Then Jericho and Matt Bianco. Our show was more scripted, with something vaguely resembling a storyline, but I like to think we were ahead of our time with the format. We just needed to brush up on our execution a little.

The pilot was successful in a very unexpected way: it didn't get a series commissioned, but it did run as a B-movie (remember those?) in cinemas up and down the country for months. It was also bizarrely surreal, due to the firemen.

We were in the middle of filming, with plenty of dry ice and theatrical smoke to add to the ambience, when the fire alarm went off. We didn't hear it because it was linked directly to the fire-station, so the show carried on oblivious to the fact that down the road a dozen or so firemen were leaping into their big red truck and hurtling towards us with the intent of putting us out.

About halfway through the show – cameras rolling and music playing – they burst into the venue, all yellow hats, big black donkey jackets and respirators, and started trying to evacuate the building. It would have completely ruined any other show, but since everyone was already dressed up in the most ridiculous costumes anyway, and the whole thing had an air of barely constrained chaos about it, it simply looked like part of the act. So we kept it in. The show also had another very minor claim to fame: it was Minnie Driver's first-ever film appearance (she was one of the clubbers in the front row of the audience).

Talking of *TFI Friday*, there's another Chris Evans connection that helped put *The Cha Cha Club* well and truly on the map. When we were touring later in the year we went on a publicity drive which included a spot on Manchester's Piccadilly Radio, where I was to be interviewed about the act. I was in the studio with the band Hue and Cry, and had the lyrics to one of the songs for the show with me: a take on Elvis's 'Are you Lonesome Tonight'. Twenty minutes into the one-hour show, I decided to sing it. It went something like this:

Are you lonesome tonight?
Do you miss me tonight? Are you sorry we drifted apart?

Does your memory stray, to that bright summer day,
When I whipped you and called you sweetheart?

Do the chains in your bedroom hang empty and bare?
Do you fondle your handcuffs and wish I was there?
Are you missing the pain? Shall I whip you again?
Tell me dear are you lonesome tonight?

Within minutes the switchboard was jammed with calls from outraged listeners – mostly parents who thought that since their children were listening to the show, the song was 'highly inappropriate', and mortified Elvis fans who felt I'd besmirched the memory of The King (oh, big goof). When I sang the song the DJ wasn't overly outraged. However, his boss was so mad at the reaction that he called security, had me removed from the studio and frog-marched me to the front gates, where I was offered sacrificially to the mob outside (largely Elvis impersonators in spangly suits).

And who was the little known DJ presiding over this indefensible slide in broadcasting standards? None other than the ginger maestro himself, Chris Evans. Chris had to make a statement to the press immediately afterwards about how he was 'terribly embarrassed' by the whole thing, but this was more for his boss's benefit than anyone else's.

While I was jeopardising the career of an upcoming media mogul, Kenny threw himself into all manner of projects, most memorably *That's Showbiz*, which he did for four series with Gloria Hunniford and Mike Smith. He had mixed feeling about the show, but did enjoy sitting behind Gloria Hunniford and playing her hair with spoons whenever the opportunity arose.

Life for Kenny and I carried on as usual: hanging out together and gleeing around, sometimes in front of the cameras, but mostly not. In 1988 we were commissioned to work together on a new series called *Brainstorm*, and we once again managed to rock the broadcasting boat.

The show was a prime-time vehicle for the BBC to present science subjects in a way that was funny and digestible, to adults and children alike. It was based on the idea of a mad scientist (Kenny) and his bimbonic lab assistant (me) carrying out experiments and illustrating how boats float, how jet planes work, why the sky is blue and all manner of interesting scientific facts. We also had guests on every week to explain different technologies (Mary Archer appeared on one episode, I seem to remember, doing something on satellites). The show worked on a number of levels, but couldn't really be classed as a ratings success. For a start, the BBC spent an outrageous amount of money on props: over £50,000 I think. This set expectations for the show's success very high indeed. And secondly, I managed to get us on to *Points of View* almost every week with complaints of one kind or another (it became such a regular occurrence that I was disappointed if we didn't make it on the show).

The problems started fairly early on, when – in the quiz section – Kenny asked viewers to identify some odd gadget that I would then demonstrate the next week. Kenny asked what a particular dooberry was one week and I replied that it was a welly warmer: something used to warm up your wellington boots on a cold winter's day. But that's not what the viewing public heard. They thought I'd said willy warmer, and the following week *Points of View*'s mail sacks were bulging at the seams with outraged letters from Disgusted of Tunbridge Wells, Abhorred of Langton Green and Repulsed of Matfield. After that, it seemed every ad-lib I made provoked a rabid response from some moral minority, and *Brainstorm* became a byword for smutty kids' television. Quite an achievement for a show that set out to be 'educational and fun for all the family'.

It certainly exposed Kenny and me to some life-enriching experiences. In one episode I had to handle some live leeches, which I'd been assured were well and truly fattened up with something else's blood before I had to pick them up. As I 'played' with them, explaining how they anaesthetise their victims before making an incision and sucking out the blood, what should this disgusting little slug thing do? Start eating me. A thick trickle of blood ran down the back of my hand and the leech handler came on set and pulled it off.

'It's all right,' he said. 'It only makes a tiny hole. And to be honest, that blood is something else's. It's just regurgitating.'

Oh yeuch!

I also managed to nearly kill Kenny demonstrating a stretching machine. It was like a table that lay flat, with ankle grips into which your legs were locked. A big handle then swung the table upright and you were left dangling by your ankles in the hope of walking off a few feet taller afterwards. As the lab assistant it was my job to lock Kenny into it and swing him upside down. As he lay down we had a little on-screen banter about not trying this at home, and how dangerous it might be if you didn't lock the ankle clips properly.

'That's right,' said Kenny to camera. 'Falling off on to your head can be extremely risky, especially when you're as brainy as me! Luckily I've got a super-clever lab assistant who's made sure I'm buckled in and ready to stretch. Shall we swing away?'

'Yes Professor!'

'Then let's get stretching!'

I grabbed the handle, gave two firm turns and the table went upright. Kenny slid straight off and landed on his head.

They didn't commission another series.

13 We're all Going on a Summer Holiday (in February)

THERE'S SOMETHING DEVILISHLY DIFFICULT ABOUT writing something like this, and that's trying to work out what happened when. I've never kept a diary (that's always seemed a terribly dangerous thing to do: what would happen if it got into the wrong hands?), so pinpointing dates and events is a torturous process of looking through press clippings and trying to fill in the blanks. But there are some days that stand out like beacons through the fog of the years, fixed points of such significance that their memory stays with you forever. The day Kenny first invited me on holiday with him was one such event.

As I mentioned earlier, Kenny was perpetually trying to draw me into his holidays in the most oblique fashion, always telling me how nice it would be if I could journey with him, without actually taking the plunge and asking me outright. And I was similarly reluctant to take the plunge from the other side by asking him if he wanted me to come with him. It had begun to get a little silly, as he'd ended numerous trips prematurely by turning up on my doorstep with bundles of holiday presents, full of regrets that I hadn't come with him.

But on Wednesday 17 February 1988, shortly after 6 p.m., he changed all that with a single telephone call to the house that I shared with my mother.

We were in the kitchen making dinner when the phone rang. I picked it up, and there was Kenny, all breathless and full of excitement. We chatted about the usual bananary things and then he went momentarily silent.

'Clee,' he said coyly. 'Are you doing anything on Saturday?'

'Not really,' I replied. 'What have you got in mind?'

'Well, my curly yellow friend,' he drawled, 'how do you fancy spending a few relaxing, carefree and fun-filled days in Spain with Francis and me?'

My heart leapt into my throat. Francis Butler was a friend of ours who had just bought an avocado farm in the south of Spain. He is one of two handsome, dashing and extremely witty brothers. The other, Alex, I'd originally met through Kenny. Francis and I had spent many an evening out dancing, and along with their beautiful sister Penny – who is as equally fantastic as her brothers – the Butler Brothers are a guaranteed, bona fide, Grade A, fun time out.

I was poleaxed. He'd done it! Kenny had invited me on holiday. In shock, I managed calmly to accept, declaring that I could do with a few days away from London. All those years when he had gone away on trips and had said how lovely it would have been if I had been there, and how much he had missed me, and now he'd plucked up the courage to ask me along. Not only that, but he'd done so with the same composure as if asking me around for a cup of tea and a custard cream. He went on to say that he would let me know about the tickets and travel details and would make all the arrangements. When I put the phone down I leapt in the air, then grabbed my mother and twirled her around in dizzying circles.

'Guess what! Guess what!' I cried, swinging her around my head like the proverbial cat. She, of course, had no idea why I was so peculiarly elated, but maintained her sense of calm with a sort of benign amusement (aren't mums great?).

'You'd better tell me before I die of asphyxiation,' she cried.

I let go and allowed her to catch her breath before going on to tell her that Kenny had just asked me to go to Spain with him for five days. I was beside myself with excitement.

'I can't believe it!' I said. 'He's invited me. Me! No one else, just me. All these years and he's finally plucked up the courage to invite me away!'

By this time I had worked myself into a crescendo of antici-pation. Having never trodden in this area of our friendship before, Kenny had finally taken the initiative and realised that I felt the same affection for him. All he had to do was ask: there was absolutely zero chance of rejection.

I gleefully went on to recount the entire conversation word for word, blow for blow. What I didn't realise was that I hadn't put the phone down properly and Kenny – who was trying to make another call from his house – heard every single word I said. I didn't find this out until a couple of days later when he made a few tongue-in-cheek remarks about how long it had taken us to organise a holiday together and gave me a prankish grin. I was mortified, but didn't let him see. I simply said that I couldn't remember saying anything very interesting (a lie). It obviously didn't matter, because a week later we were off to Spain: our first holiday together!

Our departure had a slightly surreal note to it, since all of our friends knew what a big deal it was that we were finally travelling together, so they organised a seeing-off party the likes of which was last seen when the *Titanic* left Liverpool. We arrived at the airport completely mob-handed, and after all the usually airport faffing about, Kenny and I eventually boarded the plane to a distant chorus of goodbyes and the intermittent popping of champagne corks. We were off.

The flight was short and giggly, and we were met at the Spanish end by Francis, who'd driven to the airport in his little sporty red number (that's a car, not underwear). It was early evening by the time we cleared customs, and in no time at all were soon speeding along the Carretera, a terrifying stretch of road which, allegedly, has the dubious reputation as the most dangerous highway in Europe. Francis, who was obviously an old hand at this route, decided to give us a commentary of the sights as we hurtled around corners and overtook little farming vans with carefree abandon.

'It's like driving on a giant Scalectrix set,' he bellowed, looking over his shoulder at me in the back seat, clearly unconcerned with small matters like oncoming vehicles or traffic signals. 'Mind you, you don't get many cars coming at you the other way on a Scalectrix set.'

He laughed reassuringly, only it couldn't have been that reassuring because Kenny sat in the front seat gripping the door handle with one hand and his seat belt with the other. His knuckles were quite white and there was a sheen of fear-induced sweat on his brow.

'For God's sake, slow down will you!' He was hyperventilating like a landed fish, and his humour had strangely deserted him. Francis took his driving hand off the wheel and slapped Kenny heartily on the shoulder.

'Don't be so nervous old chap,' he roared, laughing. 'They all drive like this round here. If you go sensibly they'll run you off the road quicker than you can say *gracias amigo*.'

We went around another bend on two wheels and Kenny went a deeper shade of green. The funny thing was there was a strange logic to Francis's explanation, since everybody seemed to be driving with the same lunatic desire to hit other cars, which seemed to cancel out Francis's own homicidal efforts.

'Please, Francis,' pleaded Kenny. 'I'm really not enjoying this very much.'

Francis was momentarily distracted by the need to get out the way of an oncoming lorry.

'What was that?' he shouted.

'Nothing,' mumbled Kenny, deciding that the best policy was to let Francis devote whatever small concentration he had to the matter of getting us all to the farm in one piece, instead of distracting him with useless pleas for our lives. Kenny shut his eyes and gripped the door handle even harder until the plastic cracked. After what seemed like a fortnight, we eventually arrived at Francis's 'farm', which should more aptly have been described as 'huge rambling palatial place'. We were alive, but deeply psychologically scarred. I expected to have to unpeel Kenny's fingers from the door handle and wave smelling salts under his nose before we could get him out of the car.

Unlike all our other friends who'd been trying for years to

get Kenny and I sleeping together, Francis took an alternative approach and decided to separate us as much as possible, putting Kenny in the west wing and me in the east wing. The house was so big I was hoping Francis would issue us with floor plans and an orienteering compass so we could find the bathroom during the night, or at least put signs up on the wall like you get at hotels: DINING ROOM, POOL, RECEPTION – that sort of thing. It was a truly beautiful house, all white walls, Spanish curly bits and terracotta tiles.

After a quick shower and tour of the house (I made secret chalk marks on the walls so I could find my way back), we rendezvoused in Reception Area Four and set off to go to dinner, and so meet up with the rest of the holiday crew. We were a bit late, as it took us quite a while to entice Kenny back into the car, but after a thankfully short drive we were soon at the expensive, but style-challenged, part of town called Puerto Banus: home to leather-trimmed T-shirts and greasy blonde perms. Once brimming with some of the best paella I've ever had, we ambled off to a nightclub where Francis had arranged for us to meet up with Alex and some other friends.

The club was at street level, overlooking the port, and only a short walk from the restaurant. Kenny had perked up considerably by now, and seemed to have forgiven Francis for his creative driving. Alex and three other chums were already there when we arrived, so we decided to take a table outside since the weather was balmy and the cool breeze from the sea wonderfully refreshing.

We hadn't been seated for more than ten minutes when I felt my chair jerk beneath me. I turned, and there – rapidly disappearing down the street – were two teenage gypsy boys clutching my evening bag. I let loose a cry of 'gypsies!', much as you'd cry 'elephants!' on a safari game hunt, and gave chase in my see-through and slightly beaded tango dress. Alex – ever the gentleman and always up for a bit of big-game hunting – also leapt to his feet and dashed off down a side alley, with the intent of heading them off at the pass. At the moment it all went off, Kenny and the rest of the crew were inside getting drinks, but the other customers froze at their tables like some

Renaissance painting, glasses of wine half-raised to their lips and forks stopped in mid-air.

As the boys made off at some considerable pace, I saw an opportunity to take a short cut by leaping over a low wall. Well, it was a low wall on my side, anyway. I vaulted over it only to plunge an extra few feet, finding myself landing clumsily on a restaurant table in between a couple trying to have a romantic night out for two (now a romantic night out for three). Their jaws dropped into their laps. I smiled apologetically, carefully picking my way through plates of mussels in white-wine sauce, before jumping gracefully off the table and resuming the chase. I hurtled down an alleyway that seemed to be pointing in the right direction, and, with Alex's voice echoing from some indeterminate point in the distance, rounded a corner into the slavering jaws of two devil dogs.

They were Dobermans: big, lean and, judging by their demeanour, really, really unhappy about something. I skidded to a halt and felt every muscle in my body go 'eeeek! run away!' We stood there facing each other for what seemed like hours: a comical Polaroid of tourist meets local wildlife. They were growling at me with a deep baritone rumble, lips curled back from their million-spiky-teethed jaws, as if deciding which bits were going to make the juiciest part of their dinner (I was panting like a loon). I tried to look at them with as much *bonhomie* and tenderness as I could, but this obviously had no effect, as they both took a step closer, growling even louder and dribbling alarmingly. I was about to throw myself on the ground and play dead (I read somewhere that dogs won't eat dead things) when Alex suddenly appeared at the end of the alley, behind the dogs.

Now it was two against two, and you could see the bloodthirsty glint in their eyes diminish by about, er, zero. And why should it? They were two highly evolved slaughtering machines, designed to rip the throats out of their prey with a single muscly wrench of their jaws. We were two out-of-shape humans with bellies full of wine and no gun. The odds were badly stacked against us. But what they hadn't reckoned on was our cunningly evolved ability to run away very fast indeed.

Alex jumped up in the air and started screaming at the dogs.

My friend April and I bunking off school to watch filming in west London.,
with producer Hunt Downs.

A medley of
party moments.

At Charles Althorp's 21st birthday party, with Nikolai creeping in at the side.

Meeting Prince Philip at the Berkeley Square Ball, with David and Elizabeth Emanuel.

On holiday in
Ronda, Spain.

Life with Kenny off
the set was often
similar to life on it.

Heading for
Gibraltar: posing
for Kenny...

...and with Francis.

Marcel Wave.

Cupid Stunt.

Gizzard Puke.

Sid Snot.

The Princess of Wales's favourite impression of Prince Charles.

Ray Cameron, keen to encourage a romantic liaison between Kenny and me, started writing more and more bed scenes for us.

Miss Whiplash.

Forever together in our own film.

Momentarily distracted by the sight of a demented Englishman doing a rain dance, they stood looking from him to me, clearly confused as to who would make the easiest dinner.

'Cleo . . . run away!' he shouted. I took this as my cue and turned tail, running as fast as I could back towards the restaurant. Behind me I could hear the snarling of the dogs mingled with deranged screams from Alex, and then the pounding of Alex's footsteps catching up with mine.

He pulled up beside me, both of us still racing like mad things.

'Keep going, Clee,' he panted. 'They're not far behind!'

We doubled back a couple of times, the sound of claws on cobbles gradually receding into the distance, until we popped out from between two buildings like a cork from a bottle, straight into the laps of Francis, Kenny and co., who were sitting at our table admiring the sea view.

We sat down at the table, gasping for air, and recounted our two-for-the-price-of-one story, starting with being hounded by villains and then chased by villainous hounds. Our friends sat and listened, slack-jawed. When we'd finished Kenny put down his glass of wine and waved his hands about as if trying to grapple the words from thin air. Eventually he just burst out laughing.

'Clee, I just . . . I mean . . . *how*? You've only been gone five minutes. Why doesn't anything normal ever happen to you?'

'What do you mean?' I said. 'That was normal.' We looked at each other and laughed.

By the end of the meal, Kenny was feeling very tired and said he wanted to go back to the farm to catch up on some sleep. He'd already arranged a hire car for us earlier in the evening, so planned to leave us at the restaurant and make his own way back. I don't think he relished the thought of getting back into the car with Francis again.

Francis was being slightly naughty and had taken it into his head to try to wind Kenny up by flirting outrageously with me, more for his own amusement than anything else. I think because he was so tired Kenny took it all a bit too seriously, and left in a huff, after arranging with me to meet him at 6 a.m. the next morning so we could sneak off early to Rhonda on our own. Having taken years to pluck up the courage to ask me on holiday, I think he had expected to have me all to himself, and Francis – who would get a gold medal in flirting if it was made into an Olympic sport – was very expertly diverting my attention in the most charming manner.

The next morning I got dressed quietly and crept out the front door. The sun was just up and had started to burn some of the dampness out of the cool, crisp air. It was February and so still quite chilly, but you could see it was going to be a truly beautiful morning. I was really looking forward to Kenny and I spending a day together. As I walked up to the gates, Kenny appeared from behind a bush, dangling the car keys and clutching a road map under his arm. He ran over to me kicking his heels in the air like some jolly Dick Van Dyke.

'Come on, Clee,' he chirped. 'Let's get out of here before Francis sees us.'

We jumped into the car and pulled out of the driveway, heading towards Rhonda, a beautiful town on the mountain road between Algeciras and Antequera. I wound the window down a little and let the scented air blow into the car. As we drove along, we had a post-mortem on the night before, and I could tell Kenny was feeling slightly sheepish about his peevishness at the restaurant.

'I'm sorry, Clee,' he said. 'I love Francis, but now and again he's too much.'

'He was only doing it to annoy you,' I said, touched and amused by the little green tint in Kenny's eyes.

'Precisely!' said Kenny. 'That's what makes him so irritating sometimes!'

Without warning, a grunting sound came from behind us – in the car! I swung around and looked over my shoulder at the blanketed mound on the back seat, which neither of us had paid any attention to when we got in. It was moving. There was someone, or something, underneath it. A hand emerged, then a tousled head of hair, and then a yawning, stretching Francis emerged moth-like from his blanket cocoon.

'Morning folks,' he said. 'Fancy a day at Rhonda?'

Kenny and I looked at each other, flabbergasted. Our masterful plan had been rumbled, and once again Francis had gone to considerable effort to wind Kenny up – even more than he had the night before. Francis sat up and put his head between the two front seats.

'And what precisely did you two lovebirds have planned without me? Resistance is futile!'

He was right. Resistance was futile. We looked at each other and burst out laughing. Kenny slapped Francis over the head with his map book, perhaps a bit harder than necessary, and we carried on for what actually turned out to be a very enjoyable day for all three of us. Francis had wisely decided to throttle back on the flirting and Kenny resigned himself to Francis being as generally obnoxious as possible.

Francis did manage to irritate Kenny one more time before the day was out, however. We returned that night to the farm and had a rousing opera-singing game around the piano, which Francis bashed with a demonic ferocity. Kenny was a great respecter of all things musical, and Francis's hearty efforts at demolishing the instrument upset his sensibilities terribly. I thought it was hilarious: not only Francis's violent attack on an otherwise innocent piano, but that Kenny should get so upset by it. We retired to bed in the small hours of the morning all excited about our plans for the following day. Francis had decided we should hire a yacht and sail to Gibraltar: a bally good day out on the high seas with plenty of bubbly and suntan oil (he'd tired of irritating Kenny and decided to channel his energies into something else).

I had it in my head that a day sailing would mean we'd be on some sort of royal *Britannia* yacht, all white and chrome, with a swimming pool, deck quoits and lots of over-attentive stewards rushing around in crisp sailor uniforms pandering to our every whim. With this in mind, I dressed in what I thought was an appropriate outfit: a plungy dress and polka-dot sling backs. It was only when we arrived at the marina that I realised I'd made a terrible mistake. We walked along the quay, admiring gin-palace after gin-palace, with me tugging Francis's sleeve saying 'Is this the one? Is *this* the one? *Is this the one?*'

We came to a gap in this monstrous display of disposable income, and came face to face with a tiny little rickety wooden boat that was so small it should have been operated from shore by remote control. The 'captain' clambered out of the deck and came to meet us. He was a rugged, windswept Englishman who regarded us as a cat might regard a cornered mouse: interested, but in a detached, sinister sort of way. I couldn't put my finger on it, but there was something not quite right about him. He didn't even have a uniform, not so much as a peaked cap with an anchor on it. I found this very disappointing.

As we clambered on board clutching our bottles of champagne, he took one look at my shoes and politely, but firmly, refused me on to his boat.

'You'll injure yourself and the boat in those things,' he said distantly, spitting something foul over the side of the ship. 'Go buy some sensible shoes and then you can join us.'

So Kenny and I trudged back along the quay until we found one of those inflatable-lilos-and-bucket-and-spade shops where we bought a pair of deck shoes. Kenny, who was always such an excellent mimic, machoed his way along the dockside, curling his lips and doing a hammy impression of the captain all the way to the shops and back. I was shrieking with laughter.

'Don't laugh,' he said, sounding exactly like our sinister sailor. 'You'll injure yourself. Go buy a sensible sense of humour, and then you can join us.'

By the time we returned my sides ached with laughter.

The ship's crew had swelled to two with the arrival of the captain's best mate, or whatever they're called. He looked even more shady than the captain himself, with hazy, drugged eyeballs that were slightly off kilter, so when you spoke to him you didn't know which eyeball to look at, if any. He also had a tendency to reply to any question about ten minutes after you asked him – and then in slow and carefully constructed sentences. Talking to him was like having a telephone conversation with someone in Australia: there was this agonising pause as the words went from his ears to his brain, and a time lag between his brain and his mouth.

Our vague sense of disquiet was soon dispelled once we set sail, where we spent the journey singing naughty verses to the Popeye song and making up rude lyrics to Captain Pugwash. Gibraltar was a wheeze – full of monkeys and lemon trees –

and after refuelling our champagne supplies, we clambered aboard the HMS Bathtoy to go home.

About an hour into the return journey a Spanish police boat appeared off our port side (am I sounding like a proper sailor yet?), and the police captain yelled something in Spanish at us through his loud hailer. Our skipper spasmed into a full-on clenchy-buttock attack, and First Lieutenant Druggie dissolved into a pool of clamminess. They looked at each other like French aristocrats must have done when they heard there'd been a revolution, and started making nervous preparations for the police to board the boat. Alarm bells were ringing in all of our heads and we shot each other bewildered glances. We got even more panicky when, as the boat approached us, our captain hissed between his teeth that 'it would be best for all concerned if everyone remained silent and acted normally.' Normal? Gulp-a-rooney!

The police boat pulled alongside and two stern-looking policemen climbed on board. They looked very menacing, but it was a relief to see some real uniforms at last. They demanded to look at all of our passports – which of course we'd needed to get into Gibraltar – and then they started half-heartedly prodding around the ship, lifting coils of rope and lengths of chain in the hope of finding goodness knows what underneath.

They had no interest in us – a bunch of tiddly English tourists out on a day trip – but plenty of interest in the boat. They both went to the back of the yacht and started talking intensely, pointing to different parts of it and describing its shape in the air with their hands. It seemed obvious they were planning how to rip it apart. It was a very tense moment. I couldn't bear the stress any longer, so I leapt to my feet and delivered one of the few Spanish phrases I know: 'ta gusta mi vestido?', which means 'do you like my dress?' I was a bit doolalee and over-happy, but the scene was in dire need of a rewrite and the two previously stern-looking policemen just threw back their heads and laughed unguardedly. They returned a few Spanish phrases, which I didn't understand, but they sounded like compliments so I dissolved in a melty fashion and offered them a glass of champagne. They politely declined, and then obviously decided they didn't want to rip the yacht apart after all, because they climbed back on to their own boat, shooting a withering look at our captain and his mate. Once their vessel was untied it roared off across the waves and the captain visibly wilted with relief. He came up to me and made a small, courteous bow.

'Madam, I must thank you for your intervention,' he said with great formality. 'You prevented a most difficult situation.' At this point Alex appeared behind me.

'I think you owe us an explanation,' he said, in firm British tones, like some John Hannah character from a 1930s murder mystery. 'I don't know what you characters have got stashed away on this boat of yours, but I think I speak for all of us when I say we don't want to find we've got ourselves involved in any sort of drug-smuggling scenario.'

Alex was right. It's one thing having a bit of an adventure on a day trip to Gibraltar, quite another getting caught up with Mediterranean drugglers – especially being shiny sort of people as far as the press was concerned. I could see the headlines immediately: Kenny Everett and Miss Whiplash in Spanish Smack Scam.

The skipper stood looking at Alex and then nodded. He turned, walked up the yacht, then bent down and lifted a trapdoor in what looked like the floorboards of the deck. From the hole emerged a woman – Vietnamese at a guess – blinking in the light and clutching a small baby to her chest. She looked very frightened.

'Bloody hell,' said Kenny. 'It's a boat person.'

'Two actually,' said Alex.

The captain said something to the woman, she gave us a thin smile, then she ducked down again and disappeared from view. He replaced the floorboards and threw some rope over the trapdoor.

'There are no drugs,' he said. 'Just some extra passengers.'

'No drugs? I wouldn't bet on it,' mumbled Kenny. 'Not if his first mate's anything to go by. I don't think he even knows we're at sea.'

Francis leant over and whispered to Kenny and me:

'I think we'd better stop asking questions now,' he said. 'The least we know about this the better. Let's just head back and forget about it all, heh?' We agreed that was probably the wisest course of action.

When we arrived back at port, our captain insisted, with some forcefulness, that he take us all to dinner in gratitude for us being 'such good passengers'. I suspect he thought that being indebted to him for a meal would guarantee our silence, but he didn't have to worry. He may well have had a kilo or two of something interesting and expensive stashed away in addition to the Vietnamese woman, but quite frankly it was none of our business and we had no intention of telling anyone (does publishing the story in a book count as telling anyone?). At dinner we didn't really want to ask too many questions (like I said, there was something very unsettling about him), so we had a polite tapas and quickly made our excuses. We headed back to the farm and saw the evening off with a valiant attempt to make a dent in the stock of Francis's wine cellar.

The next day Kenny and I had a second go at spending time on our own. We packed a picnic basket and set off up into the mountains to find a scenic walk and, after driving for an hour or so, found the perfect spot. It was a wide, lazy river with a row of stepping stones joining the two rocky banks. We parked the car and unloaded our fruit and wine, and set off across the stones.

Kenny and I used to go walking together all the time, and some of my best memories are from our hikes together. Kenny found the tranquillity and solitude of the countryside very calming; away from all the pressures and complications of life he found a great inner peace. Whenever we were with friends or in a crowd, Kenny always tried to keep everyone happy and be upward-inflectiony. But when we walked, whether it was on a carpet of needles in a quiet pine forest, or trekking across a wind-scrubbed expanse of heathland, he was able to stop being what others expected of him and just enjoy life for its simple pleasures.

It was at times like this we were most intimate: sharing our hopes, our secrets and our possibilities for the future – some feasible, some not. Often we would talk about things we might do in the full knowledge that they would never be, skirting around reality. It was a fantasy we would construct, and for a brief time immerse ourselves in it like children playing make-believe. As we picked our way through the Spanish countryside, the sun rising in the sky and the air slowly warming us, we talked about buying a big yacht and just sailing off into the sunset – he and I together forever, living a peripatetic existence like a couple of nautical adventurers. It was pure daydreaming of course, but sharing the image together was fun anyway.

We'd been walking for a couple of hours in what we'd perceived to be a roughly circular route, when I suggested we go back to the village we'd passed through, shortly before parking the car to, have some lunch. The only problem was, we couldn't find the stepping stones to get us back to the other side. We walked along the river bank until we came to a bit that looked shallow enough to paddle across. Kenny was wearing a new pair of brogues, and I had my peep-toes on – neither very suitable for river crossing – so we took off our shoes and hitched up our clothes to go across. I was holding the shoes, Kenny had the wine and the camera, and with my skirt around my waist I stepped in. It was actually quite shallow, and I was only up to my knees in water. Then suddenly I wasn't. I was up to my shoulders, holding the shoes above my head and gasping for air because the water was so fantastically freezing.

Kenny was close behind, but not that close. He hadn't plunged as I had, and, seeing the shock and disbelief on my face, shrieked uncontrollably with laughter, nearly dropping the wine. I couldn't move I was so horrified. He quickly came up beside me and pulled me out of the hole. He only got his legs wet. I had managed to fall into the one and only deep spot in the entire river.

We made it to the car and I sat on a towel, my dress clinging to me, soaking wet and miles from another outfit. Despite his initial reaction to my predicament, Kenny was very concerned and decided to take me to the windiest restaurant he could find so I would blow dry while we ate. We found a lovely little place with a sunny roof where they were serving food, and where I got a few funny looks from the other customers when I entered all cold, clingy-dressed and dripping. But we didn't care; nothing could have touched us that day.

This had been a very private and romantic day for us. We

were relaxed and happy, and I was just starting to get comfortable as my dress dried out, when out of nowhere who should bound into view but Francis, in all his noticeable, exuberant glory. Kenny's mouth dropped to his ankles. Here we were, in a tiny village miles from anywhere, not having told anyone of our destination and suddenly: Francis! This was getting silly.

I have to say that Francis is very good company, and much sought after among the female fraternity, unwittingly leaving a trail of broken hearts behind him. But he made Kenny jealous with his confidence and good looks, and his concerted campaign to materialise whenever we were alone. As far as I was concerned, as much as I adored Francis, Kenny's worries were unnecessary. I had told Kenny this, but Francis's appearance changed the atmosphere. So we finished lunch and made our way back to the farm. Kenny was very quiet.

That night Kenny and I did dine alone (we had a mouth-marriage of a pizza in a smelly local restaurant, I seem to remember), and over dinner had a chat that took us deep into all the corners and secrety bits. Kenny had been taken by surprise by the extent of his jealousy, and was trying to come to terms with the way he felt. After a long and intimate conversation we realised that we adored each other as much as we dared believe, and that it was nothing to be frightened of. Saying this to each other was like opening a gigantic present that we had both wanted so desperately.

Our friendship deepened into something truly wonderful, and the rest of holiday went without any further emotional strains or upsets. Kenny and I, in all our years together, never had a physical relationship, but we were as close as true lovers could be. Closer maybe.

14 Fairy Tale

NINETEEN-EIGHTY-NINE WAS A SPECIAL YEAR for us both in so many ways, and Kenny often remarked that it was the favourite year of his entire life. I feel very proud to have been such an integral part of his happy memories, and for me 1989 stands out as the year when our relationship truly cemented.

Spring set in and we started to venture into our summer wardrobes. It was around this time that Kenny and I discovered a little Latin sweatbox of a restaurant with a live band – a wonderfully friendly (and back then, slightly shabby) place called Mourinos in Bayswater. Kenny had always been very shy of dancing, although he enjoyed it immensely. Whenever we went to clubs he would only venture out on to the dance floor on three conditions. First, he needed to have a few drinks inside to rev up his footwork. Second, the dance floor had to be really packed, so no one could see him, and third I'd have to dance with him so he didn't feel self-conscious. A typical man then. . .

But in our newly discovered restaurant, Kenny stumbled across a new passion: the samba. He loved Latin rhythms and, after a taste of dancing in the basement of this wonderfully hot and sweaty club, plus a few top samba tips from me, he took to it like a duck to water. He'd suddenly found a dance that didn't make him feel embarrassed and at which he was very good.

We promptly went out and bought him a pair of leather-soled brown and white correspondent shoes so he could spin on the dance floor with consummate ease. Kenny wasn't too big on footwear and spent most of his time in a pair of battered old trainers – shoes that make it very hard to perform a dazzling routine of slidy steps because the rubber soles keep sticking to the floor. But with his new foot attire he could slide around like Michael Jackson on an ice rink. He loved it! Twice a week we'd get all dressed up and head for the club, ready to strut our funky stuff. This was before the place was renovated, and it had an authentic 'raw' feel to it that you just didn't get in the West End. It was all cracks and leaky bits, but we adored it. Almost all of the customers were of Latin origin – there wasn't a photographer or pointy showbiz person in sight – and we could go unnoticed, dancing ourselves inside out until we were sparkling pools of warm water on the floor. I would wear tight polka-dot dresses of course, and Kenny would wear a white shirt with his sleeves rolled up and cotton drill trousers. We were the *best*. The club may have been full of people born to samba, but Kenny and I eclipsed them all. At least once a night we'd empty the dance floor, and an audience would gather around us, cheering us on while we bubbled ourselves in our own private world of music, buttock-juggling ecstasy and each other.

Not only could we laugh together, but we could dance together too. It was a whole different love affair all on its own, a physical expression of our relationship that in many respects took the place of sexuality in other couples. We were joined at the soul, totally in synch with each other physically and mentally. And what's more, other people could see it, and they would instinctively back away in a natural gesture of respect, giving us space. I shall never forget the happiness on Kenny's face as we spun in and out of each other's arms, never missing a beat, never putting a foot wrong.

Nobody ever seemed to recognise us there, or if they did, they didn't say anything. They just let us come and join in, exuding nothing but warmth and welcome towards us. We secretly danced there every week for a couple of months, as well as widening our net to other Spanish sweatboxes like the Bar Madrid off Oxford Street. We were in our favourite film and the storyline was perfect. Kenny would be so excited by our nights out that he always asked me to turn up at his flat as early as possible, so we could jiggle our giblets to a thumping fandango on his gramophone before we left. It was a special personal time we enjoyed then, a time to talk, as well as to dance and to tune into each other's moods and thoughts before hitting the dance floor for real. It was perfection: no one knew who we were and we could just be Kenny and Cleo. There would be no one trying to interfere on any level, whoever they were and no matter how well-meaning they were.

On nights like this Kenny would often look me straight in the eyes, hold me close and say that he had never been happier or felt more comfortable and confident in his life than when we were together.

One night we came back to his apartment after a late-night dancing session, and Kenny went straight to the kitchen to pour a couple of nightcaps. I went upstairs to his roof garden. It was a wonderfully clear and warm night, and although living in London means you don't get to see as much of the heavens as you can when you're away from the city, I was sitting on the steps looking at the brightest of the stars through the faint orange glow of the night sky. It was June 21 – midsummer's night – and already you could sense dawn gathering its strength below the skyline. I felt pleasantly exhausted after several hours of Latin twirling, and deeply content with the life I had, and with my love and security with Kenny.

The door to the roof opened and Kenny appeared with two champagne cocktails. He closed the door behind him and sat next to me on the step. We said nothing for a moment. We just sat there looking at the sky and soaking up the night. Then Kenny slipped down on to one knee and knelt beside me, taking my hand.

'I love being with you, Clee, you know that don't you?' he said. I nodded and smiled at him. Nothing needed to be said. He paused, then went on:

'We have so much fun together. I'm so happy. You're the only person I trust. I never want to be away from you, not even for a second.' He gripped my hand a little tighter. 'Clee, will you marry me?'

I looked at him, not really believing what I had heard, totally lost for words. Kenny sensed I was dumbstruck and smiled at me.

'You do like being with me, don't you?' he said.

'Of course I do,' I replied, my head swimming. It was a good job I was sitting down because I think my legs would have given out. 'I love being with you, Kenny. I love being with you more than anyone in the world.' He looked at me with great intensity.

'Clee, I even miss you when I have to go for a pee.' I laughed and asked him if he was really sure he meant it. Really, *really* sure. It was, after all, quite a spectacularly massive thing to ask someone. He said yes, of course he meant it.

'Let's get married Clee. As soon as possible.' I smiled and gave him a huge hug.

'I'd love to marry you,' I said.

Kenny leapt to his feet and planted a kiss on my face.

'Well, let's get things organised,' he said.

He grabbed my hand and dragged me into his living room, brimming with glee, and without any warning picked up the phone, dialling furiously. I could hear it ringing at the other end and then the voice of someone answering it. It was 4.30 a.m., so I was really hoping it was somebody likely to be up at such an unsociable hour.

It wasn't. It was my mother.

'Hello, Mrs C?' said Kenny looking at me. 'It's me, Ken. Sorry to wake you up but I've got some good news for you. No, nothing horrible, it's good news. Well, yes, it is about Clee. About both of us really. We're getting married. Yes, married!'

He handed the phone over to me and I told my mother the whole story. She was very excited for us.

When we finished the call (she wanted to congratulate Kenny again after her initial shock had worn off), Kenny took me by the hand and led me back on to the roof garden. He pointed to his huge satellite dish, exclaiming proudly:

'Half of that is yours.' He ran to the chair. 'Half of that is yours. All of this is half yours.' He stopped and took a step towards me. 'Except for me. I'm all yours.'

I smiled, my heart pounding: physically and emotionally. I wanted to freeze-frame every moment and put it in my pocket to look at later, just to make sure it was really happening.

We went back inside and Kenny closed the curtains ('that

way the night'll last longer'), put on the stereo and danced. We danced and talked until about 10 a.m., when we both admitted to ourselves we needed some sleep. In all the years Kenny and I were together, I never once slept over at his house. It just seemed improper. So I did what I usually did and ordered a cab, which got me home in a matter of minutes.

Once home, I washed and changed, then climbed into bed and tried to get some sleep. But my mind was a whirl and I don't think I could have slept if you'd bagged me with an elephant tranquiliser. I tossed and turned for a couple of hours and then gave up and decided to make myself a breakfasty-lunch arrangement. I was just making some coffee when the phone rang. It was Kenny.

'Clee,' he said. 'I haven't slept a wink. Are we still engaged? Are you still sure?'

I was overjoyed. It had happened!

'Of course I'm sure,' I said.

'I've been thinking about it since the moment you left – where we should get married, who we should invite. All that weddingy stuff. I think we should do it as soon as possible.'

He went on to tell me about a beautiful, small country church that he had connections with, and asked if I liked the idea of getting married there. I said it sounded perfect. Kenny had already phoned around a lot of our friends – including Simon Booker, a wonderful comedy-writing partner of his; Barry Cryer; Eric and Jane Gear; George and Bette Gear; and Jo Gurnett – to tell them the news. You can imagine the great excitement.

There was only to be a handful of people who would know – people we could trust so that we could be private. Jo Gurnett was thrilled and was going to be the maiden of honour 'because you get to carry big bundles of flowers and wear a fabulous hat' she told me on the phone when she called later to congratulate.

We were going ahead.

The next day we went to George and Bette's house in Trewin. They'd invited us for lunch by the pool to celebrate. It was when I was swimming and talking with Bette – Kenny and George had gone off to play badminton – that something in my gut went twang. The feeling came from nowhere, and I suddenly felt very much like crying, but didn't. Something felt wrong. I said nothing and put it down to nerves, because our plans were rolling ahead with unstoppable momentum, and we were already receiving happy engagement cards from the inner circle we'd informed. But I knew something, somewhere, was rolling backwards.

I dried myself from my swim, excused myself with Bette and went upstairs to one of the bedrooms. I sat on the bed trying to make sense of the sudden swarm of overwhelming confusion that had engulfed me, feeling almost nauseous with worry. I knew what the cause of my concerns were, and I felt that up until that moment the issue had been reconciled. But the more I thought about it, the more untenable the situation seemed to be in reality.

Kenny and I had already had a conversation about the fact that ours would not be a sexual relationship. This was fine with me, and I had no illusions as to the nature of any future relationship we might have. But it mattered to Kenny more than I had at first admitted to myself, or understood. He wanted children: my children. But how? He hated himself in this dilemma, and this development was bringing to his mind all those old insecurities and sense of personal frustration at his sexuality. I didn't want to bring that pain back into his life again.

Over the course of the next four days my joy and elation became increasingly edged out by a gnawing and persistent doubt. I could see that Kenny too was struggling with some great crux. After four days of engagement, things came to a point when we were sitting opposite each other at lunch. I could see the despair that had crept into his eyes, so I broke the silence that we had both respectively kept.

'Well,' I said to him, knowing what he was feeling, but couldn't say. 'It was fun being engaged, wasn't it?' I tried to keep my voice light and breezy, but I could feel the emotion welling up inside. 'I really would have married you, only I think we are beyond marriage, don't you?'

He looked at me with huge tears in his eyes, but I could sense there was an element of relief for him as well. I smiled, trying not to cry.

'Besides,' I added, 'marriage is for earthlings, isn't it?'

He took my hand and quietly started to say that he was sorry, but I wouldn't let him finish. Not only did I not want him to feel bad, but it was also such a horrible moment – like having your heart grated – that I just wanted it to be over so we could get on with having happy times again. We finished lunch with our emotions badly shored up and then put together a plan to un-tell everyone. Many lunches and dinners were to follow.

After a time, we went back to just the way we had been before, with one noticeable difference. We had found something in our relationship that resembled a limit. Until then we hadn't noticed limits. We didn't fail. We just skirted around the subject of marriage and left it conveniently to one side. But the engagement forced us to deal with the issues that we had deftly sidestepped, and brought a maturity and personal honesty to our relationship that had been absent before.

In many ways we were already quite married to each other, and a wedding – in the long run – would have only brought uninvited attention and comments from people not qualified to make them. We concluded that all round, our engagement had been a huge success, even a triumph actually. But we never talked about it again. We never needed to.

It's all so simple really.

15 Twisted Fire Starter

THERE'S A DANGER IN TELLING all the stories of our Big Nights Out that it looks as if our lives together were one enchanting round of champagne reception after party after splash. But these are highlights in an otherwise fairly normal everyday existence. We used to go shopping together, go to the cinema, watch television or just flump around all day like a couple of goofs: the usual things that people do when they're not working and they want to enjoy each other's company.

Kenny loved getting out of the city just like anyone else, and when he really wanted to take a break from all things showbiz, it was to his most trusted friend, ally and bank manager Eric Gear, that he turned. Eric was like a brother to Kenny, and one of the very few people who never, ever let him down. Kenny would have put his life in Eric's hands if need be, and the two had a deep and respectful bond that stretched back years and years.

Some of Kenny's favourite times were when we all went on walking holidays in Derbyshire with Jane (Eric's wife), George (Eric's brother) and George's wife Bette. I can't say enough nice things about this little group of friends. They are some of the most genuine, funny and generous people I know, and they did nothing but make Kenny happy, and me feel part of the group from day one.

Eric (in Kenny's words) is a 'wonderful teapotty sort of fellow', although I was never quite sure if this referred to his shape, his body temperature or the fact that he always had a hand in his jacket pocket. His lovely wife Jane is Irish, and (by everyone else's standards anyway) quite a grown-up. Kenny used to try to tease her, but she was completely unfazed by it all and would remain affectionately aloof, like a much-loved auntie indulging her favourite nephew. Kenny's standard joke was at breakfast when Jane would invariably have green figs in syrup. She'd be eating and Kenny would start making the most repulsive, schoolboy descriptions of what figs did to your digestive system. But she was completely unscathed by the whole thing. And when she got up from the table he'd start doing wet, flatulenty sound effects in an effort to make her blush, but all to no avail. The more she ignored him, the more grotesque he became until eventually even we had to ask him to stop, despite the fact we'd all be crying with laughter by then.

George is one of those old-fashioned raconteurs; an enormously entertaining man with a gregarious fun-loving nature that has quite a touch of the devil-may-care about it. He's highly skilled in the ancient and much-respected craft of ye olde naughty limerick telling, and he's a got a black belt in shaggy dog stories. His wife Bette has (lucky for her given the ebullience of her husband and brother-in-law) been blessed with the patience of a saint,* a graceful strength of character and a colossal sense of humour. Together we made a fine walking group and bunch of friends. With Eric at the helm, our treks were adventurous and so picturesque that we always seemed to be ambling on the fringes of heaven. Going walking with them was not unlike stepping into an Enid Blyton story, with plenty of fresh air, laughter galore and lashings of ginger beer. Well, that last bit was almost right. It was more like lashings of Nuits St-George.

Whenever we went hiking we would make our way from the hotel in the morning and stand on the steps gathering ourselves before the walk. We'd all be decked out in sensible walking boots and jackets made out of durable, non-sweaty material that breathed but didn't get you wet (how does fabric breathe?). Kenny would spread his arms, sniff the clean morning air and smile like a loon, while the rest of us would shoulder our little packs and set off down the path of the hotel.

---

* I'm fairly certain it's not St Hurryup or St Getonwithit.

By the time we'd reached the gate, George would usually take a good look around and announce boldly that this would be a fine place to take the first refreshment of the day.

'But we haven't even left the hotel yet,' was Bette's usual response.

'All the more reason to refresh before we get too tired.'

Then George would pull a bottle of wine from his rucksack, sit on the grass six feet from the hotel's front door, and pour everyone a drink. We'd continue, with regular refreshment stops to ensure we kept our energy up, and make it back in the afternoon after clocking up a modest eight to ten miles or so. The only aching we ever suffered from was because of too much laughing.

Kenny was not religious in an active way, but he did feel that going on those walks was about as close to God as you could get. Sometimes we'd be walking up a hill, crest the brow to be presented with a magnificent view of rolling dales and hedged patchwork, and Kenny would break into spontaneous applause.

'Good work, God,' he'd cry, admiring the view. 'Nine out of ten for that one.' He'd stand admiring the sight for a moment then carry on, a little smile on his face.

We all knew how lucky we were to have such friends as each other, and how valuable and irreplaceable those days would be. Those times were special times for Kenny. He was safe, loved and could be himself completely. Later he was to have some of his ashes sprinkled in Derbyshire on these very hills (at his request).

There are too many good times with Eric and family to recount here, but one stands out more vividly than the rest. It was 5 November, and Eric and Jane had arranged a bonfire night at their house in Kent. It was only a small party, but Eric had built this funeral pyre of pyramidesque proportions in his back garden. It was so big there was snow on its peak, and parties of skiers trooped past us to climb up to the top and go off-piste. OK, that was a bit of an exaggeration, but it was a magnificently monumental fire, made with trees, garden shed and anything combustible within a three-mile radius of the house. One noticeable feature of Eric's parties was the generous flow of alcoholic beverages, and tonight's gathering was no exception. We let off a few fireworks – whizzing explodey affairs you could buy in a newsagent's – and by the time the fire was lit we were all well and truly into the spirit of the occasion. The bonfire caught immediately, and within twenty minutes it was a roaring furnace singeing the grass all around and sending volcanic showers of sparks into the sky that were far more impressive than any of the fireworks we'd bought. The heat was quite terrific, and Kenny took his shirt off to bask in the radiance. There was a dull crash from the fire as a few of the large bits of wood in the middle collapsed inwards, sending even more fiery red sparks up into the wind, so instead of looking like Mount Everest it now resembled Mont Blanc.

'There are never any damned witches around when you need them,' mumbled Eric, munching on a baked potato.

'Or suicidal fire-walkers,' said George, helping himself to another glass of wine.

'But darlings,' said Kenny. 'There's always a suicidal fire-walker around when you need one. Don't you know?'

'I don't see any,' I said, looking under the garden bench. 'Unless they're really small, or stuck . . .' I didn't get a chance to finish my sentence. Kenny had dropped his food on the lawn and was running like mad straight for the furnace.

'God Almighty Kenny,' shouted George. 'What the bloody hell are you playing at?'

Too late. Kenny flung himself into the fire, climbing through the flames, up and over the burning wood with the agility of a mountain goat and the self-preservation instinct of a lemming. He was very fast and very agile, and jumped out the other side like a skilled stuntman. There was a moment of stunned silence and then the garden erupted into raucous applause. Kenny appeared from behind the fire, beaming from ear to ear and dusting bits of charcoal off his chest and out of his hair. 'Bravo, bravo' we all shouted as he took a little bow. As an act of impetuous lunacy it was very impressive, but a little scary. If he'd lost his footing for just a second, he'd have plunged into the burning fire and instead of us toasting Kenny, we would have had toasted Kenny.

Then, to our amazement, he did it again. But this time he took a smaller run up and just sort of jumped into the fire waving his arms above his head, hoping, I'm sure, to add a bit of lift by trying to fly through. There was a collective gasp as Kenny emerged from the other side, smoking more than he had the first time and slapping his jeans, which seemed to be smouldering a bit. This time the applause was deafening and the cheers seemed to rouse him no end. He walked back to where I was and took my drink out of my hand.

'Cheers, Clee,' he twinkled, taking a swig of wine. 'That was good fun.' I laughed.

'Fantastic, Kenny, but probably best if you don't do it again, heh?'

'What?' he said. 'Like thiiiiiiiiiiiiiisssssssssssssss?'

To my horror he thrust the glass back in my hand and did it again. It was no less terrifying than the first two occasions: more so if the truth be known. The fire was just as homicidal, and you can only get away with things like this a few times before the laws of probability strike you down out of sheer cussedness. This time we reined in the applause: it was only encouraging him and none of us wanted Kenny to end up as a Guy Fawkes night statistic. I looked over at Jane, who stood clutching a bowl of chilli, watching Kenny, and shaking her head.

'I don't know what we're going to do with him,' I said.

'Serve him with the salad if he's not careful,' said Jane, smiling.

One of our favourite haunts was a secret, candley Russian restaurant call Nikita's in Iffield Road, Chelsea. It's a very old, well-established place that has a beguiling air of mystery about it. The restaurant has regular tables and chairs, as well as these small, private booths that each have a heavy, red velvet curtain across the entrance. You can pull the curtains shut and cut yourself off completely from other diners, the waiters and people who want to give you the bill. When you need service there's an old Victorian-style doorbell fixed to the wall inside the booth, which you ring like a butler's summoning bell-cord. A waiter then emerges to clear your table or whatever (head bowed so you get the feeling he's not even looking at you) and then as quickly as he appears he evaporates off into thin air, the curtain falls back into place, and you're once again severed from the outside world. It has a unique *Dr Zhivago* feel to it, and every time we'd eat there I would step out on to the pavement afterwards humming 'Lara's Theme' to myself, despite the fact that they hadn't played it in the restaurant. But best of all, because the booths are all side by side, you never get to see anyone in the other booths, and they never see you. We'd wonder who might be behind the other curtains. Adulterous couples carrying out illicit affairs? Philandering politicians with their research assistants? Bolshevik revolutionaries planning a winter uprising? It was all very clandestine and brimming with character.

At the time, I hadn't cut my hair for a few years and, unsurprisingly, it had grown to a very impressive length. I'd got bored with the pseudo-punky look I'd sported for the early years of the television show, and to be honest it was quite nice not having to spike it up every morning. A night out at with Kenny at Nikita's soon put paid to that.

It was a Thursday, and we'd already got the ball rolling with a few whisky and gingers before leaving the house. You know sometimes when you go out you're all listless and wilted and it takes a few fizzy things to get you perked up? And then on other occasions you're bursting with so much berdoingyness it's all you can do to sit still? This evening was one of the latter.

We arrived at Nikita's in filigree spirits and, as was our wont, we started sampling the various vodkas the restaurant sold. This was in the days before Absolut made flavoured vodka rather trendy, but of course, being Russian this restaurant had a seemingly endless array of highly dangerous drinks that silently crept up on you throughout the evening and then whacked you over the head when you least expected it.

We'd taken our favourite booth and were indulging in some illegally rich and gloriously unhealthy Russian food when I started to suffer from happiness overdose and went into Active Anecdote Mode. It was quite a visual story, I seem to remember, and involved me waving my arms about and jumping up and down excitedly in my seat a lot. I was getting to the crescendo of the tale when my wild gesticulating got a little out of hand and I swung an entrail of my lovely long locks over the top of the candelabra in the middle of the table. I hadn't noticed anything was amiss, but Kenny suddenly leapt out of his seat and started slapping my head.

'Kenny, Kenny, what are you doing,' I shrieked, shocked at his reaction to my story.

'Clee, oh my God. Clee, you're on fire!' shouted Kenny.

His eyes stood out of his head like ping-pong balls on springs, and he was quite beside himself with panic, thumping me with anything he could lay his hands on, from the cushion on his seat to the napkin off my lap. It was obvious he wasn't getting things under control and our booth was rapidly filling up with an acrid, stenchy smoke. By now he'd run out of things with which to whack me, and was frantically scanning the table for anything that might help.

'Don't panic Clee,' he said 'I'll put you out. . . .'

Then: a brainwave. He grabbed a glass of water and threw it over my head. Good initiative, I thought. At least, it would have been good initiative, if the glass had actually contained water.

It was my vodka.

This – as anyone with O level physics or a pyromaniac in the family will tell you – did not help matters one little bit. Fire and inflammable spirits are not good bedfellows (unless you actually want more fire of course). I was very grateful that I couldn't see what was happening on my head, because Kenny recoiled with a rallying cry of 'FIRE!'

Although we hadn't rung the bell, the waiters obviously assumed something was amiss in our booth, probably due to the smell, the screaming and the clouds of smoke. The curtain was flung back and two waiters appeared, fireman style, with two big jugs of water, which they promptly threw over me. There was some fizzling, a cloud of steam and everything went deadly silent. People were peering out from behind their curtains to see what was going on.

I put my hands to my head. I didn't feel any burns, but then I didn't feel much hair either. I was stunned. The thought that I was inevitably prepared for every eventuality by always wearing waterproof make-up was my only comfort. Kenny reached over and fondly dabbed my face with the singed napkin.

'Oh Clee,' he said. 'Are you all right?'

I nodded. 'Yes, I think so.'

He wiped away something from my face. 'You still look lovely and glamorous if that's what's worrying you,' he said.

At that point, in a moment of surreal irony, a waiter appeared with the two flaming Sambuccas we'd ordered five minutes before. Completely oblivious to the drama that had just unfolded under his very nose, he put them on the table in front of us among the burnt napkins and soggy clumps of barbecued hair.

'Your drinks,' he said proudly.

At this point Kenny leant forward in his seat, caught the Sambuccas with his elbow and tipped them both straight into my lap. Now I had a wall of blue flame leaping straight up the front of my dress. I threw myself backward while Kenny, who was still clutching the napkin, started beating my lap wildly with it, screaming loudly. But the Sambucca was not to be outdone. It stuck to the flailing cloth and within seconds the napkin was alight, as was the curtain to the booth, and bits of the tablecloth.

By now I was laughing hysterically. The Sambucca wasn't burning me at all: the heat was going straight up, away from my lap and not even warming me up. But it looked spectacular. The waiters were quicker off the mark this time and suddenly both Kenny and I were drenched by a tidal wave of water from three oceanesque jugs.

Once again an unearthly hush descended on the restaurant, the only noises being the gentle trickle of water off the table on to the floor and Kenny's laboured breathing.

Kenny was clearly quite shaken and upset by the whole thing, and the fact that I wasn't actually hurt didn't seem to make him feel better.

'What if you'd been burnt?' he kept saying. 'I couldn't bear it.'

I cheerily furnished him with a selection of comforting comments and then laughed wildly, saying that I thought we should probably go back to his house after all the excitement and he could trim my hair into a new shape for me.

'It feels a bit tufty,' I said.

We paid our bill, apologised profusely, and went back to Kenny's house, where he proceeded to prune my hair with his rose clippers. For the rest of the evening he kept holding my cheeks and kissing my face.

'I would have died if I'd hurt you,' he said repeatedly.

'Don't worry about it, Kenny,' I replied, looking in the mirror. 'But I'll tell you one thing. Don't ever take up hair-dressing.'

16 Sucker, and Other Stories

OLLOWING THE ENGAGEMENT WE HAD a lovely summer together. Most weeks we would go up to Capital Radio (where Kenny had his show on Capital Gold) play Frisbee in the park before he started work, and then take a leisurely stroll to the studios. Kenny maintained more than ever that this was the best he'd ever felt in his life. During this time we'd talk about his family, his parents in particular. Kenny started to phone them regularly, in Australia, and have long curly chats with them – something he used never to do. At first he would only call when I was there, and I would speak at length with them about what he and I had been up to. They are wonderfully warm people and soon Kenny started to talk about visiting them in Australia for Christmas that year. The atlas became a permanent fixture on his coffee table, forever open at the Australia page, becoming increasingly grubby as Kenny spent hours poring over all the exotic names.

One day, when we sat in his living room having a chat, Kenny hunched over the atlas like some geographical alchemist, he slammed the book shut and looked up.

'How about it, Clee?' he said. 'Shall we go? It'll be summer there, and we can get a ticket that takes us around the world. We can stop off in all these fabulous places on the way.'

'It sounds wonderful, Kenny,' I replied, but I didn't really give it much serious thought. Kenny was so often firing off these random thoughts that you'd go mad if you actually scheduled them all into your diary. And sure enough, the atlas soon found its way back on to the bookshelves and that was pretty much the last I heard of it.

Then, in October, Kenny – in a typical act of flamboyant

generosity – turned up at my house with two first-class tickets to Australia. Throughout all of the summer he had become increasingly closer to his family, so much so that Kate (his sister) and her family had come all the way over from Perth to visit him. They had a great time together, and Kate invited us both to Australia for Christmas, an offer that tied in perfectly with Kenny's idea to spend our winter somewhere hot and sunny. It was all agreed. We would fly out shortly before Christmas and spend Christmas Day with Kate and the family in their beautiful house across the road from a quiet, golden Australian beach.

In the run-up to the trip, Kenny and I spent a lot of time (and money) doing the most extravagant Christmas shopping, fuelled by the effervescent company of Messrs Moët and Chandon. Between wrapping the presents, drinking the champagne, dancing and watching our favourite television show (*Empty Nest*), life couldn't get much better. Looking back, it didn't. It really was the most special year.

No matter how well you organise yourself for a trip, the day before you go is always a mad rush of slopping, packing, washing, ironing and low-level panic. Kenny and I decided to forgo all the usual last-minute rushing around for a marathon present-wrapping and grand-toasting session. Round at Kenny's we slung what clothes we thought he might need into two oversized suitcases, laid the rest of the presents out in a disorganised jumble of Sellotape and acres of Santa wrapping paper, and then opened a bottle of champagne to toast our trip. Then we opened another bottle and toasted the health of Kenny's family. Then we opened another and toasted the Wright brothers for so kindly inventing the aeroplane. Then we toasted the movement of the tectonic plates for making Australia. Then, well, I can't remember to be honest. It all got a bit blurry from that point onward. Many fine drinks later I think we ended up toasting the lampshade, but for what particular achievement, I'm not sure. Being lampshadey probably. I went home that night feeling very floaty and excited.

I woke up the next morning feeling mostly floaty. In fact I felt extremely sideways, as I fumbled my way through the taxing job of getting dressed and collecting my luggage together. It was all I could do to organise a cab around to Kenny's house. With a head that felt like it had been stuffed into a small shoe and a stomach that was turning like a washing machine on fast spin, I must have looked quite a treat when I turned up at Kenny's house: grey around the gills and red around the eyes. Kenny brought his luggage down to the taxi, and, looking markedly better than I felt, got our trip off to a rousing start with a chirpy quip to the taxi driver and a cab full of sparkly holiday banter.

When we arrived at the airport, we had another interesting surprise, this time in the shape of a pack of reporters and paparazzi. Someone in our circle of friends must have accidentally given them a whiff of our trip to Australia, and more interestingly for the press, had hinted at the engagement. They'd put two and two together and made seven. We stepped from the cab and were met with a barrage of questions. Since I was barely capable of speaking my own name (my tongue seemed the wrong size for my mouth, and every time I tried to say something, the words all crashed into each other), Kenny took over and fielded all the questions with the air of a consummate professional. He handled it in a very humorous, non-committal way, relishing the fact that, in the flurry of questions, no one mentioned his homosexuality. In the end, all he said was that he was taking me to Australia to meet his parents. That seemed to satisfy most of the reporters and they left us to get on with the arduous business of getting on board the plane. I needed a press conference like I needed a plate of jellied eels, so once we'd cleared customs and passport control, Kenny led us to the executive lounge where he set about trying to get a one-man recovery system up and running.

He sat me down in a dimly lit corner and disappeared towards the bar, returning a few minutes later with an impressive array of hangover cures spanning fruit juice, Alka Seltzer, milk, mineral water, tonic water, and (yuk) more champagne. He was brimming with confidence, safe in the knowledge that at least one of them would do the trick. I was just about getting to grips with my delicate condition when I inhaled a lungful of plane fuel through the ventilation system. That was it. A wave of nausea hit me and I wouldn't have been able to move if someone had set the lounge on fire. Actually, I don't think I would even have noticed. I was held together entirely by waterproof make-up and a pair of sunglasses. This would all have been academic of course had it not been for the fact that they were closing the gate for the flight and we had fifteen minutes before they shut the doors and went without us.

Desperate times call for desperate measures. I popped two Dramamine in my mouth and downed the obligatory glass of champagne. Almost immediately my nausea and pounding headache fled, leaving my stomach and brain to foregather. I felt one-third human again, and within ten minutes had got myself together enough to stand up, take my hand luggage and walk towards the plane. My excitement, which had been been conspicuous by its absence that morning, reappeared as Kenny and I took our seats on the plane. We got out our itinerary and thumbed through the plans again, and Kenny briefly showed me all the places he'd booked and our schedule for hotels, etc.

We'd decided to take a circuitous route to Kate's, going first to New York, then the Grand Canyon, Los Angeles, Sydney, Perth, across to Singapore and finally back to London. It was a mammoth trip – a monster of a holiday – and we couldn't wait to get to our first staging post: New York. We had just watched the video of the film *Big*, starring Tom Hanks, and decided that our first stop was to be FAO Schwartz, where characters in the film had danced on the giant keyboard. So, throwing our last scruple to the wind, we ordered our food and settled in for the journey.

But there were two notable factors I'd forgotten: the Dramamine and the champagne.

'Hey, Kenny, look at that,' I said, pointing to a gap in the clouds below us. 'I think that's . . .'

The next thing I knew Kenny was shaking me and laughing.

'Earth to Cleo, earth to Cleo,' he tittered. 'Anyone home?'

'Oh, sorry, I must have dozed off,' I said, suddenly feeling mightily peculiar indeed. 'I was just saying I thoug . . .' Mmmm. Mellifluous velvety sleep.

'Clee? Hello? Clee?'

'Oh yes . . . I was just . . .' Back to a subterranean lull. I felt something shake me again but was in too deep to respond.

The next thing I knew, we were circling New York waiting to land. Apparently I'd fallen asleep during my lunch seven hours previously and hadn't stirred since.

It was mid-afternoon by the time we landed at JFK and took a cab to the hotel. I'd woken from my Dramamine and champagne stupor and was pleased to discover Kenny in full organisational mode. He said he didn't want me to worry about a thing: he was in charge and would deal with all the plans. This was fine by me, and I could see Kenny swell with machismo as he excelled in the role of chivalrous gentleman. We checked into the hotel, a fairly typical New York building with a man on the door and flags and trees out the front, and made our way to our rooms, which were opposite each other. I'd hardly got my suitcase on the bed when the phone rang.

'Time for a scotchypoos, Clee,' said Kenny. 'And then . . . FAO Schwartz!'

I put on a thick jumper and my heavy overcoat (it was mid-December, absolutely freezing and snowing heavily), nipped across the hall for a quick drink with Kenny and we were off.

Have you ever had a dream of how something will be, only to live the dream and find it a million times better than you ever thought it could be? New York is one of those places that most of us hold dear even though we've never been there. From *Kojak* to *Taxi*, the city is scorched on our minds as the place of yellow cabs, rising steam vents, hot-dog stands and chewing-gum accents. And we saw it all. We'd taken a step through the looking-glass and gone straight into the heart of all our favourite films. But in real life it was so much better, so much more unpredictable. So New York.

Question: why does steam come out of manhole covers in New York? You watch it in the movies and just take it for granted; 'well, that's what happens in New York'. But when you're there, it suddenly seems so absurd. Almost volcanic and strangely mythical. It's like watching *LA Law* and then going to California and marvelling at the palm trees everywhere. Anyway, Kenny and I were having exactly this conversation when a car came around a corner too fast and, in the snow and ice, spun into a long, leisurely skid. It sailed past us and I could see the driver wrenching the steering wheel from side to side with an expression of sheer panic. His fear was matched only by the look on the face of the small, rotund man behind a hot-dog stand on the street opposite who stood with his mouth open, bun in one hand, spoonful of onions in the other. With the languorous inevitability of a supertanker, the car sailed across two lanes of traffic, spinning majestically towards the hot-dog cart. The hot-dog man realising too late that he was in the path of an unstoppable object, leapt out of the way as the whirling car clipped the edge of his cart and sent its contents exploding into the air in a mortar blast of hot dogs, onions rings, buns and mustard.* They fell to earth with a dull splatter, some on windscreens, car roofs and pedestrians. Rather than prompting a rush to check for victims or injuries, the accident merely provoked all those caught in the melee to wind down their windows and shout abuse at the hot-dog man and his motorised assailant. Everyone else honked their horns just for the fun of it. What a loony bin! Kenny and I stood watching this with our jaws agape, turned to look at each other in complete amazement at what we'd just seen, and collapsed into a helpless heap of laughter.

It was lucky no one was hurt. The streets were alive with the animation of Christmas shoppers and, as we walked away from the commotion, we passed a couple of old men with horse-drawn carts at the side of Central Park. They were wrapped up to their eyeballs in warm clothing, peering over the heads of the shoppers to get a glimpse of the hot-dog hoo-ha. One turned to the other, and in an accent that was pure Sgt Bilko, said:

'Whole lotta shit goin' down today, Harry.' It was so perfect.

I don't think there's a place in the world that does Christmas better than New York. Every street corner has a Santa on it; every department store has a brass band or a choir out front. And with the snow and the cold weather it was more cliché than the clichés. We lapped it up.

---

* Isn't that a meat-eorite?

We continued towards FAO Schwartz, and once inside headed straight for the giant piano keyboard that we had seen in *Big* (if you haven't seen the film, it's a long, narrow plastic carpet of piano keys so large that you play it by running up and down the carpet and jumping from key to key).* For a couple of professional adolescents, we were unashamedly having fun. We danced up and down on it making tunes for what felt like hours, until one of the shop assistants finally came up and politely pointed out that some children wanted to have a go and would we mind letting them on.

We reluctantly vacated the keyboard and went on another present-buying binge for Kenny's family. By this time we were feeling fairly tired, grubby and hungry, we so decided to return to the hotel for a shower and then to go on for some dinner. We got to the sidewalk outside the store and I hailed a cab. One pulled up almost immediately and I leant down to speak to the cabbie through the window.

'Hi,' I said. 'Could you take us to . . .' I frowned. What was the name of our hotel? I couldn't remember it. In fact, I didn't think I even knew it in the first place. 'Hold on a sec,' I said. I turned to Kenny. 'What was the name of our hotel?'

'Oh, it was the, er, Imperial? Emporia? Egg-Nog? God, I can't remember.' I could see the thought-lines etched on his face. 'Clee, I don't have a clue.'

Uh-oh, I thought. This could be fun. Suddenly I had an idea. The keys! Kenny seemed to have exactly the same thought as me, and simultaneously we dived into our pockets and pulled our room keys out.

'Here we are,' I said to the cab driver. 'We're staying at the hotel . . . 1147.'

'Apparently I'm staying at the hotel 1148,' said Kenny, over my shoulder.

We looked at each other and gulped. Room numbers, but no hotel name. How hugely useful. The taxi driver leant across the seat and stared up at us.

'So you friggin' idiots ain't got no friggin' idea of what hotel you're at huh?'

---

* If you really haven't seen the film, rent it tonight. It's the best film ever.

'Er, no,' Kenny answered sheepishly. 'But it was quite a big building, with a man at the front and some flags. Oh, there were these trees as well. And it wasn't too far from the park.'

'You just described half a friggin' New York mister,' said the cabbie, spitting something disgusting out of his mouth that flew past my leg and landed soggily in the snow on the sidewalk. 'I guess you're in deep friggin' shit now, aintcha?' he added, a bit unnecessarily. He waved his fist, threw in a few more verbally flamboyant expressions, then popped the clutch on the cab and zoomed off into the traffic in a cloud of exhaust fumes.

We wondered what to do next and went to a restaurant to work out a plan. I suggested we look in the Yellow Pages under hotels, hoping something would ring a bell, but nothing did. (Have you any idea how big the hotel section is in the New York Yellow Pages? It's the size of the entire Shropshire phonebook.) We ate a light dinner but our hearts weren't really in it. We were feeling very cold and tired.

Everyone around us began to look like clones of movie stars: all perfect dental work, sunbed suntans and Blake Carrington hairdos. I said to Kenny that maybe we were stuck in a time warp, and that we'd be lost forever – nobody would ever find us unless they entered the Twilight Zone. I laughed and tried to make light of it, but Kenny was on the verge of a major sense of humour failure. He looked unhappy, worried and very, very exhausted. I attempted to reassure him that it would all be all right somehow, but he wasn't convinced. We couldn't call the travel agent in England who had booked our tickets because they were five hours ahead, which made it about midnight their time. That left us with . . . no options whatsoever. We left the restaurant, carrying all these bulky shopping bags, and started walking the streets. Things were getting desperate. Then Kenny saw a policeman and a little light went on over his head.

'I know, Clee,' he said. 'This policeman'll help us. I'll describe the hotel to him. He's bound to know.' Kenny ran up to him with renewed energy and explained that we were lost.

'Where are you staying?' asked the cop, only half interested in our predicament.

'Well, that's the problem,' said Kenny. 'We can't remember.

And it's not on our keys and we haven't got any of the paper-work from when we checked in.'

The cop looked at us like we'd just stuck two huge signs over our heads that said 'Stupid Tourists', but Kenny carried on regardless, getting more and more keen by the minute. He started describing the hotel in the most fantastic detail.

'There were two small trees outside the entrance,' he said, handing me the shopping bags and getting highly animated with his gesticulations as he tried to get the cop to visualise it. 'They were small and round with bobbly green bushy bits on sticks.'

The policeman looked increasingly baffled as Kenny did impressions of the trees. People walking past on the sidewalk started giving us a wide berth. Kenny was clearly clutching at straws by this time and I thought it was really quite funny in a sweet sort of way, but he had this mad look in his eyes that obviously unsettled the policeman. He told us we were crazy, and with a dismissive shake of his head, turned tail and simply walked off, leaving Kenny halfway through a Marcel Marceau impression of an ornamental shrub.

Kenny was crushed, which in all fairness he had every right to be. All our tickets and money were in our hotel, including our passports, and our flight to the Grand Canyon was the next morning. If we couldn't get to the hotel tonight, the holiday was rapidly going to turn into a bobsleigh to hell.

By this time it was about 10 p.m., but we just kept walking and having coffees for the next two hours. I could see that Kenny was beginning to look very pale and unwell: what I thought to be part worry, part caffeine overdose. He turned to me and pleaded desperately:

'What are we going to do, Clee?'

We were very close to walking into the nearest hotel and booking two rooms for the night, leaving our search until the morning. But that was admitting failure, which always sticks in the throat. So I took us into another coffee bar, sat in the quietest corner possible, and tried to remember if I had seen the name of the hotel anywhere. Kenny had told the cabbie at the airport which hotel it was while he helped him put the bags in the trunk, so I didn't hear it then. When we got to the hotel I didn't even look up to see its name on the front, because it was so cold, I just ran straight in. Kenny checked in for us, and once we were in our rooms I didn't even have time to read the room-service menu before we went out. I don't think I ever knew the name of the hotel.

But then it came back to me. Moments before I had drifted into my Dramamine coma on the plane, Kenny had shown me the itinerary with our entire schedule laid out. Had I seen the name of the hotel? I shut my eyes and recreated the moment in my head. I was sitting next to the window, and Kenny opened the travel wallet and laid it out on the small table of his chair. There was a piece of paper from a computer printer with our names on it stapled to the corner of the wallet. The picture floated in front of my eyes. Nearly there, but not quite. I'd always been blessed with a very pictorial memory: I could look at 'Spot the Difference' puzzles and see the discrepancies immediately. If only I could pull in some of that talent now.

'Ssh Kenny,' I said. 'I've nearly got it.' The picture went from hazy to solid and suddenly it was like I was reading it in front of me. 'Kenny, I can see the page. We're staying at the . . . Mayfair Regent Hotel.' He grabbed my hand and squeezed it.

'Are you sure?' he said, not daring to think I might be right. I opened my eyes and gleed at him.

'Sure I'm sure,' I said. 'Let's go.'

I was right. The next cab we hailed knew exactly which hotel I meant and the sense of relief was like coming up for air after deep-sea pearl fishing. When we pulled up outside the hotel twenty minutes later, Kenny leapt from the cab and hugged one of the trees out front. The doorman looked at us like we were Martians.

If only he knew.

The next day we were off to the Grand Canyon. Kenny was sporting all the symptoms of a bad head cold, and in the cab to the airport every pothole and bump made him hold his head and wince in pain. He was very pale, almost white, and sweating profusely. Flying proved particularly traumatic for him. His fever got worse and he asked the stewardesses to keep bringing him icepacks, which we pressed to his head throughout the flight, but which seemed to do nothing except offer temporary relief. He was too ill even to talk.

The flight landed in Phoenix. It was to continue to Los Angeles, but we were getting off in Phoenix. We'd booked a hotel near the Grand Canyon, but there was no way we were going to make it that night. Kenny was so ill it was decided that we should get him off the plane immediately and into the care of some professional medics. By this time he was so dizzy I virtually had to carry him off, and as we walked along the exit tunnel one of the airport staff came up to us with a wheelchair. Kenny refused to sit, and I had to battle with him to get him in. He claimed he didn't want to look ill (he was as grey as beef dripping and sweating profusely by this time, so he wasn't fooling anyone). In the end, it wasn't much of a contest. He was so sick that if I didn't carry him or put him in the chair he'd have stayed exactly where he was, so he flumped (secretly grateful) into the chair. I'd already requested that the airport doctor examine him, and asked the airline to collect our luggage for us.

Two minutes after we stepped off the plane the paramedics arrived. A team of six-foot tall, chiselled, handsome, strapping doctors appeared in these rather snazzy medical overalls carrying their equipment in silvery, sci-fi-like hard cases. They wheeled Kenny into a room and beckoned me in with him, questioning me about his condition and his symptoms. They laid him down on a trolley and within seconds there was a doctor at every corner, looking in his ears, down his mouth, in his eyes, testing reflexes, pushing on his stomach, taking notes, measuring the curtains and asking him a million questions. They were all so efficient it was amazing, and so charming with it. (Since insurance pays for everything in the US, they can afford to be extravagant with their healthcare.) After testing everything except the water pressure in the drinking fountain, they proclaimed Kenny to be Free Of Anything Fatal. The conclusion they drew was that Kenny had contracted a severe viral head cold, exacerbated by the stress of walking around New York in the freezing cold for three hours. He was to be put to bed immediately and could not fly until the next day.

Any motion for Kenny was agony, so I found a hotel as near to the airport as possible, got him wrapped up as warm as I could, and had a cab drive us there as slowly and calmly as you can in a country where pothole manufacturing is the nation's third largest industry. Airport hotels are a nightmare at the best of times, but in the States they have a real parallel-universe feel to them. Ours was called the Not Very Welcoming Inn or something, and was decorated in the style of a lightly furnished underground car park. These places are unforgivingly dismal. They're sleep-only staging posts on journeys most people don't want to make, to destinations they'd rather not be heading for. But in the US, they seem to attract an especially odd breed of traveller, people who actually choose the kind of hotel you or I would only stay in when there's absolutely no other choice (short of sleeping on the freeway). And this was no different.

We pulled up outside and I dragged Kenny into the foyer, which was full of 'guests' with no teeth and strangely deformed faces, all mumbling crazy things to themselves and staring at us with poppy-out bloodshot eyes. It was like something out of *Deliverance*. I was half-expecting a bald kid with a banjo to appear behind the front desk and grin toothlessly at me while the guests in the foyer drank moonshine to the steady beat of rocking chairs in the front car park. Oooh, it was creepy.

I had booked us into separate rooms (of course) and when I went in to check on Kenny the next morning, his fever had broken and he was feeling much more his usual self. He didn't remember much of the night before, although he had a strong recollection of people with no teeth. I told him we were staying in an airport hotel and he nodded sagely. Nothing else needed to be said.

We got our stuff together and had the courtesy coach take us to a car rental lot behind the airport. There we picked up a comfortable, spacious red thing that looked like the sort of usual family saloon car you might get in England, but exactly twice as large. It looked like the illegitimate offspring of a Ford Mondeo and an oversized London black cab.

We drove to Flagstaff, and then on to our next hotel, which appeared to be teetering on the edge of the Grand Canyon. I was sure that all it would take would be someone to sneeze on the front balcony at the same time as there was a strong westerly breeze and the whole thing would slide over the edge, like a milk crate off Beachy Head. Thankfully it was so unlike the Unwelcoming Inn it was wonderful. Not a slab of concrete in sight, but instead big, heavy wooden beams and a rocket-sized Christmas tree in the foyer, with the kind of O.T.T. American Christmas decorations that make the Regent Street lights look like something you put on your car dashboard. It was very story book, and just what we needed.

Kenny was still feeling slightly delicate from his 'bad turn', so we had a very leisurely day just pottering around the hotel, soaking up the atmosphere and planning our trek into the canyon the next day. This is what you do when you go to the Grand Canyon. You potter about at the top, thinking to yourself 'uckin' Ada, I bet it takes ages to get down there', then you jump into a good stout pair of walking boots and do it just to prove yourself right. We even had an early night and didn't drink too much so that we'd be good and fresh for the rigours of our trip the next day.

As always, we'd thrown ourselves into our adventure with a touch more enthusiasm than common sense. Too much common sense can make you very boring, and if you had to do all the things in life the way you're supposed to, you'd never bother getting out of bed in the morning. The day of the trip, we woke up and had breakfast together in the dining room of the hotel. It was a beautiful morning, the sun already blazing low in an azure sky. In December, Arizona is much like many other high deserts: bitterly cold at night and then, if there are no storm clouds, warm during the day. We put on our best walking boots, grabbed a small guide map and set off down the pathway.

Kenny was feeling back to normal, and the joy of not being sick and sweaty put him in a jubilant mood. We skipped down the path singing all the naughtiest limericks we could think of, and then making some up for good measure. We'd been walking for about half an hour when the path became decidedly steeper. There was a huge sign next to the path warning walkers of all the do's and don'ts of climbing into the Grand Canyon. The general gist of the sign seemed to be that if you weren't an Olympian athlete you shouldn't even think about looking over the edge, let alone walking into the jaws of 'the Valley of Death'. Since neither of us had high blood pressure, angina, false limbs, any form of pregnancy, a slight cough or the need to wear reading glasses, we decided we weren't in any danger. At the bottom of the sign – in big, bold red capital letters twice the size of anything else on the board – was a warning about water and your need to take lots of it into the canyon with you. It was a long, long, hot walk apparently, and without water you might spontaneously combust out of sheer dehydration.

Did Kenny and I bring water with us? What is this thing they drink called 'water'? We looked back up the path towards the hotel. We'd descended one hell of long way down since we left, which meant – if we wanted to return for water – we'd need to ascend one hell of a long way up. And to be honest, the allure of more down was far more attractive. We shrugged, and carried on.

About fifteen minutes after the sign, we came across a little cave where a bunch of icicles hung from a small rock promontory protected from the Sun. I was already feeling a bit thirsty, so I broke a couple off and offered one to Kenny in case he too was thirsty. I knew about all this survival stuff: when you come badly prepared to deal with Mother Nature, you take what Mother Nature has to offer. And on this occasion I thought she was being quite generous, considering.

'No thanks, Clee,' said Kenny. 'Not unless you've got some scotchypoos to put it in.'

I laughed, and we carried on walking, me sucking my icicle like a lollipop and feeling very pleased with myself for being so ingenious.

It's impossible to describe how gargantuously, epically, monstrously vast the Grand Canyon is. It's beyond the power of words. The first settlers arriving in the American West must have ambled leisurely across the flat Arizona desert and then just stopped in their tracks with a croaky cry of 'I say . . . what the bloody hell is that?' As you climb down into it, one canyon wall slowly rears up above and behind, while the other seems to edge ever closer from across the ravine, a roaring tidal wave of rock that threatens to crash towards you and flatten you like a bug on a windscreen. Going into the canyon at a walking pace somehow increases this sense of scale, because you come to realise how insignificant and minute you are against this backdrop of nature's awesome majesty. And when your pace is slow, it gives the brain time to get adjusted to the size in a way that driving or flying down just couldn't do. It really is the most intimidating experience, and Kenny and I were beside ourselves with the sheer exhilaration of it all.

Apart from its size, the canyon is simply breathtakingly beautiful. It contains towering buttes, mesas and separate little valleys all within the titanic grip of its magnificent stone walls. It is also dotted with old lava flows, hills composed of volcanic debris, and sudden intrusions of dark and crumbling igneous rock. As you walk down into the canyon, you go through nine different layers of rock that resemble an unfathomable stack of pancakes arbitrarily ripped into two by some ravenous rock giant. Walking down into the canyon is like taking a day trip back through time as you ooze slowly downward into ever older rock deposits. At the very bottom the rocks are estimated to be almost a billion years old. The walk had the feeling of a journey to the centre of the earth, where forever began.

They weren't wrong when they said it was a strenuous and difficult walk. Luckily Kenny and I were in good shape, having done our fair share of hill walking over the years, and by lunch time we'd made it to the bottom. We rested for a while, tried to unscramble our brains from the mind-boggling effects of the view, and then turned around and headed back the way we came.

We thought the walk down had been hard work. Hah! What fools. From top to bottom, the canyon is almost a mile deep. Now a mile may not seem that much when you're walking in a generally flat direction, but when you're walking up, it's one hell of a distance. Every step up takes an effort of mind as well as body. You stop looking around and admiring the view and start thinking about getting one foot above the other, one foot above the other, one foot above the other. Your head bows and you focus on the steady aching rhythm of creaking knees and throbbing thighs. By this stage the day was becoming dry and relentlessly parching. The higher we climbed, the more we left behind us the cool floor of the canyon and edged further into the arid, dusty heat of the Grand Canyon National Park plateau.

By late afternoon we'd made it back to the small cave with the icicles, which were still in the shade and still gloriously icy. My throat was dry and my tonsils were cracked and shrivelled. I felt gritty and dusty in every pore and my lips had chapped with the heat. I ran ahead of Kenny, snapped off the biggest icicle I could find and sucked at it like a kid with their first ever ice cream. I offered the icicle to Kenny but he declined. We'd come this far, he argued, so he might as well hold out for a bucket of ice-cold lemonade followed by a swimming pool of champagne.

An hour or so later, dragging ourselves up the slowly flattening hill towards the top, we crested a small rise and saw the balcony of the hotel appear above us. We clawed our way like a couple of dementeds and made the final push home.

'The bar,' croaked Kenny, sounding just like Peter O'Toole in *Lawrence of Arabia*. 'I need a drink. I need anything except walking upwards.'

We staggered into the hotel and headed straight for the bar, where a sympathetic-looking barman asked if our climb had worn us out.

'I've never been so thirsty in my life,' said Kenny, small dusty clouds falling off his beard and dulling the shiny bartop. 'Can I have a huge glass of iced water please?'

'Certainly,' said the barman, putting the glass in front of him as if he had it ready prepared under the counter. 'And madam? Are you just as thirsty?'

'Not quite,' I said. 'I drank a few of those icicles on the way down, and just finished one on the way back up again. I'm the resourceful one in the team.' The barman, who had taken to politely polishing a glass, promptly dropped it, where it shattered noisily on the stone floor.

'Icicles? From that cave near the top?' he asked, ashen faced.

'Yes, that's right,' I said.

'Oh my God!' he shrieked. 'That's the hotel's sewage overflow!'

Kenny sprayed his drink and nearly choked, guffawing uncontrollably. My giblets ruched and all the blood flowed out of my upper torso and into my shoes. I suddenly felt definitely worse than I did the day of the flight.

'But . . . but . . . Oh God,' I moaned. 'Will I die?'

The barman recomposed himself and arranged his lips into a small polite shape, obviously trying to keep some deep hysterical laughter from bubbling to the surface. He stepped carefully over the broken glass and leant over the bar to whisper in my ear.

'No, honey,' he said. 'But you'll wish you were dead.'

'Quick,' said Kenny. 'How much for that bottle of scotch?' The barman answered and Kenny told him to add it to our bill.

'Two glasses as well,' he ordered. The barman laid them out on the bar.

'OK Clee,' he said, trying as hard as the barman to keep his composure. 'You've just swallowed unspeakable tourist sewage. Two things are going to make you ill. The unspeakables themselves, and the thought of the unspeakables. Drink this. You'll disinfect your insides, and forget about how horrid it is to eat frozen poo water off a sewage pipe!' He lost control and roared with laughter. The barman snorted and rapidly disappeared out of view, under the pretence of clearing up the broken glass.

We spent the rest of the evening finishing off the scotch, and proving Kenny right. After about half a bottle I didn't care that I'd been sucking on Cesspool Popsicles, and the scotch had clearly annihilated anything unpleasant that might have been lurking in my stomach. Word obviously got out about my predicament, because every time I looked up at a member of staff walking through the bar they quickly averted their gaze and sniggered a sneaky retreat. The image of me and my lollies must have lodged firmly in Kenny's head, because no matter what we got to talk about for the rest of the evening he'd suddenly stop halfway through a sentence and burst out laughing.

'Sorry Clee, I just . . . ha ha ha . . . couldn't stop thinking . . . phfrrr!! ha! hahaha!' It would take him a few minutes to recover and we'd be off again.

By the end of the evening, with the bottle of scotch drunk, it was all a hazy, unpleasant recollection and I was half hoping it was a false memory created by the combination of too much scotch and mild sunstroke.

When we checked out the next morning – feeling frail and slightly shabby – the concierge kept giving me extra wry little looks. As we walked out the front door the barman rushed up to me – all smiles and fresh air nostrils – and handed me a farewell present.

It was a bag of ice.

Oh such weary larks.

Next stop was Los Angeles where we stayed at the Belage on Sunset. This was a real treat for me, coming back to my old stomping ground with Kenny. This was where I spent nearly two years during my break from the UK and I had a lot of friends and memories here that were very precious to share. But that wasn't why we were here. What we were really excited about was going to our all-time number one favourite place on the entire planet: Magic Mountain.

Magic Mountain is the theme park to end all theme parks. Places like Disney World have all the paraphernalia, with a few white-knuckle rides, stuff for the kids, characters in costumes and all that malarky, but Magic Mountain cuts to the chase. It's got nothing but roller coasters. There's no mincing around with this place. You go there for one reason and one reason only. To scare yourself into another pair of trousers. It's got three-hundred acres of roller coaster rides. Yup, that's three hundred acres! The year we were there they'd just opened two new rides, the Ninja and the Tidal Wave, and the year before they'd opened a ride called the Freefall, which was still the talk of California. We couldn't wait.

Off we sped, bypassing breakfast and arriving at the gates of Magic Mountain even before it had opened. By now we were feeling a bit peckish, so we made our way to a Wendy-burger just down the road and ate an interesting selection of greasy shapes and textures that came under the heading of a Wendy Breakfast. I made a mental note never to accept an invitation to Wendy's house for anything other than cheese sandwiches and a cup of tea – certainly not before she'd cleared away all the breakfast things. By this time Kenny was bouncing up and down in his seat and could barely contain his excitement. I felt like a mother taking a twelve-year-old boy on a birthday treat. Kenny scoffed his breakfast (I ate mine more out of a sense of needing to eat, rather than an over-whelming desire to increase my cholesterol) and we made it back to the gates and took our place at the front of the queue.

The park was almost empty. The weather was clear but a little chilly, and the kids were still at school, so there were hardly any queues at all. It was excellent! We went on all the biggest rides at least ten or twelve times each, and kept coming back to the Freefall, the ride that drops you the equivalent of ten floors very quickly, and very stomach churningly. Kenny was in seventh heaven and on cloud nine all at once, and after go number eight his enthusiasm had abated precisely zero. It was making me feel horrendous but he was such a kid I couldn't slow him down for a second.

'Kenny, no!' I said, after he tried to drag me back on for the ninth time.

'Oh don't be such a girl,' said Kenny, grabbing my wrist and pulling me slowly towards the entry gate. 'One more time. Please . . . *please* . . .!'

I had to refuse. I was one more gravity-defying drop away from resurrecting Wendy's breakfast shapes. Any more flying through the air in ways for which I wasn't designed would have had me carried out of there on a stretcher, trembling with severe upsidedownness. It was absolutely time to go, before I involuntarily redecorated the Magic Mountain crazy paving.

We left and pottered around Heverly Bills (as I call it), and then went to see Kenny's chum Noel Blanc, Mel Blanc's son. (Mel Blanc was the voice behind Bugs Bunny, Barney Rubble and just about every major cartoon character you care to remember.) I'd never met Noel before, but he was extremely noodley and friendly, and he showed us his incredible collection of cars (that's the real big drivable ones as opposed to small dinky toys). We spent the rest of the afternoon at his house with some of his friends and his mother, and then went off for a rhythmical Mexican dinner where we were able to catch up on some of our dancing. It had been a while since Kenny and I had rumbaed together, and it was a fantastic end to what turned out to be a very eventful trip across the US.

From Los Angeles the flight to Australia is nowhere near as brutal as it is from the UK and, after saying goodbye to friends in California, we leapt on the plane and headed towards Sydney. We were met at the airport by our friend Lawrence and his wife, who were in a very long black limousine. They took us to our hotel, The Regent, where they left us with arrangements to meet up later that evening. We checked in, dropped off our bags, and went straight to lunch at a place called Eliza's, a beautifully uncluttered, clean and gardeny place in a very fashionable part of Sydney.

While we were sitting and chatting, a sudden squall broke and the heavens opened with an intense shower of heavy rain. Kenny and I looked at each other across a plate of tagliatelle, leapt out of our seats and dashed out the back of the restaurant. We stood in the rain with our arms outstretched and our faces raised to the heavens. The rain was warm and very refreshing, and it felt so good to stand and feel the grime of the journey wash off our faces.

'You're the most beautiful creature in the world,' oozed Kenny, the water running through his beard and dripping off his face. 'No one makes me laugh like you. You know that, don't you?'

'Of course I do,' I replied, hugging him. I was very happy.

We finished our lunch, dripping on the floor and getting plenty of odd looks from the other customers in the restaurant, as was our wont. Kenny kept giving them odd looks back, as if they were quite mad not to go and stand in the rain before eating their food.

Back at the hotel, we dried off and met up with Lawrence and his family, getting back around midnight. Our rooms were next door to each other and both overlooked Sydney Harbour and the Opera House. The windows ran from floor to ceiling and I couldn't sleep that night: it was so beautiful. I left my curtains open, and from my bed just watched the stars and the boats sparkling on the bay. The management sent both Kenny and me a bottle of champagne each every day, but we couldn't drink them all, despite our best efforts.

We spent our time walking for miles around Sydney and through the surrounding countryside. Kenny was very relaxed, largely I think because we were on the other side of the world and he felt confident and unthreatened by the pressure from the media, and all those people who had a claim on his life. He never let go of my hand, and when we arrived back in the evenings we'd change into the hotel's fluffy white dressing gowns, Kenny would put on the special music tapes he'd made before we left, and we'd dance in his suite overlooking the bay.

We'd usually end up sitting in the (empty) bath, drinking fearsome cocktails, still wearing our robes. This became our favourite chortling place. What I didn't know was that he would sometimes record our conversations. It was his way of capturing and reliving our wonderful times together – an audio album of sorts. I still have those DAT tapes, and when I play them I can remember how everything felt and smelt: all wrapped in happiness. Those DAT machines record just about everything. You can almost hear around corners, and the detail is so profound it's just like being immersed in the moment all over again. I couldn't bear to listen to them for quite a while, but now they are some of my most precious possessions, a chunk of fabric cut from time and preserved intact forever.

Our last night in Sydney was Christmas Eve, the day before Kenny's birthday. We were travelling to Perth on Christmas Day, so that night I'd arranged for the hotel to bake him a cake riddled with bananas, which we ate in his room while he opened his presents. By this time we were absolutely shattered. We'd crammed more activity into the last week than we usually did in six months, and were very much looking forward to being in a normal house for a while, simply lying around and doing nothing.

The plane to Perth was quite empty (travelling on Christmas Day didn't seem to be everyone's cup of tea for some reason), and, as we sat watching the in-flight movie, who should appear walking up the aisle handing out Christmas presents but Santa Claus, albeit a huge roly-poly one whose beard looked decidedly suspect (although he made up for it with oceans of ho-ho-ho-ness). Kenny was very excited when he saw him.

'I knew he travelled by plane,' he whispered conspiratorially when Santa gave him his present. 'There isn't a reindeer in the world who can keep up with his kind of schedule. I wonder if he gets Air Miles.'

We were met at the airport by Kate, Kenny's sister, and her husband Conor. They took us to their beautiful, sprawling house, idyllically located opposite a glorious golden beach with big crashing waves. It was the middle of the summer out there of course, and the weather was unquestionably Australian. The house was full of Kenny's family, bustling with children and oozing bonhomie and familial love.

We unpacked and appeared with our presents, which the kids leapt upon within about a millisecond of us coming downstairs. Kenny had bought his mother a large white teddy bear, which she adored, and his father a pair of beautiful leather brogues to match Kenny's own pair, of which he was so fond.

Our stay in Perth was lovely. We went into the outback in a four-wheel drive to see the kangaroos and drove vertically down roads where – if left to my own devices – I'd have used a climbing rope instead of a car. We went swimming every day in the sea across from the house, which was cataclysmically refreshing, and incident-free until I lost my bikini top.

I'd dived underwater into the crashing waves, and when I came up for air, I was curiously naked up top. My bikini top had emphatically disappeared, and despite some fairly intense searching of the waves – above and below – it was nowhere to be found. The sea was awash with some very amiable Aboriginal families, so I didn't feel too inclined, in my state of semi-undress, to run up the beach. I waited until Kenny appeared and then shouted at him from the sea to come in the water.

'Quickly, Kenny,' I yelled. 'I really really want you to dive in now.'

'OK, Clee, I'm coming.'

'No, Kenny. I mean now!'

He dived in, swam up to me, immediately saw the nature of my predicament, and laughed softly.

'Oh dear, Clee, you've got no clothes on.'

'Thanks, Kenny. Now please help me get out of here will you?' He chuckled.

'This time, dearypoos, we're going to have to get terribly intimate'

He made me stand right up behind him and we walked slowly up the beach, in perfect step, Monkee-style, waving nonchalantly at all the families lying on the beach who couldn't quite believe their eyes. They couldn't work out if it was a tall half-naked girl with a small hairy man stuck to the front of her, or a small hairy man with a big half-naked girl growing out of his back. We got to the roadside, which had a fair amount of traffic on it, and every time a gap looked like it was approaching Kenny would jerk forward as if he was going to run off without me. I'd grab his shoulders and pull him back and we'd miss the gap. We were laughing wholeheartedly by now, especially since the occupants of every second or third car would toot their horn, waving and shouting at us. Either they recognised us from the television shows (which used to play down under), or they just liked tooting half-naked girls on the roadside. By the time we made it across the road and into the house we dissolved into a heap of laughter on the front porch and scrambled inside.

The days were spent lying in the garden eating delicious things and drinking fine wines. Kate and Conor had really tried to make it perfect for us. We'd visit Kenny and Kate's parents and play spoons with them (a musical chairs game with spoons on the dining room table). We had the best time, and on New Year's Eve Kate threw a party at the house. Kenny was of course in charge of the music and filled the room with flamboyant Latin rhythms. He took his mother by the hand, his father invited me to the dance floor, and we all danced together, twirling in and out of each other's arms. Kenny couldn't believe that his mother could samba so well. He was amazed because it was the first time he had ever danced with her, and she was equally bowled over by Kenny's impressive dance steps. Her eyes misted over with happiness and pride to be dancing with her son, and it was truly touching to see such unconditional love in her eyes.

This was one of Kenny's most important moments that he loved and treasured in the time ahead. After all the difficulties in communicating with his parents for so long, he embraced his father in a way that swept away the years of pain. He was finally allowing himself to be accepted by his parents, who had always loved him, no matter what. We spent the entire holiday with his family, who treated me with total acceptance and gratitude for encouraging Kenny back towards them and for helping him to build the bridges.

Then, all too soon, it was time to leave. On our last day, Kenny took me around in the car and asked me if he bought a house here, whether I could be happy?

'Of course I could,' I replied. 'I'll be happy anywhere if we're together.'

But I knew it was just a fanciful idea. Kenny needed to be around parties and music and new things going on. Life here would be too quiet for him, and I think he knew it as well. But the holiday had given us a taste of an idyllic world that only comes alive when you're on holiday and away from home, where reality takes a vacation as well. He didn't buy a house there, and that was the last time we ever went to Australia together.

There was something else that also defined our time in Australia, something that I didn't discover until much later. When I did know, looking back on those few weeks, everything Kenny said and did made so much sense that I wondered why I hadn't realised at the time: building bridges with his family, expressing emotions that he usually kept to himself, his joy and childish enthusiasm at being away from the real world in London, his desire to capture every moment with photographs and tapes. They were all the actions of a man facing up to his mortality, looking at his life and trying to make sense of relationships with those he loved, and finding his true place in a world which was now finite.

The acts of a man who knew he was going to die.

Kenny had discovered he was HIV positive.

17 When Harry Met Sally

W E LIVE IN AN AGE where we put enormous faith in medicine and in the powers of doctors to cure us of our ills. My generation has grown up without a real fear or understanding of sickness and death, and, with the exception of cancer, we have had little to be afraid of as far as Mother Nature is concerned.

Not any more.

The arrival of so terrible a disease as AIDS has cast a long shadow over many of us, especially those in the communities that have borne the brunt of its wrath. It has brought illness back into the realm of the young, and reminded us that none of us will live forever. For those in and around the gay community during the eighties, the outbreak of this plague was a terrible shock as it began to claim victim after victim.

In four years, from 1989 to 1993, I lost 23 friends to this dreadful disease. We all knew someone who was HIV positive, or who had full-blown AIDS. Each day seemed to bring another bit of bad news, all against a whispered backdrop of 'there but for the grace of God.'

You don't have to be promiscuous to catch AIDS. You only have to sleep with one promiscuous person and by default you've slept with every single person they've slept with. The public-health adverts at the time tried to scare us with frightening images, but it wasn't the pictures that were frightening, it was the mathematics of sexual contact. Two partners meant ten partners. Ten partners meant a hundred partners. A hundred partners meant a thousand partners. The awful tragedy of this disease was that its arrival coincided with sexual and social liberation, a pattern of behaviour that started in the sixties and was reinforced in the hedonistic days of the seventies and early eighties. But because of its long gestation period, enormous numbers of men and women became infected long before they even knew the risks, or before the disease seemed a reality rather than empty hysteria. It was complacency that took so many good people away from us. And it was complacency that killed Kenny.

Kenny, as I said before, was not promiscuous. But he wasn't celibate either, and it would be wrong of me to pretend he caught AIDS by playing Scrabble (I can't think of anything you catch from Scrabble, except sleeping sickness perhaps). He had a regular boyfriend in the shape of Nikolai, but Nikolai was profligate. Nikolai had a rapacious sexual appetite, not caring if he was bedding man, woman, animal, mineral, vegetable or bicycle. And it only takes one profligate to cause an epidemic.

Kenny and I rarely discussed the ins and outs of his sex life – it was his business and something he kept very much to himself – but I did have a deep residual worry about how well he was 'looking after himself' in the bedroom. Like so many other gay men he had a vague appreciation of the risks of unsafe sex, but in the early eighties few had even heard of someone who was ill. It seemed – like the threat of a new ice age – just another scientific scare story that had blown out of all proportion.

Kenny had discovered he was HIV positive shortly after our engagement, and before we went to Australia, but it took him a long time to work out how he could tell me, or any of his close friends. It's something that I have given a lot of thought to over the years: if you knew your time was limited, how would you handle it? Is it fairer to tell those who love you, or not tell them? Do you try to make your time with them special, and unmarred by the shadow of death, or do you let honesty be the best policy and offer them the chance to come to terms with your loss while you are still there? This must have been something that Kenny troubled over for a long time.

In 1989, there was something different about Kenny that I couldn't put my finger on. The Australian trip threw this difference into much greater relief, but it was the kind of subtle and profound change that you can only rationalise retrospectively.

Why go on a picnic to the outback and hide a tape recorder under a rock to record the most mundane of conversations? Why take photograph after photograph like a demented Japanese tourist? Why try to cram so much into each day like a madman on ProPlus? He seemed more intense, more intent on savouring every little experience and every taste of life. He laughed louder, he danced longer, he worked harder. And he often said later that 1989 was the best year of his life. I think in that first year of knowing, as he struggled to come to terms with a sense of closure, Kenny's senses expanded and he became more alive than he'd ever been before. I've heard this from others, that facing your mortality makes the joy of simply being alive seem more tangible and more valuable. The air smells fresher, birdsong is more melodic, sunsets are more divine. And I can understand this completely. Most of us go through life with our eyes closed off to the beauty and majesty around us. Having that veil drop must be a most profound experience, and I believe this is precisely what happened to Kenny once he'd discovered he was harbouring this deadly time bomb.

By now Kenny and I were inseparable. We had discovered truths about ourselves that only the closest of lovers glimpse, and in our sense of other worldliness we had found a companionship that was as solid as stone. We were – as I felt on the very first day we met – Martians whose trajectories had crossed and who'd clung on to each other through all manner of experiences. People simply couldn't understand our relationship and the depths of our feelings for each other; in their eyes our bond couldn't be compartmentalised, and we didn't fit any established model of how two people with such a deep commitment to each other 'worked'. This just reinforced our sense of togetherness, because it drew the walls closer around us. But soon something else was about to enter the enclave, something neither of us had expected or knew how to handle. There was an interloper in the happy house.

In the spring of 1990, a while after we'd returned from our Australian holiday, Kenny rang me up at home.

'Clee,' he said. 'You've just got to come around to the flat right away. They've made a film about us!'

'Hi, Kenny,' I said. 'What do you mean they've made a film about us? Is this a television show or something?'

'No, I mean a proper film. It's got actors and everything. They've changed the names – obviously to keep us a big secret, but it's definitely us.'

'OK, Kenny,' I chuckled. 'I'll humour you. I'll be round in a jiffy.'

I leapt into a jacket (it was a bit chilly I remember) and walked around to his house, a brisk ten minutes away. Kenny buzzed me up and met me at the door to his flat with a warm hug and a glass of whisky.

'Take a seat, dearypoos,' he said, waving a video cassette teasingly under my nose. 'This is *our* story. I've just finished watching this, and I'm going to watch it all over again. But I think I'll spend most of my time looking at your face.' I raised an eyebrow and he laughed.

'Put it on then,' I said.

Kenny slid the tape into the machine and we settled back into his all-enveloping sofa to watch the film. It was called *When Harry Met Sally*. We didn't go to the cinema much, preferring instead to wait for films to come out on video, so the hoo-ha around Meg Ryan's fake orgasm had largely passed us by when the film was released. The plot was all something of a surprise for me. But Kenny was right: the storyline was immediately recognisable.

If you haven't seen the film (and I can't believe there's many out there who haven't), the movie's all about a man and a woman very much in love with each other as friends, but who struggle trying to make their relationship 'normal' by becoming a proper 'couple'. Sound familiar? We thought so, and connected immediately to a number of scenes that made us laugh and then go suitably quiet.

When the film finished, Kenny got up and turned the television off, went to the kitchen and came back with two more tumblers brimming with whisky. He handed me one and sat next to me, taking my hand in his. He said nothing for a while, merely sat swirling his drink around his glass and I suddenly felt a deep and dreadful panic begin to well up inside me. Something was desperately wrong. I could tell from his eyes that he was gathering the strength to tell me something I didn't want to hear. At the very back of my mind, far away in a corner to which I was turning my back, was a notion of what it might be. But this thought was too terrible to even glance at, and I ignored the distant beating of its black, bleak wings.

'Clee,' he said slowly, as if choosing his next words with great deliberation. 'I have something to tell you.'

I knew exactly what he was going to say. I held his hand tighter, wishing and praying that I could just whisk us away from all of this, to make it not real, to stop him from saying it and so stop it from becoming a reality. If he didn't tell me, it wouldn't happen. Kenny continued.

'I don't know how to say this. I don't think there's an easy way to say it at all, so I'm just going to have to spit it out.'

He paused, hunched over his glass, his face pinched and taut. His eyes looked haunted and tired, and time seemed to atrophy around us, each second stretching painfully outward until it seemed as if we'd been sitting motionless for hours. He put his glass on the floor and turned to look at me.

'Clee . . . I'm HIV positive.'

I felt a wave of weakness, and nausea rushed through me. If we hadn't been sitting I think I would have fallen to the ground. Kenny was HIV positive. It was too terrible to contemplate. All too terrible. Kenny bowed his head.

'I'm sorry Clee,' he said, so quietly I could barely hear him.

What did I feel? My every emotion had been knocked out of me: I felt like a husk. And then, anger. Anger that Kenny should have been so careless. Anger that it was all so avoidable. Anger that he'd been selfish and stupid and lazy and had thrown everything away for reasons that were so unnecessary. It took nothing to practice safe sex. Now this disease was going to take everything. We'd overcome so much together, shared so many problems, supported each other in times of darkness as well as creating so much light. But now . . . now here was something that we couldn't solve, something that – no matter how hard we tried, no matter how much we cared about each other – was insurmountable.

What can you say to someone who's just told you they're HIV positive? There are no words that can protect them from the brutal truth, no soothing balm for the soul. The inescapable reality is that it is a disease that cannot be cured, a condition that offers no morsel of hope, no crumb of restitution. It devours hope, and leaves in its place barren submission.

I can't remember what I said to be honest. I think I made empty noises about it not turning into AIDS, about there still being a chance, about how – if he looked after himself – he could hold off for years and years and years. But they had no meaning, these platitudes. They held no promise or truth. It was a mantra, a meaningless prayer that offered comfort only in its saying, not its meaning.

Kenny knew this. He'd come to terms with this over the previous months – not his dying exactly – but that things had changed irrevocably. The rules that applied yesterday no longer had any relevance today. He had ahead of him a new chapter in his life, a chapter where he'd have to rewrite the characters and redefine the lives contained within. Warm, cosy escapism was a luxury now. The truth would always be there.

'Does it change anything?' he asked, looking at me with a deep disquiet. He sounded so vulnerable, so exposed, that my anger instantly evaporated. 'Between us I mean? Will we be the same?' I held him tight.

'If you mean will I stop loving you? No, of course it changes nothing.' I looked into his eyes, so full of sadness and fear. 'I'll always be here, and I'll always love you. Nothing will change.'

I was right, but I was also wrong. I never stopped loving Kenny, I never have. But things did change, of course they did. Where once we were two, we were now three. This malevolent, dark disease would always be there, always between us: unspoken, unseen, unacknowledged, but still there – casting its dismal shadow on every laugh and every moment of happiness.

We held each other and talked through the night; the first of many long and painful conversations that opened us both to the bone. But every time we had these discussions – when Kenny was frightened, or tearful, or angry – we would draw a line under them and move on, trying to shake off any lingering maudlin sentiments. Kenny had no time in his life for self-pity, and I couldn't let him slip into the depression, which, in his youth, had proved so debilitating and all consuming.

He was still Kenny. He was funny, and sensitive, and inventive, and silly and all the qualities for which I loved him. But there was something else in his eyes now, a *gravitas* that had never been present before. It wasn't a maturity as such (Kenny was never, ever mature, thank heavens), rather a sense of having taken some ballast on board, of being less flighty and more considered in what he said and what he did. It was the closest Kenny would ever come to being a grown-up.

Above all things, Kenny didn't want people to feel sympathy for him or to be awkward in his company. So, for a long time he kept his illness a secret, and those of us who knew kept it a secret with him. This was a deeply private matter, and the thought of battling his illness while having to deal with the scrutiny and judgement of the public was too much for him to cope with just yet.

This disease had robbed him of his hope. He wasn't going to let it rob him of his dignity as well.

Later that year, as I was waiting to cross a road in Kensington, a tall thin man stood next to me as the cars sped by and we waited for the traffic lights to go red. I only saw him out of the corner of my eye but there was something about his aura, an intangible sense of being, that made me turn and look at him. At first I had no idea who it was, but then he winced as a truck thundered by and I recognised – of all things – his teeth. The shock was so profound I lost my breath.

It was Nikolai. He and Kenny had long ago parted company, and I had not seen him for a couple of years. Nik was a massive bear of a man when we were all together in our gang. His presence filled a room, physically as well as charismatically. But now, I saw before me a wisp of the man I once knew. He was once larger than life, but now it looked as if death was about to cut him down to size. His cheeks were sunken and sallow, his hair was thinned and retreating and his face was creased with deep dark lines. We all knew that the plague had claimed him, and that he had taken himself to a private nursing home to see out his last days in solitude. But seeing this reduction in him, face to face, was shocking and frightening. This malignant virus had fast-forwarded his life: he was 39 but looked 93 – a cruel and shrivelled caricature of the man he had once been.

He felt me staring at him and turned to look at me. On recognising me, a flash of fear and horror crossed his face. He immediately turned his head away, and marched off as fast as he could, his steps clumsy and measured. I watched him disappear around the corner and felt a great sadness, not just for him, but for everything he had come to represent. The end of an era. The lights up at the end of the party when the real world intrudes and you have to pay the price for your fun. Payback time.

Nikolai was once fuelled by other people's adoration for him. His energy came about from his charisma and the effect it had on others. This terrible disease had robbed him of his magnetism and his power, and he had hidden himself away from everyone so that they would never see him degraded like this. But I *had* seen him, and he'd run shamefully away: ashamed at the illness in himself, and maybe ashamed at the illness in others. I knew he'd heard about Kenny.

Nikolai died six weeks later.

Kenny lived with HIV for six years. He came to terms with its message, and used his time to do the things he'd always wanted to do. He also learnt to make decisions that affected his life much more carefully than he had before. It seems a heretical thing to say, but it made him a better person. It made him more honest with himself, it helped him focus on the things that really mattered and it forced him to rebuild the bridges that, in the past, he had burnt recklessly behind him.

'I'm lucky in a perverse sort of way,' he said one night, when he rang me at four in the morning with the night terrors. (This was a regular occurrence about which we often joked. 'I'm here anytime for you Kenny,' I said one night, 'but does it always have to be four o'clock in the morning? Can't you get the night terrors at lunch time?')

'What do you mean, you're lucky?' I mumbled, fumbling for the light by the bed. 'You're HIV positive. What's so lucky about that?'

'Most people don't get a chance to put things right,' he said.

'One day you're thinking of your pension, you step out in the road and before you know it you've been squished by a number 47 bus. All those loose ends, unpaid gas bills, messy relationships, unfinished letters. I've been given a chance to get it all sorted out before I go.'

'Yes, I suppose you're right. Are you OK now?'

'Yes. Thank you,' he replied.

'Good,' I said. 'Now how about putting things right and letting me go back to sleep?'

'Of course. Good night, Clee. Thanks.'

'Goodnight Kenny. I'll ring you tomorrow.'

Life went on.

18 Snarks and Narcs

THE NEW KENNY TOOK TO life with gusto and enthusiasm. He started doing things he'd never done before: like eating salads, going to the gym, and wearing pyjamas to bed. And where once he would have balked at some of the ideas people were throwing his way, he began to consider doing things that – had he not known that his life were to be condensed – he would otherwise have passed up. One of these was his debut stage appearance in Mike Batt's *The Hunting of the Snark*, a musical based on the nonsense poetry of Lewis Carrol. It was the perfect vehicle for Kenny, who had been a professional nonsense-maker for 30 years. Mike Batt, most famous as the musical creator of the Wombles, had written the tunes and got the backing to put the show on at the Prince Edward Theatre in the West End. He immediately approached Kenny to embrace one of the roles, but it took him a number of approaches before Kenny eventually agreed.

It's almost impossible to get across how brave a step this was for Kenny. He was terrified of performing live in front of people. The radio was his preferred medium because he could hide behind the voices and the production and go into his flights of fancy without ever exposing the real Kenny Everett to the audience. When Kenny stepped into a recording studio, he became a different person. The glass walls became like a second, thicker, skin that he did not have. It allowed him to expand his personality and become the bold and audacious person he felt he wanted to be. But there are no glass walls when you perform live: you have to give something of yourself. For someone as shy as Kenny, it was like asking an agoraphobic to go for a walk in Lincolnshire. But his illness had given

197

him new courage, and as he'd always wanted to do a live performance, he'd decided to do it whatever the consequences. And why not? The worst that could have happened would have been bad reviews. When you're coping with the day-to-day stress and reality of being HIV positive, the possibility of bad reviews tends to pale into insignificance. As a form of mental preparation for the show, Kenny actually convinced himself that he preferred working on the stage to working on television, but this was a kind of karma preparation that helped him feel more comfortable with the project. And, by any stretch of the imagination, it was a brave thing to do – from a standing start to a full West End musical production.

'It's like hanging over the edge of the Empire State Building,' said Kenny in the run-up to the show. 'Exhilarating and terrifying at the same time.' (A reference to our New York trip where Kenny had done exactly that: hung over the edge of the Empire State Building. 'This is my favourite building on the planet,' he exclaimed. 'King Kong's sat on this.')

Watching Kenny prepare for the part was wonderful. He played the billiard maker, a happy-go-lucky character who sang, and danced and did lots of twirly things with a polished cue. If you ever saw Kenny work, you'd realise how much he had an eye for detail. All of the jingly bits that he did on his radio show were highly crafted pieces of production, and he revelled in making even the smallest of jobs absolutely perfect. When you listen to a lot of the singing harmonies from his television show – particularly the choir sketches and mimicry of the Bee Gees – you grasp how much he strived to make his work not just good, but excellently perfect.

And so he approached his part in *The Snark* with exactly the same commitment and drive for perfection that he did with everything else. He had a beautiful voice that was very adept at harmonising and he was very used to singing as part of the television and radio shows. But dancing – that was a different matter altogether.

He'd done a lot of choreographed sketches with the dance troupe on the television show, but being filmed meant he'd only have to get a few steps right at any one time before they changed cameras and he could start again. And although he was a highly accomplished samba and rumba dancer, those steps are very fluid and spontaneous, whereas a choreographed routine has to be the same every time. Going on stage and doing a whole routine meant getting it absolutely perfect in one go: there's no 'take two' when you're in front of 2,000 theatre goers.

Once rehearsals started and he'd learnt his basic steps, I would go round to his flat and we'd practise them for hours and hours and hours. He'd move all the furniture out of the way and clear a large space in his sitting room, put on the music that Mike had written for the show, and we'd spend the evening doing spinning biz with billiard cues and getting Kenny to sing and dance at the same time.

In the run-up to the launch of the show, the theatre put Kenny through a lot of pre-show publicity, which he wasn't very comfortable about. Some of the interviewers were very astute indeed, and although none of them asked him outright if he was HIV positive, there were certainly some heavily suggestive questions about whether he was afraid of death, and why he'd taken up eating healthy food and going to the gym regularly. Angela Levin's interview in *You* magazine the week before *The Snark* opened was the most perceptive of them all, although Kenny fended off her questions very adeptly. But it was obvious that – since Nikolai's death had made the newspapers the year before – many were beginning to suspect something was amiss.

On the opening night at the Prince Edward Theatre I went with my mother and Eric and Jane, and was more nervous than I had been at the opening night of my own show. Kenny had put so much effort in, and had invested so much emotional energy, that I don't think I could have coped at if it had all gone horribly wrong.

When Kenny came on stage the audience erupted. They loved him – it was obvious, – and immediately I could see the applause swell Kenny's chest and give him an extra boost of self-confidence. I looked around the theatre and every face had lit up. It was like they were all watching a friend on stage, that they all had this bond with Kenny that went beyond the usual appreciation most television stars get from their fans. He had the entire audience willing him to do well.

Kenny did a great job. He never set out to be musical hall star, but nevertheless he threw himself into the role like a classic 'trooper'. He didn't put a foot wrong or sing a note out of key. It was like watching a small child at their first school play, where they've learnt their lines and practised so hard to get it perfect. I could see the concentration on his face throughout the whole show, and when he came on for the curtain call at the end, he got the biggest round of applause. We went backstage afterwards and Kenny was so alive with the performance he was crackling with energy and excitement. He kept asking me 'did you like it? Was I any good,' and again the picture of him as a small boy after the first night of the school play kept popping into my head. Everyone else in the production knew how much effort Kenny had put into his part and he was awash with kind-hearted congratulations.

The reviews the next day were all fairly negative about the show, but were not so bad for Kenny. (It's odd how some productions – seemingly no better than others – catch the imagination of the critics and the public, while others, which seem equally as good, end up going to the great opening night in the sky.) Bar a couple of reviews from people lodged firmly up their own colon (no names mentioned, but Kenny never read the *Daily Telegraph* again), what shone through all of the copy in the following day's papers was the affection that the reviewers had for Kenny. It was the exact same reaction I'd seen in the eyes of the audience the night before: when Kenny came on stage they so badly wanted him to do well it was a tangible feeling of support. Kenny was very pleased overall with the result, and for someone who – as he was so often quoted as saying – was so thin-skinned he was completely raw, it was a triumph of spirit over adversity. The show ran for a number of months, but unfortunately wasn't a commercial success, so Mike Batt eventually closed it down and went off to think about the Wombles for a bit.

Kenny wasn't unduly upset about its closure. For him going out on that stage the first night had been the real challenge, and after that it didn't really matter whether he continued doing it for a long time or not. In fact, Kenny had such a low boredom threshold that I think his interest was already beginning to wane a little before the show closed down. So, in many respects it was probably an act of good timing. But whatever anyone said of the show afterwards, Kenny felt good about having done it, and we were all very proud of him for having made such a bold step.

Life outside of work continued pretty much as usual, except that Kenny had a tendency to get tired quicker than he had before he was ill. He'd also given up drinking to excess, and by the time *The Snark* went on stage, we hadn't been roaringly sideways together for well over a year, all as part of Kenny's health drive. He'd even taken to filling himself with those heavy-duty protein drinks that bodybuilders use when they're trying to get muscly. These things combined with Kenny's (previously unheard of) thrice-weekly visits to the gymnasium, meant he looked fitter and better than he'd done in years. Captain Kremmen had always been Kenny's macho alter ego. As a smallish man with a smallish physique he'd forever wanted to be a beefcake, and Kremmen allowed Kenny to indulge his superhero fantasies very adequately. But now, with all this healthy living and exercise, he was starting to look very Kremmenesque himself.

'Look at me, Clee,' he said proudly one evening when he stepped out of the bathroom in his fluffy bathrobe. He adopted a bodybuilder's stance. 'I've got muscles! I've never had these before. Don't they look fantastic!'

The one vice to which Kenny did take a shine (and this is probably going to cause all sorts of ructions, but here goes anyway) was ecstasy. Kenny had dabbled with drugs in the sixties (he'd gone on a few trips with friends, and had even had some acid trips with John Lennon, one of which was quite a negative experience, so he abandoned them after that), but had steered clear of most narcotics since the late seventies. But along came ecstasy and Kenny loved it. For someone who was so naturally touchy-feely anyway, it was pennies from heaven. It would be very wrong of me to condone any kind of drug use (don't try this at home kids . . .), but I would be lying if I didn't say that some of the emotional insights Kenny experienced when he took E was carried over into his everyday life, helping him to find the courage he needed to face his illness. I would try to convince him that he shouldn't really be doing Class As in his condition – knowing that the immune system is highly susceptible to chemicals and toxins, especially E (where you don't really know what is in them) – and would often hide his stash so he couldn't take any. But in the end I gave up. They made Kenny feel great, and since he already had a terminal illness, he reckoned the risk of taking one and dropping dead on the spot wasn't actually that relevant. It's like giving up smoking after finding out you've got six months to live: a bit after-the-event and hardly likely to make any difference in the long run anyway. But for the benefit of any children who might be reading this:

DON'T DO DRUGS

There.

19 The Long Goodbye

WHILE KENNY KEPT AN INCREDIBLY positive attitude throughout this fallow period in his illness, there were still things that made our times together occasionally painful. We couldn't hide anything emotional from each other at all: I could read what was going on behind his eyes as much as he could read behind mine. This meant that when he was feeling scared or overwhelmed, he couldn't keep it from me. This upset him ('I don't want to give you the willies,' he'd say) and also me, because I could see the pain and fear that always lurked not far beneath the surface. Now and again it would burst through and I'd get calls in the middle of the night, or Kenny would appear on my doorstep unexpectedly, as if he'd just woken from a bad dream and needed comforting. These times were the hardest. When he was vulnerable and frightened and he would take my hand and whisper 'I'm falling apart, Clee.'

There was nothing I could say that would make it right.

Kenny's night calls became a regular fixture, and this became our new time for talking to each other. We'd stopped joking about them after a while, because they really were the moments – in the darkest hours – when Kenny's courage and certainty would desert him, and there'd be no comfort in humour or dismissive one-liners. In the middle of the night, when the distractions of life were at their most distant, Kenny would see the shadowy outline of Death standing patiently in the corner of his room, and it would terrify him.

Once, he rang me at about 3.30 a.m. in the middle of winter: cold and miserable, and the night was depressingly heavy with a dismal rain. We'd been talking for a while when he paused and then asked:

'Is there a heaven?'

'Of course there's a heaven Kenny,' I said. 'You'll be there, meeting all those fabulous people you've known, and all the others you haven't met yet. You can meet Mozart and Brahms. John Lennon's up there. Your dogs'll be up there; think how good it'll be to see those boys again. They've missed you, I bet.' There was pause. I could almost hear Kenny thinking.

'But will they let me in, Clee?' he said eventually.

This was such a worry for Kenny. As a Catholic, no matter how lapsed, he was educated by the Church to believe that homosexuality was a mortal sin, and I think this was what bothered him. It meant no matter how much he repented, he would never get to heaven. But this went against Kenny's belief that 'God wasn't a vindictive git', and that as someone who'd tried to be a good person, and tried to do the right thing by other people, or put right any wrongs he may have committed, he deserved a place in God's flowery garden.

'You've got nothing to worry about, I promise you.' We talked some more, until I could hear the fear had left his voice, and his breathing had calmed. 'Can you sleep now, Kenny?' I asked.

'Yes, Clee. Thank you.'

I said my goodnights, and verbally tucked him up into bed. This was our life now.

These fears were deeply private ones for Kenny, and he hid the terror of his condition from both himself and those he loved. When the story broke of him being HIV positive, he handled it in a wonderfully farcical way that ensured no one pitied him or felt uncomfortable in his company.

I can't remember who ran the story first, but the journalistic community had been slowly closing in on him for some time. After Nikolai's death, it didn't take long for them to work out that he and Kenny had been together while Nikolai was HIV positive. After that, all they needed was some proof, which they eventually secured from an undisclosed source.

It was our regular routine to go together to Capital Radio's studios near Euston when Kenny broadcast his show. Often we'd go to the park first and play Frisbee or have a picnic, then I would either sit and watch him doing the show or do some shopping. When the show finished we would go off and eat or return home to dance. The day the story broke was no different, except that Kenny rang me at home before to make sure I was going to join him at Capital.

'Meet me at the studio, darling,' he said. 'They'll be after me today.'

Sure enough when Kenny got to the Euston Tower in his mac and baseball cap the press had set up camp outside, waiting for him to arrive. The journalists were joined by a group of fans who'd read the morning papers and wanted to wish him well. The extent of the public support quite took his breath away; on his walk to the studio that morning three people had come up and hugged him in the street. 'I should do this more often,' he said to the cameramen before he went in. Once inside, he had to deal with friends and colleagues who had heard the news from the media, and were feeling slightly self-conscious about asking how he was (except Dave Cash, the DJ at Capital who was probably Kenny's closest colleague and work friend, whom Kenny had told some time before).

David Hamilton and David Jensen popped their heads around the studio door during a record on Kenny's show to say hello.

'Hi Ken,' said David Hamilton. 'How are you?' Kenny contorted his face, wrapped his hands around his neck and slid slowly down his chair.

'Haven't you heard?' he rasped, gasping for breath and falling to the floor, flapping like a landed fish. 'I'm dyyyyyyiiiiiinnnnngggg . . . urghhhghhh . . . I'm going . . . I'm fading . . . Quick . . . get my wooden overcoat, it's all over.' He made one last hammy gesture and flopped lifeless onto the floor.

The two Davids stood in the doorway, their mouths open, both speechless. I clamped my hands over my mouth to stop myself from laughing.

'Oh ermm yes,' said David Hamilton eventually.

'OK,' added David Jensen. 'We'll, er, see you later then Ken.

I hope everything's all right.' They all looked at each other and burst out laughing. Kenny got back into his chair and winked at me.

When the show was over we went down into the foyer, came out of the lift and spotted some films crews that hadn't got any footage of Kenny coming into the building earlier. They saw him, and wanted to know how he was feeling. He turned to me.

'Watch this, Clee,' he said. 'Let's have some fun.'

He grabbed a bunch of flowers from the reception desk and went and laid on the floor in the middle of the film crews. He crossed his hands over his chest and put the flowers on his stomach. In a loud, Kennyesque voice he moaned, 'oohhh it's very close now, any minute now, I can feel it coming . . .'

People laughed. That was all Kenny wanted from those around him, to appreciate him, and feel that he'd made them happy. His condition threatened to take away his ability to make others feel gleeful, so he met it head on by turning it into a joke. It was a brave thing to do, because once you do that, you make your illness public property. No matter how private he wanted things to be, that privacy had been stolen by whoever leaked the story. So Kenny did the only thing he could and turned it around into something funny.

For many people the news coverage of Kenny's illness came as a shock. Not only did they have no inkling that he might have contracted HIV, but when he appeared on the television he was already starting to look frail. He had shaved off his beard, leaving himself with a moustache (which actually made him look very handsome, but quite different from how the public remembered him from the television show), and during the question and answer session before he went into the building his voice faltered twice.

Now everyone knew.

Kenny was frightened of dying, and so was I. He was inside of me now, and I knew that when he died he would take a large part of me with him. Kenny could see this, and as I comforted him, he in turn comforted me.

When we used to dance together, before he announced his

illness, our steps were joyous sambas or berdoingee erotic rumbas, glittery bouncy numbers where we would shimmer and shake to Latin rhythms and find a connection that closed us off from the world around us. Now when we danced, Kenny mostly played slow tracks. We would hug each other and sway to the music for hours on end, holding each other tight and pulling ourselves into a deeply private world that was ours alone. I knew what was in his head as we danced, and he would squeeze me tighter when thoughts of our parting crossed into his mind. And I would nuzzle into his neck and breathe him into me, trying to grasp the incomprehensible idea that one day this smell would be gone forever, that this flesh would no longer be here and that everything that we had built between us would be cut in half and destroyed.

'I'd give you anything, Kenny,' I said one night. 'If I could rip out my liver and my kidneys and my heart and give them to you to make you better, I would. I wish I could.' Kenny kissed my hair.

'I don't want to go, Clee,' he said. 'I wish there was something to be done, but there isn't. There just isn't.'

Kenny never cried in front of me. He was courageous and brave, and – as he said on numerous occasions – he was falling apart. But he never cried.

That must have taken such enormous strength.

One night, close to Christmas 1994, we sat on Kenny's sofa listening to some music and talking. He'd been feeling progressively more and more tired in recent weeks, although he'd have occasional days when he'd bounce back and be full of vigour and energy. But those seemed fewer and further apart now. His pace of life was gradually slowing down as he had more and more early nights and spent more time at home.

He got up and went into the kitchen, returning with two tumblers of whisky.

'I worry about you, Clee,' he said, once he'd sat down. 'When I'm gone, I mean.'

This theme was running increasingly through Kenny's thoughts: about how his death would affect those he loved. He didn't want to be a cause of others' unhappiness, and it was so typical of him to be thinking of others and not himself.

'Don't worry about me, Kenny,' I said, as I had done many times before. 'I'm a Martian remember?' And then Kenny said one of the most astonishing things he'd ever said to me, something that struck at the very heart of our relationship.

'No, Cleo. You're not Martian. You can't think like that any more. Soon I'm not going to be here and I don't want you to be alone. Do you understand, Clee? You *can't* be a Martian now.'

I looked at him in horror. How could he say this? How could he possibly try to change me now, after all these years?

'Of course I'm a Martian, Kenny. And so are you. You've always said so. I don't want to fit in. I can't even try to fit in.' I picked up a banana from the fruit bowl on the coffee table and waved it in front of his face. 'What's this, Kenny?'

'It's a banana, Cleo.' He was smiling.

'Of course it's a banana,' I replied. I brought it to my face and shouted at it. 'You're an apple now, understand? Stop being yellow and curly. You have to be round and red from now on, Kenny says so.'

Kenny laughed and pulled me to his chest, stroking my head. He whispered in my ear, 'I'm so glad we met, aren't you?'

'I'd change nothing,' I replied. 'And I wish we could do it all again.'

In January 1995, Kenny and I met for lunch in a restaurant around the corner from his house. He had lost a lot of weight, and his illness – now full-blown AIDS – was making rapid inroads into his health. His ears were troubling him (he already suffered from tinitus), and he was becoming dizzy and uncoordinated – knocking things over, bumping into furniture, breaking dishes. This troubled him a lot. He was such a detail man – in his work especially – and losing the ability to do intricate, delicate tasks made him very frustrated.

He took my hand, and I could see on his arm a lesion: an area of skin damage that virtually all AIDS sufferers eventually get as the immune system crumbles. But there was a sparkle in his eye, a twinkle that hadn't faded one bit. He smiled at me and squeezed my hand.

'Clee,' he said, 'we've been so perfect with each other, haven't we?'

'Yes, Kenny.'

'And do you know what? In the fifteen years we've been together, I've never once seen you without your make-up on.' He chuckled. 'Never. Not even after I set light to your head. Or when you were so sick the day we flew to New York.' I thought about it and agreed.

'You're right,' I said. 'We're pretty damn fabulous people Kenny. We couldn't possibly see each other without our make-up. It wouldn't be right.'

He paused to take a drink of water, looking out over my shoulder to the people walking by on the pavement outside. He turned back to me.

'Clee . . .' he said, very deliberately and slowly. 'I'm getting ill now. I really am falling apart this time, and things are going to get a lot worse. But the thing is . . . I don't want you to see me without *my* make-up on. Do you understand? That wouldn't be right either. You realise what I'm saying, don't you, Clee?'

I did understand. I knew exactly what Kenny meant. Over the last year or so, I had just about come to terms with Kenny's departure. We'd said all the things that had to be said, and we were ready to say goodbye. There would be no tears, no anguish, no misery. Just gratitude that we'd found each other, and a farewell that wasn't submerged in sickness and death.

This was to be the last time we'd see each other.

We talked some more – about quiet, personal things – and then we made each other some promises. The kind of promises you don't tell other people. The kind that stay with you forever.

I walked him back to the flat, and there we said our final goodbyes.

I did not see Kenny alive again. He died three months later, in the arms of his family.

20 Dark Days

KENNY DIED AT 10.43 A.M. ON 4 April 1995, in his flat at Lexham Gardens. He had refused to be admitted to hospital, preferring to have full-time care facilities set up in his flat. By his side was Kate, his sister, who had put her life on hold for the previous months and dedicated herself to nursing Kenny through his final days. She and Kenny rediscovered themselves in those weeks and months. They hardly knew each other as adults – their lives had gone in very different directions – but this was a time to learn about themselves and face Kenny's destiny with the kind of bond and intimacy that only family can offer.

Lots of people have claimed a kind of martyrdom for 'nursing' Kenny during those last months, but there is only one person who deserves full credit and that is Kate. She looked terrible after Kenny died: the strain and stress had taken a heavy toll, and the pain was etched in her face for the world to see. Hers was a courageous final act for a brother she'd never got a real chance to know until then.

I was told of Kenny's death that same day, by one of those who was in the flat when he finally slipped away. I cannot describe those first few hours that I knew. My grief took me into a deep abyss, a terrible hellish place where I was blind and breathless. Kenny had gone, and despite all my preparations, all my mental groundwork, the heart had been ripped from my life and I saw no reason to go on. I rang his answerphone time after time after time, sometimes four or five times an hour, just to hear his voice. I thought that if I left a message it would break the curse, rewind the clock and have him alive and well and laughing again. They were dark, dreadful hours. I was pinned down by a paralysing grief that left nothing of me in its grip.

Two days later, still barely connected to the real world, I went to say a final farewell to Kenny as his body lay at a funeral parlour in Westbourne Grove. Although I had made a promise to him that I wouldn't see him once the illness had taken hold, I had to see him just one more time. I didn't think he'd have minded too much: he was no longer in pain, and I was sure he would look dignified and at peace.

When I arrived, the undertaker – a short kindly man with grey, gentle eyes – led me down a long corridor to where Kenny was lying. The door was opened and there he was, lying peacefully in an open coffin with flowers all around the room. He had his hands on top of his chest, and was dressed in his favourite jacket. When I saw him, I cried out his name and ran to his side, taking his face into my hands and weeping at the sight of his small, boyish figure, now so still and silent. I took his hands in mine, interlocking our fingers as we had done thousands of times before.

It was then that I noticed his nails were slightly raggedy, which is something Kenny would have hated. He was such a tidy man that things like this would irritate him enormously. I took out a small pair of nail scissors and an emery board from my bag and sat and gave him a manicure, talking to him all the time about how I felt for him; how many ways I loved him and how much he had enriched my life and made me into the person I was today.

Once his nails looked smooth and smart, I gave him a head massage – as I had done a million times before. Kenny had always had a little nobbly bit on his scalp that we used to joke about being the beginnings of his horns growing through. When I felt the lump on his icy head I was suddenly overwhelmed by a sense of loss and betrayal. Here was Kenny: gone, stolen. He'd been taken rudely from a life he still had to live and a love that would always be there for him. It was unfair. It was wrong. I wept wildly and held his hand to my cheek. I just wanted to be with him, wherever he was. If I could have stepped out of myself there and then, I would not have hesitated. I wanted to be with him so badly.

But then a sense of calm came over me and I stopped weeping. I looked down at Kenny's face and saw how peaceful he looked. I realised how wrong it was of me to want him back. He was gone, and now he was somewhere supremely perfect. I told him not to worry about me, that I would be all right. That life would go on, and so would I.

I took a strand of my hair and cut it with the nail scissors. I tucked it deep into the pocket of his jacket and then I cut a small lock of Kenny's hair to keep with me. I figured, since it contained all of his DNA, the blueprint to Kenny, that I'd always have a small complete version of him with me forever.

I'd been with Kenny for a half hour or so when the undertaker came into the room. He closed the door behind him and asked if I would like a cup of coffee. I was about to reply when there was a loud rapping on the door he'd just shut. He turned, opened it and looked up and down the long corridor. There was nobody there, nor was there anywhere for anyone to have gone had they knocked on the door.

He turned and smiled in a resigned kind of way.

'That must have been Kenny,' he said quietly. He saw the expression on my face and sat down next to me.

'You needn't look so shocked my dear,' he said. 'I've worked here all my life, as have many of my colleagues, and we'll all tell you the same. Things like this happen all the time. I wish I could tell people so they weren't so upset when they lose their loved ones. They're still around, you know, watching and hearing. Never far away. You haven't lost Kenny. He's just gone somewhere else. You'll see him one day.' He smiled, touched my shoulder and left the room.

I stayed a while longer, kissed Kenny goodbye, and left.

I did not go to the funeral. It was not an event for Kenny, it was an event for those who thought they knew him, and I couldn't be part of such an empty and hypocritical charade. The service was held in a small church in Farm Street, Mayfair, where Kenny and I had attended Edward Duke's funeral a couple of years before. Kenny had fallen in love with the place then, and told me that this was where he wanted to have his service when it was his turn.

Up until the morning of the funeral, I was determined to go, despite the fact that the whole thing was spiralling downward into some kind of plasticky showbiz affair that bore little or no resemblance to what Kenny would have wanted had he been around to contribute. But on the morning of the funeral something happened that I can forgive, but I will never forget. An act so petty and pointed that it still makes me angry to think about it now.

Kenny had often told me that he wanted to drive a red Porsche for a week – one of those marvellously opulent affairs with gleaming paintwork and smooth sleaky shapes. I'd kept telling him to just go out and hire one, but being Kenny he never got round to it, and it remained his one outstanding 'little ambition'. So, on the morning of the funeral, I went to Harrods and bought a children's pedal Porsche – bright red and perfect – and filled it to the very top with as many bananas as I could, all tied up in a big yellow ribbon. It was my final goodbye, my last gesture to Kenny that said I'd remember him for the fun, and the laughter and the irreverence. I wanted my goodbye to be cheery and uplifting, not some dreary wreath or dismal bunch of flowers. I wanted it to be *Kenny*.

I took it along to the funeral parlour for the undertakers to take to the church. They were very sweet, and said that although it was an unusual tribute (and why not? Kenny was an unusual man), they'd be happy to have it at the church ready for the service. I left them, and went home to get ready.

Half an hour later the phone rang. It was the undertaker. He was very apologetic, but wanted me to know that Kenny's sister Kate had forbidden them to take my tribute to the church. She felt it was 'inappropriate' (but not inappropriate enough not to give my personal message written on the card to the press for them to print). I was so shocked I couldn't speak, and simply hung up the phone. How could she? She knew Kenny had no time for 'appropriate' gestures: that simply wasn't what he was all about. She knew what our banana code meant. But above all she knew how close Kenny and I were, and that by refusing the tribute she was snubbing me in the most brutal and cruel fashion.

I know what grief can do to people, how it can affect their

judgement and make them do things that in saner times they would not do. But I felt Kate had no right to do this.

I don't know if Kate realises how hurt and wounded I was by that one thoughtless act. As I said earlier, I have forgiven her, because that's what you do. But it is forgiveness without understanding or empathy. I was denied my final farewell to Kenny.

I was so upset and beside myself with fury, almost beyond my control, that I realised if I went to the funeral I would say something awful or make a terrible scene. I truly felt like killing someone. I know, looking back, that this was how the anger of my own grief was bubbling malignantly to the surface, and I didn't want to turn Kenny's funeral into any more of a farce than it was already becoming. I've always felt that funerals should be something to honour the dead, not to please the living. After my tribute was shunned I did not want to condone the hypocrisy by being part of it.

I left for the countryside as his funeral was taking place. My will to breathe lay scattered in his ashes. I didn't want to try to feel good or happy. It hurt, and I felt the pain to my core. But in amongst this terrible pain was a tiny sliver of salvation: Kenny and I had shared so much, and been so close, that those memories were untouchable. Nothing would ever change what had passed between us – no funeral hoo-ha or last minute snubs. It was all irrelevant. Kenny and I would be bananas forever.

As each day came and went, and Kenny's death edged another day into the past, the pain did not recede. In many ways it got worse. Sometimes I'd be watering the garden and I'd hear a song on the radio, or I'd come across one of his notes, or I'd smell Badedas bath gel and I would fall to pieces. It was all too much. I was fearless with despair, and entered a period that is a dark and miserable memory for me, a deep depression that seemed to sap my very will to get out of bed in the morning and simply breathe.

I was beginning to concern my friends because I just couldn't seem to shake myself from this grieving stupor. But then, months later, long after Kenny's death, one of my closest friends and I sat down in her garden, the smell of cut grass fresh in the air and the evening birdsong loud and raucous, and she told me not to expect to get over it.

'What do you mean?' I asked. 'Am I going to feel like this forever?'

'No,' she said. 'Not if you learn to accept what's been taken away. You'll get used to it, eventually. You'll even learn how to live with this hole inside you. But don't expect the hole to be filled. If you spend your life waiting for it to heal over, you'll never be happy again. Once you know where that hole is, you just learn to stop walking into it every day. Look at it from a distance if you have to, but don't walk into it.'

That was the most helpful piece of advice I received. It truly helped me come to terms with losing Kenny, and slowly, imperceptibly, the colour began to leach back into the world.

I've accepted the void, but I have no expectations of it ever being filled.

21 Sunshine

'M SITTING HERE, LOOKING AT a photo of Kenny and I together, with a great joy in my heart. The darkness has lifted, and I can see the past not with sorrow or regret, but with a wonderful feeling of gratitude. For the first fifteen years of my life, I had an awful sense of displacement with the world, a feeling of not belonging. But when I first saw Kenny in that silly general's outfit, wilting under the studio lights, I knew I'd never be alone again. He was a kindred spirit, a soul mate who knew me as well as I knew myself, who knew what I was thinking without me saying a word. And although he was complex, with worries that stayed with him throughout his life, he was such a good man, a man with an immense capacity to love and to give. He gave me fifteen years of laughter and delight, and helped me come to terms with a world in which I didn't fit.

And even though Kenny has gone, I'm not alone. I still talk to him every day, but in a different voice. I know he's never far away, and on some occasions I can turn and feel him standing beside me or laughing quietly in my ear. One of the promises he made me, on the steps of his house the last time we saw each other, was that he'd let me know he was happy.

Two years after his death, he did exactly that.

It was 4 April 1997, the second anniversary of Kenny's death, and we were on a weekend break in the West Country with some friends. It is a day of very mixed emotions for me: one of the few times when the sorrow of his death makes an unwelcome return, but mixed with a great sense of gratitude and fondness. My mother – who was such a support to me when Kenny died – knew that this was a special day, and suggested we go for a walk in the countryside.

'Kenny would have liked to do that today,' she said softly, standing and looking at the weak spring sunshine burning off a light mist from the garden as we had our breakfast. She suggested we gather our friends and drive out to a forest that she knew. It was 7.30 a.m.

The morning was bright but a bit chilly. When we parked the car and walked into the forest, the sunshine was still struggling to warm away a thin ground mist that was floating around the trees. It was a beautiful forest: big broad oaks and gnarly chestnuts bursting with springtime vigour, the canopy of leaves thick and heavy with growth. There was a cacophony of birdsong (one of Kenny's favourite words, I thought to myself, smiling) and here and there the odd daffodil was poking through the leafy forest floor, making random splashes of yellow on the deep green and brown background. We walked and talked for a while, going deeper into the forest, which had a real fairy-tale feel to it. I half expected Little Red Riding Hood to dash past any minute asking if anyone had see her grandma (it was far too pleasant for the wolf to be any-where in sight). We crossed a small wooden bridge over a stream and my mother and our friends sat down on a fallen tree to catch their breath and soak up the atmosphere. I glanced at my watch. It was nearly ten o'clock. I caught my mother's eye. She smiled at me wisely and nodded at me. I gave her a little wave and carried on walking, taking myself away from the group and leaving the path, pushing deeper into the forest. I wanted to be on my own for a while, and she understood perfectly.

My mind was wonderfully tranquil. I was thinking of Kenny. I could see his smile, and hear his laugh. I was back in time: walking with him down into the Grand Canyon, climbing out of a window into the top of a bus wearing a ball gown, dancing with him in a sweaty nightclub to a thumping Latin beat, our feet a blur and our hearts thundering.

So many good times, so many happy memories.

I pushed my way past a holly bush that was growing between the trunks of two old and crusty looking trees and I felt a shiver run up my spine. It was the same sensation I had when Kenny and I had moments of telepathy, when we would look at one another and know exactly what the other was thinking without having to say a word. I carried on, pushing past the bush and found myself staring at a small clearing in the forest.

From the canopy of foliage high above me, a single beam of sunlight had burst through the leaves and was shining down through the trees. It was so bright it was almost dazzling – a golden pole of glittering brilliance that caught every mote in the air like a million microscopic diamonds hanging suspended in space. And there, where the sunlight hit the forest floor, was a single, brand new pound coin, reflecting the light into my eyes so strongly I had to squint as I knelt down to look at it.

Kenny was beside me. I could smell his skin and hear his breathing. His presence was totally real and palpable, and as I closed my eyes I could feel his love and warmth sweep into me, a wave of tenderness and laughter that made my skin tingle and my arms and neck come up in goosebumps.

I opened my eyes and looked at my watch.

It was exactly 10.43 a.m.

I felt Kenny smile.

Life is good. I'm working a lot; I've discovered a new self-confidence, and I'm ready to take whatever's thrown at me. As a 'showbiz' couple Kenny and I were in the public eye for a long time, but no one ever knew how much we meant to each other or what our relationship symbolised. Much was written about Kenny after he died, mostly focusing on the problems he had in life and making him appear so much smaller than he was – denigrating what he brought to the world. I wanted this book to redress the balance a bit, to show what a capacity Kenny had for love. To show that beyond the laughter and silliness was a man of great depth and intelligence, a man who always put others before himself. He deserved better than the publications that came out after his death, and I hope this book has bestowed something on all those people who gave – and still give – their warmest affection towards Kenny.

Right to the end, Kenny doubted his talents and how much of a genius he was. But now, at long last, I think he knows.

He's gone back to that pink fluffy planet that they should have taken him to when he accidentally got dropped on earth. And he's happy.

I will love him and miss him forever.

Cleo's Glossary

Publisher's Note – few have done more in recent years to enliven the English language than Cleo Rocos, so much so that her extended vocabulary has even managed to garner coverage in the press ('A new word, "bimbonic" enters the language thanks to actress Cleo Rocos...' Daily Telegraph, 22 Feb, 1993). To help you get to grips with adjectives that have flourished from nouns, nouns that have sprung from verbs, and verbs that are completely made up, we've compiled a short glossary. This is by no means exhaustive, so if you come across any more bananary linguistics, Cleo recommends you just go with the flow. It makes gleeing so much easier.

Ariba	Cries of joy and feeling happy and fruity
Bananary	Yellow, curly, and very very cheery
Berdoingee	Bursting with energy and bouncing like a rubber ball
Bimbonic	Fluffy blondes of few years and fewer brain cells
Bongly/Bongliness	Surreal and enjoyable lunacy
Buttock juggling	Dancing
Cartoonular	Of a cartoon – brightly coloured, caricatured, and having an innate sense of silliness
Chesticles	Ladies bosoms
Clenchy-Buttocked	Uptight and anxious
Crunkled	Like crinkled, only dirtier
Doolalee	Raving mad
Earringy	Token bright adornment
To Faff	To prevaricate

Bananas Forever

Floaty	That lovely feeling of dislocation you get after drinking three bottles of champagne
Floaty	That awful feeling of dislocation you get the morning after drinking three bottles of champagne
To Flump	To collapse in a boneless fashion into a comfortable chair
Jiggling giblets	Just having a good time, often while dancing
Marshmallowy	Harmless mouth clouds
Noodley	Delicious, friendly and loveable
Sideways	Anything intervening with the normal balance of the brain, ie too much alcohol or being unwell
Spangly	See 'Earingy'
Stareen	Glamorous young star (female)
Surficular	Shallow
To Glee	To enjoy self-indulgent merriment. To spread a little happiness
Up-And-Downy People	See 'Clenchy-buttocked'
Upsidedownness	An intense and overwhelming nausea caused by stupidly agreeing to go on 67 roller-coaster rides with your best friend Kenny Everett

Other titles available from Virgin

Losing My Virginity
The Autobiography

Richard Branson

Full of Richard Branson's controversial views on everything from
Margaret Thatcher to British Airways, this long-awaited
autobiography of Britain's best-known and most respected
entrepeneur opens the book on Branson's ethos of family, work
and life on the edge. A captivating read that's destined to be a
major international best-seller.

£20 HB
ISBN 1 85227 684 3

Dad's Army
The Lost Episodes

Jimmy Perry and David Croft

When all but one of six early episodes of the British comedy classic *Dad's Army* were accidently wiped after their first broadcast in 1969, it was thought they had been lost forever. Now Croft and Perry have unearthed the scripts for those long-lost episodes, dusted them off and specially adapted them for publication. With previously unpublished photographs, this is a perfect lasting memento for fans.

£14.99 HB
ISBN 1 85227 757 2

Robin Hood According to Spike Milligan

Spike Milligan

Paying scant regard to any previous versions of the age-old folktale of Robin Hood, Spike Milligan thunders through the lastest in his rollicking reworks of classic literature like a runaway horse through Sherwood Forest. Another classic gets Spiked . . .

£10.99 HB
ISBN 1 85227 732 7

Billy Bragg
Still Suitable for Miners
The Official Biography

Andrew Collins

This riveting book tells the life story of the maverick and idiosyncratic icon of leftfield pop. Exploring Bragg's involvement with Red Wedge throughout the 80s, the book also discusses his role as the 'spiritual heir' to 50s protest singer Woody Guthrie and reveals his political views.

£12.99 PB
ISBN 0 7535 0232 1